BY LINDA HOWARD AND LINDA JONES

Blood Born

Running Wild

Frost Line

BY LINDA HOWARD

Shadow Woman

Prey

Veil of Night

Ice

Burn

Death Angel

Up Close and Dangerous

Cover of Night

Drop Dead Gorgeous

Killing Time

To Die For

Kiss Me While I Sleep

Cry No More

Frost Line

BY LINDA JONES

Frost Line

Linda Howard
and Linda Jones

HARPER

An Imprint of HarperCollins*Publishers*

FROST LINE. Copyright © 2016 by Linda Howington and Linda Winstead Jones. All rights reserved. Printed in the United States of America. No part of this book may be used or reproduced in any manner whatsoever without written permission except in the case of brief quotations embodied in critical articles and reviews. For information address HarperCollins Publishers, 195 Broadway, New York, NY 10007.

HarperCollins books may be purchased for educational, business, or sales promotional use. For information please e-mail the Special Markets Department at SPsales@harpercollins.com.

FIRST HARPERLUXE EDITION

ISBN: 978-0-06-246721-8

HarperLuxe™ is a trademark of HarperCollins Publishers.

16 17 18 19 20   ID/RRD   10 9 8 7 6 5 4 3 2 1

Chapter 1

Elijah's nose was running. He used the sheet to wipe it, knowing Mom wouldn't like it. He was mad at her so he didn't care. It was her fault he was crying, anyway, and if he wasn't crying his nose wouldn't be running. His bottom lip stuck out a little as he sniffed resentfully, almost hoping there would be more snot so he could wipe his nose on the sheet again.

It wasn't fair she'd sent him to bed. He wanted to play with Uncle Bobby. Tomorrow wasn't a school day, they had another week of Christmas vacation, and Mom always let him stay up later on the weekends. But tonight she'd sent him to bed even before his bedtime, when Sammy came over. Now Sammy was gone, Uncle Bobby was here, and she still wouldn't let him stay up. He was seven years old, not a little baby. It wasn't fair!

He knuckled the wetness from his eyes, his heart swelling with outrage. He always got to play with Uncle Bobby, who got down on the floor with him to wrestle and brought him candy and cool stuff to play with, and when Mom fussed about it always said, "Now, Amber—" that was Mom's name "—a boy's got to have some fun." Then he'd ruffle Elijah's hair and say, "Right, son?"

It always made Elijah feel happy inside when Uncle Bobby called him "son." No one else did. Uncle Bobby had even given him a Christmas present! A Captain America, a big one. It wasn't a doll, either; it was an action figure. Girls played with dolls; boys had action figures.

He'd asked his mom a couple of times about his real dad but she'd always say they were better off without him and look mad, so he'd stopped asking her even though he'd really like to see his dad one day. The other boys in his class had dads, even if they didn't live in the same house. None of Mom's other boyfriends ever called him "son" the way Uncle Bobby did. Mom said he couldn't talk about them, though, especially when Uncle Bobby was here, but he liked Uncle Bobby way better than he did that jerk Sammy. Sammy was never nice to him, and his mom always sent him upstairs to play when Sammy was there, and told him not to come down or she'd spank him. She never said that when Uncle Bobby came.

Sammy had been here just a little while ago, which was why Elijah had been sent to bed the first time. But he hadn't gone to sleep; after Mom left his room, he got up, turned on the light, and played with his Transformers instead. He'd sent the Transformers against the Avengers; usually he liked the Avengers best and let them win, but this time he'd played a different game and after a long battle the Transformers had come out on top.

Sammy hadn't even bought him a present for Christmas.

Then Sammy had left, and Uncle Bobby had come to visit. When Elijah heard his voice he'd raced downstairs, excited and sure Mom would let him stay up now, but instead she'd gotten mad and sent him back to bed.

He was so preoccupied with his sense of ill-usage that at first he didn't pay any attention to the thumping noise from downstairs. A second thump made him raise his head and listen intently. Mom better not be wrestling with Uncle Bobby, he thought fiercely. Wrestling was what Uncle Bobby did with him. But that's what it sounded like, and the injustice of it propelled him out of bed. He stood in the dark—well, almost dark, because the basketball night-light kept it from ever being really dark. He'd told Mom he was too old for a night-light, but he was secretly glad she'd left it.

He heard some sounds that he couldn't identify, kind of yelling but not yelling, maybe some coughing, then finally the unmistakable sound of breaking glass.

They were definitely wrestling! They'd broken something. He never broke anything!

He tiptoed to the door and eased it open, listening intently. The light from the living room spilled up the stairs and across the hall. His bare feet didn't make any noise as he crept down the stairs. He was just going to peek around the corner to see if they were wrestling, and if they were he . . . he didn't know what he'd do. Maybe he'd break something, to show Mom how mad he was.

Christmas was over, but the tree was still up and the tiny white lights were on. He could see just the edge of the tree as he reached the foot of the stairs. The tree made him feel good, as if he could hold on to Christmas for a while longer even though he was mad because he couldn't play with Uncle Bobby.

There was a drumming sound, as if something was beating against the floor. Elijah knew how to sneak, because he'd seen it in the movies. The sneaking people always got close to the wall, and kind of slid closer. He couldn't get right against the wall because there was a table there, so instead he got down on his hands and knees and crawled. Slowly he eased his head around the corner just enough to see what they were doing.

Confused, he stared at them. He didn't know if they were wrestling or not. Mom was on the floor, flat on her back, and her heels were making that drumming sound, beating slowly up and down. Uncle Bobby was on top of her, his hands around her throat, and he was kind of shaking her. Mom's face was a strange dark color, so dark at first he wasn't sure it was her. What was wrong with her? Her head moved to the side and she saw him—he thought she saw him, only she didn't say anything.

Her hands were around Uncle Bobby's wrists but then her fingers opened and she kind of slapped at his arms a little, mostly missing, and her arms fell down to her side. She kicked slower and slower, only one foot moving now in a thunk . . . thunk . . . thunk. Then the sound stopped, and her feet were still. Her tongue stuck out a little, and her eyes . . .

Her eyes looked like his dog Bosco's had when he got hit by that car last year, open but not seeing anything.

Elijah knew what "dead" was. Bosco had been dead.

Uncle Bobby was breathing hard, sweat running down his face. He looked really mad, his lips pursed together, his eyes squinty. He didn't stop squeezing

Mom's neck. He slammed her head against the floor, twice.

Mom was dead.

Uncle Bobby had hurt her, and Mom was dead.

Sheer panic flooded Elijah's body. What would he do without Mom? He wanted her to get up and laugh and say she'd just been fooling; he wanted her to give him one of her special extra hard hugs, the one that always made him laugh as she swung him back and forth. His mom couldn't be dead.

But she was.

He didn't want to see her dead eyes anymore. Slowly, barely able to move, still on his hands and knees, he backed away from the living room. He didn't look where he was going. He meant to go upstairs and hide in his room, but suddenly there was cool tile under his hands and he knew he was in the kitchen. The light was off, but there were electric clocks on the microwave and on the oven so he could see a little bit. Wildly he looked around, not knowing why he was here. Could he get to his bedroom?

Then a shadow loomed across the tile, and Uncle Bobby's heavy footsteps sounded as he came out of the living room and started up the stairs.

Elijah almost squealed with terror, but he pressed his lips hard against the sound. He could hear himself breathing. Could Uncle Bobby hear him breathing? Would he put his big hands around Elijah's throat and squeeze and shake the way he'd done to Mom?

He couldn't go upstairs. Uncle Bobby was up there. He had to run, and hide; he had to hide really good or Uncle Bobby would find him and then he'd have dead eyes like Mom and Bosco.

Dead.

Mom was dead.

Elijah's chest heaved but he didn't let himself cry. He had to be quiet, and he had to be brave and fast. He had to be like Captain America.

He stood up and crept to the kitchen door. He stretched on tiptoe to reach the latch Mom always fastened as soon as it got dark, and slid it back. It made a metallic click and he froze, unable to look around in case he saw Uncle Bobby reaching for him. Nothing happened, though, and with trembling hands he turned the lock in the doorknob. As quietly as possible he opened the door. Cold air poured in through the widening slot. He was skinny—Mom always said so—and he didn't need a big opening to get through. As soon as possible he squeezed through. The chill of the concrete porch bit into his bare feet, but he couldn't go back inside. He darted across the porch and into the backyard.

Elijah ran. The grass was stiff with frost and scratched, and his feet were really cold, but he wouldn't stop. He couldn't go back. Couldn't, wouldn't. His heart was pounding so hard his chest ached from it and he thought he might burst from the tears inside but he held them back. Captain America, he thought desperately. Captain America wouldn't cry.

Instead of thinking about what he'd seen, he focused straight ahead. It was dark, and he was scared. He was never outside after dark; Mom wouldn't allow it. But he knew his way around the neighborhood, even this late at night. He ran through Miss Sally's backyard, past the spot where her stupid flowers had been before the cold had come and they'd died. She'd yelled at him when his ball had landed in her stupid flowers. She was probably home, but he didn't want to knock on her back door or go around front and ring her doorbell. The house was dark. She might be asleep. She'd yell at him again.

Besides, he knew where to go. Through that backyard, then cutting across to the sidewalk since the old people that lived in the next house had a fenced yard. They had a dog, and he wondered if the dog would start barking, but it didn't. He crossed the street at a run, looking left and then right. A few Christmas lights were still on, but most houses were dark. No one saw him; he was sure of that.

Elijah passed under a streetlight and wondered, too late, if Uncle Bobby was already looking for him. He didn't want Uncle Bobby to find him, especially not in the dark.

Maybe he should have knocked on Miss Sally's door, after all.

Panic made him run harder; a few steps and he was in darkness again. He felt safer in the dark, where no one could see him. Elijah cut into a yard he knew well, skirted the darkest edges of the two-story house that was a lot like his own, and opened the gate that led to the backyard. He left the gate open, then stopped to turn around and close it, his cold fingers shaking as he slipped the lock into place.

He ran to the back door that opened onto the kitchen, just like at his house. Shaking with cold, he tried to turn the doorknob. It was locked, and he whimpered in fear. Then he remembered the doggy door; Zack's Cookie was pretty big, not one of the biggest dogs in the neighborhood, but not a little yapper, either. Maybe he could get through the doggy door.

Elijah got on his hands and knees and pushed against the thick plastic of the door. Maybe Cookie wasn't as big as he'd thought, because the opening seemed awful little. He pushed his head inside, and warm air hit him in the face. He sobbed, swamped with relief, terror, and confusion all at once. Wiggling his shoulders and turning a little sideways, he slid through the door, scraping his side just a little as he tumbled into the warm kitchen. He rolled across the tile to get away from the cold and the dark and Uncle Bobby.

The dark silence of the house scared him. Zack and his family were gone for the weekend, having another Christmas with his granny. Cookie was at what Zack's mom called doggy day care. Elijah sat on the floor hugging his knees, unnerved by being alone in someone else's house. At least . . . at least he was safe here. Uncle Bobby was too big to get through the doggy door.

His lips trembled. He saw it in his head again, what had happened at his house. It didn't make sense, but he hadn't been dreaming. Uncle Bobby had been so mad. His mom . . . Tears welled up in Elijah's eyes. Mom was dead. He wanted his mom, but he didn't want to be dead, too.

When the red haze cleared from State Senator Robert Markham's gaze, when the lava-hot rage cooled enough that he could think again, he looked down at his hands still clenched around Amber's throat. He felt so distant, so dazed, that for a moment he didn't recognize the hands as his own. But they had to be, because they were at the ends of his arms. Everything was just so unreal; he couldn't believe what his eyes were telling him. He had to concentrate to move, to slowly force his fingers to relax. Numbly he stared at the dark red marks left on her flesh.

He was astride her on the floor. He didn't remember how they'd gotten down there; the last thing he clearly remembered, she'd spat in his face, and he'd felt as if he were turning inside out with rage.

She was dead. Her eyes were open and blank, her tongue sticking out a little. He'd killed her.

Shock hit him, an almost physical force that made him sag sideways. His ass hit the floor with a thud. He sat there staring stupidly at Amber's body, trying to grasp what had happened, trying to think.

The first coherent thought to surface was: What should I do?

It went without saying that the underlying meaning of that was how to get away with what he'd done.

He'd killed his mistress, but he couldn't find even a shred of regret for the fact that she was dead, only anxiety that he might be found out. Vaguely he looked around, as if he might find inspiration in the overturned coffee table, the shards of glass from the broken picture frame, the cell phone lying half under the couch.

Robert reached out and picked up the cell phone, and his hand shook. If it hadn't been for the phone none of this would have happened. Amber would still be fucking her other boyfriend, and both of them would be laughing at him for being such a doofus that he thought a woman as pretty as Amber would care about him. But the asshole boyfriend had forgotten his phone, and on the phone was a video he'd made of himself and Amber having sex, and laughing about Robert for being naive enough to provide this house for her, Amber calling him "LD" and the boyfriend laughing like a hyena when she explained that it stood for "little dick."

It was all so unreal. The evening had started quietly enough. He hadn't intended to stop by, but had a last minute impulse to get in some time with her, because around Christmas it was tough getting away from the family. Damn holidays; he hated them. He was later than usual, so late Elijah was already in bed, though the kid had gotten up when he'd heard "Uncle Bobby" downstairs, and definitely been unhappy when Amber had sternly insisted he go back upstairs, which now in hindsight Robert knew was because she was afraid the kid would say something about her earlier visitor that night. The bitch—that was how he thought of her now, after seeing that video—had excused herself to the bathroom, probably to clean up from having sex with the guy who had left just before he arrived.

That idea now seared him like acid, but at the time he hadn't thought anything about it. He'd been sitting there, clicking through the television channels, when he'd glanced down and seen the corner of the phone sticking up from between the cushion and the arm of the couch.

He'd pulled it out, and stared curiously at it. He knew it wasn't Amber's phone; hers was an Android, with a flowered case. This was an iPhone, and it had a chunky black case, the kind people bought to protect the phone from rough handling. He thumbed the home button and the screen lit, inviting him to swipe it. He did, expecting to see the security code screen, but instead the regular screen came up; whoever the phone belonged to hadn't put in a security code.

He felt an illicit thrill; finding an unsecured phone was like looking through someone's bedroom window after dark. The first thing he did was check the text messages. The screen hadn't been closed, and the most recent texts popped up.

u at home, baby
yes, *Amber had replied.*
old fart coming over 2nite?
no Im free
b there in 30

The times on the texts were earlier that evening. Robert had stared at the string of messages, cold anger building. He wasn't stupid; obviously he was the "old fart," and whoever owned the phone had called Amber "baby."

Quickly he scrolled through the other messages, finding others to and from Amber, and the intimate tone of the texts said it all. She'd been cheating on him all along. He shook with anger, but he tried to control it. He was married, and a state senator; Amber could do a lot of damage to his career if she got mad. He had ambitions, goals, and she could ruin it all.

He wanted to know who the asshole was, what he looked like. Robert didn't love Amber—that would be stupid, she was just a young(er) and pretty piece of ass—but if the guy was also married and was sneaking around with her, maybe he could leverage that to keep her from raising hell.

Next he went to the photos, flicking through them. Most of them were selfies, of the guy by himself, or goofing around with friends, some of them with Amber. He looked about Amber's age, dark-haired, on the skinny side, sometimes wearing a blue shirt with the logo of an auto repair company above the left pocket. Okay, he didn't know the guy's name yet, but now he knew where he worked.

There were some videos, and he tapped the most recent one.

It was of the guy and Amber fucking, right here on the couch. Their voices came clearly through the phone's speaker:

"Do you like it? Can the old fart fuck you like this? Can he?"

"His dick's too little," Amber had replied, laughing.

There was more—more laughing, more insults. His ears started buzzing, and he felt a strange sense of disconnection. No one laughed at him like that. He was State Senator Robert Markham, head of the Senate Appropriations Committee, the most powerful man in the Georgia capital because if you controlled the money you controlled everything—and they were laughing at him as if he were nobody.

Then Amber flew at him from the left, slapping the phone from his hands, slapping, slapping, hitting him in the face, on the side of the head. She hadn't screamed, probably because of the kid asleep upstairs, but she'd been spitting words at him from between clenched teeth, her pretty face red and twisted with fury as if she was the injured party, as if she was the one who had been cheated on.

Then she spat in his face, and without thinking he punched her, sending her slamming into the lamp table, knocking over a picture of her and the kid. That was his last clear memory. He just wanted to make her shut up; he wanted to make her pay for everything she'd said, for making him look like a fool. He couldn't hear anything other than the buzzing in his ears, and what he remembered was more like a flurry of snapshots than memories: frozen images of her face, strangely purple, a sharp stinging on his wrists, her hand clawing at the floor.

He sat beside her body for a numb few seconds that felt like an hour, then a sense of urgency stirred him.

He had to do something.

No one knew he was here, except for the kid. Elijah was just seven and he didn't even know Robert's full name, just called him "Uncle Bobby." But a decent cop might figure Bobby was a nickname for Robert, and maybe a neighbor had noticed his car pulling into Amber's driveway a time or two before, though he was always careful to park in the garage. With damn cell phones someone could have taken a picture with his car in the background—that would be bad luck, but it happened.

But evidently there were other cars that parked in Amber's driveway, and one other for certain had been here tonight, earlier, when it was more likely to be seen. That was pure luck on his part, and bad luck for the other guy.

The kid was the problem, and problems had to be taken care of. He'd learned that on his way up the political ladder. If the next step—the governorship— was to be his, he had to handle this.

He kind of regretted it, because the kid was a cute little guy. Still, it wasn't as if Elijah was his kid. He doubted Amber had even known who the father was.

He'd have to think this through, cover all the details, but first things first: he had to take care of the kid.

Quietly he got to his feet and went up the stairs. He tried to think how he should do it, but the only thing that came to mind was to strangle him the same way he'd done Amber—though maybe he'd just put a pillow over the kid's face and hold it down, smother him instead of actually choking him. Not only did it seem kinder, but there was less chance of leaving a fingerprint up here. He'd never been in the kid's room before, so that was good. But he knew which one it was, because whenever he'd been in Amber's room she'd always been careful to pull Elijah's door securely shut.

With that in mind, he pulled out his shirttail and used that to cover his hand as he pushed the door open.

There was a night-light burning, so the room wasn't completely dark. Robert moved silently toward the rumpled bed, then stopped in surprise, blinking his eyes. The bed was empty; the kid wasn't there.

Swiftly he looked around; the room was a kid's usual messy jumble of toys and clothes, but that was it. Covering his hand with his shirttail again, he flipped on the light.

Definitely no kid. He looked under the bed, and in the closet, in case Elijah had been in a sulk when he was sent back to bed and had hidden, then fallen asleep.

Nothing. Shit!

Robert turned out the light. Okay, maybe he'd gone to the bathroom. But the bathroom was directly across the hall—the door was open, the light was out. He looked, anyway, in case the kid was hiding in the tub. He wasn't.

Amber's room, maybe?

Empty.

Robert went from room to room, anxiety building. He had to find that damn kid. Where the hell could he have gone?

He went back downstairs, stepping as quietly as he could, his head swiveling as he tried to catch any movement. In the living room, Amber still lay as he'd left her, sightless eyes staring.

He checked the downstairs bathroom, the laundry room, the dining room. Finally he went into the kitchen, and immediately felt the movement of cold air. He turned on the light, looked around, then fixated on the back door. It stood slightly ajar, the cold night air rushing through the opening.

Quickly he turned out the light again. His blood felt like ice, horror seizing him. The kid had seen him kill Amber, and had run to a neighbor's house for help. The cops would already be on the way. He had to leave, and leave now. But what if the neighbor was standing outside waiting for him, maybe with a gun? This was Georgia; anyone was as likely to have a gun as not.

But he couldn't just stand here like a fool; he had to do something.

He used the toe of his shoe to nudge the back door open, and slipped out into the backyard. He stood in the cold and dark, listening for a sniffle, a disturbance—anything. Lawrenceville was a nice little suburb, the houses fairly close together, but occasionally there would be a wooded lot providing some separation. This late on a Friday night it wouldn't be surprising if some of the neighbors were still awake, but maybe people were tired from all the holiday bustle because he couldn't see any lights on anywhere around.

His heart pounded heavily as he tried to think. If the kid had run to the next door neighbor, there would be lights on, voices, maybe even sirens already screaming as cops raced toward them. But the night was quiet, no voices, no sirens. There was a tree line behind the row of houses; if the kid had run into the trees, there was no way Robert could find him.

But why would Elijah do that? He was a little kid, and he'd run to other people for help. Wouldn't he?

Staying in the shadows, feeling the bite of the cold, Robert crept to the front of the house and crouched beside a bush as he looked up and down the street. Now he could see a couple of lights on, here and there, but those houses were still quiet. A few had left their Christmas lights on. That was it. There were no signs of activity, no unusual sounds, no dogs barking or porch lights coming on, and still no sirens.

The kid had gone to ground somewhere. For whatever reason, he hadn't gone for help. Who knew what the hell kids thought?

Now what did he do?

His first thought: get rid of the body. There wasn't any blood. He could clean up the broken glass, straighten the furniture, take Amber's body, and dump it somewhere. The longer it took to find her, the less evidence there would be. There were plenty of lakes and rivers around, as well as wooded areas. He'd think of somewhere, maybe even drive into another county before he dumped her.

His mind whirled with thoughts. He had to wipe everything he'd touched. He had to get Amber's cell phone and her purse, make it look as if she'd gone somewhere. Take the battery out of the phone, yeah, so it couldn't be traced by GPS. That other guy's phone, too; he had to do the same thing with it—but he'd leave the phone with Amber's body, or close by. If it was ever found, that would have the cops looking at the other guy. That meant he had to leave the battery in it, make it look as if the guy had dropped it, lost it.

But first things first: he had to get Amber's body out of the house, before the cops did show up.

Chapter 2

Elijah crawled to the kitchen table, his hands and face stinging, his feet so cold they hurt. Maybe he could hide under the table, stay right there until Zack and his parents got home. But how long were they going to stay at Zack's granny's house? Two days? Three?

Did Uncle Bobby know Elijah and Zack were best friends? Did he know where Zack lived? Would he come here?

The thought terrified him, but he didn't know what to do, where else he could go. And he was cold; he couldn't run anymore. He curled up beside the table and tried to get his feet warm, pushing the toes of first one foot then the other beneath the hem of his pajama pants, against each leg in turn. It was a while before his toes began to feel warm, before the pain started to go away.

What should he do now? A policeman had visited their class a long time ago, back at the beginning of the school year. Elijah had been new then. He'd known Zack lived on his street, but they weren't best friends yet. The policeman had talked about a lot of stuff, but what Elijah remembered was 9–1–1. Everybody knew to call 9–1–1 in an emergency, even little kids. Mom had taught him that a long time ago; he didn't need a policeman to tell him to do it.

Cautiously he stood, staring out the window to see if Uncle Bobby was out there, looking for him. He couldn't see anyone, so he eased away from the table. Where did Zack's mom keep her phone? He'd never seen her use anything but a cell phone, but that didn't mean she didn't have a big phone like Miss Sally did. Elijah looked around the kitchen, then moved into the dining room and on to the living room. Nothing. He didn't like being in the dark; he couldn't really tell if there was a phone hiding somewhere or not. A couple of times he thought about turning on a light, but every time he reached toward a light switch, he'd stop. If he turned on the light, Uncle Bobby might see it and come get him and kill him.

He didn't want Uncle Bobby to call him "son" ever again. He wasn't Uncle Bobby's son; he didn't want to be friends anymore. He wanted his mom, but Uncle Bobby had killed her.

Tears leaked out of his eyes and his nose was running again. He swiped his pajama sleeve under his nose and held his breath to stop crying. When his chest hurt and he couldn't hold back any longer, he let his breath go in a rush. He didn't have time for crying; he had to find a phone. Maybe there was one upstairs—a big phone or maybe a cell phone they'd left behind. He and Zack had laughed at Miss Sally's big old phone but he sure would like to find one now. Going to the stairs he grabbed the rail, being careful the way Mom had told him, though he forgot most of the time, but now he wanted to do as she said because it kept her there, someway. He climbed the stairs, his still-cold feet taking one step at a time.

Zack's mom had night-lights everywhere! He didn't have any trouble seeing where he was going, not with all those night-lights.

If he had his own cell phone, he would've already called 9–1–1! But Mom said he was too young, that maybe he could get one when he was twelve. Twelve! That was five years away. He'd be too old to want one by then.

When he got to the second floor, Elijah went first to Zack's room. He knew there was no phone in there, but he'd been in this room a lot, and he knew his way around. It was familiar, comforting. Bunk beds, neatly made—they weren't always—were pushed against one wall. Zack had a toy box, a dresser with a lamp on it, a dirty clothes hamper. But he couldn't stay here. There was no phone; he'd known that when he came here. He just wanted to feel a little bit happy again, and he'd always had fun in Zack's room.

From there, he went next door to Gracie's room. Gracie was old, practically grown; she was thirteen, and she did have a cell phone. It was always with her, though, so he didn't expect to find one just laying around. He wrinkled his nose; her room was a mess. He hadn't known girls could be this messy, but this was worse than Zack's room usually was. Her clothes were tossed everywhere—on the floor, on her bed, across her furniture. If there was a phone, he'd never find it.

Heaving a sigh, he trudged on down the hall. The bedroom where Zack's parents slept was huge. There was enough space for a big bed, a couple of dressers, and a treadmill that had clothes hanging on it. They had a lot of weird, old stuff that was stacked everywhere. He checked the nightstands and the tops of both dressers, patting the surface when he couldn't see well enough from the night-lights. There was a lot of old junk, but no cell phone or the other kind. There were boxes, small lamps, smelly books, carved animals—an elephant and a tiger—even a globe of the world, one that would spin when you gave it a push. He did. It didn't light up, like the one he had at home.

But no phone.

What should he do, if he couldn't call 9–1–1? Should he just stay here until Zack and his parents got home? There would be food in the kitchen. Maybe Uncle Bobby wouldn't even think about looking here. Zack's mom would know what to do. She could dial 9–1–1 on her cell phone. But that could be days.

For a moment he thought about going to another house. Miss Sally had a phone. Most houses did. But he didn't know where Uncle Bobby was, if he was on the street or just outside this very house or still at Elijah's house . . . He felt cold all over at the thought of Uncle Bobby catching him, and giving him dead eyes like Mom and Bosco. No, he wasn't leaving. He was safe here.

Elijah went back to Zack's room. He'd spent the night before; they wouldn't mind if he stayed here until they got home. He crawled into the bottom bunk bed— Zack always took the top—and put his feet beneath the covers. They were almost not-cold. He pulled the thick cover to his chin, shivering for a moment, then wallowing in the warmth.

He should sleep. If it was a school night it would be a long time past his bedtime. He remembered how mad he'd been at Mom for not letting him stay up later, but then he'd gone downstairs and seen . . .

He didn't want to think about that.

The shivers came back. Outside, the wind picked up, howling like Cookie did when the little dog next door aggravated him through the chain-link fence. The tree outside Zack's window moved, and the limbs scraped against the side of the house. That window faced the street. If he looked out that window, would he see Uncle Bobby? Looking for him, calling his name . . .

Elijah leapt from the bed and ran down the hall to Zack's parents' bedroom. It faced the backyard. There was no tree to rub against the window.

But there were windows. Windows he could see out. Windows Uncle Bobby could see in.

Still cold, Elijah grabbed a big blanket from the foot of the bed, and pulled it to the closet. No one could see him if he was in the closet. He opened the door and stepped inside, pulling the soft blanket with him. It was a big closet, with racks of clothes on both sides, and boxes and shoes lined against the walls.

When he closed the door, darkness wrapped around him like the blanket. There was no night-light in here, no moonlight or streetlights shining through the window, because there was no window. He couldn't see out. No one could see in.

For the first time in what felt like hours, Elijah felt safe. He lay down on the floor and pulled the blanket to his chin. He should've grabbed a pillow, too, but he hadn't thought about it and as much as he would've liked one, he didn't want to leave the warmth of the spot he had made for himself.

Uncle Bobby wouldn't find him here, in the dark, behind a closed closet door. No one would find him here.

Elijah slept. He dreamed.

His headlights picked up the sideways white drops and Robert's hands tightened on his steering wheel. Sleet was marginally better than snow or freezing rain; in the cold and dark, the clock ticking relentlessly, foul weather was the last thing he wanted to see. Or maybe it wasn't; maybe bad weather would make it harder for anyone to find Amber's body, and destroy more evidence as a bonus. He didn't know. All he knew was that this was a shitty end to a shitty day.

He'd driven more than half an hour north of Lawrenceville, taking dark and narrow back roads until he reached the old roadside park. He parked in the gravel lot that was littered with beer cans and discarded burger wrappers. The dented trash can was overflowing, as if it had been a while since any maintenance was done. In his half-panicked state, he wasn't any more certain if that was a good thing than he was about the bad weather. Did that mean someone would show up tomorrow? Find her body right away? That would be bad.

On the other hand, he'd like to leave her on top of the trash can. Trash in the trash; it was fitting. He'd like to, but he wouldn't.

He turned off the car's ignition, so no lights would give away his presence if anyone happened to drive by on the road, though this late—or early—and in increasingly bad weather, traffic had been very light, almost nonexistent. The clouds blocked out all starlight and the blowing sleet cut visibility down even more.

The wind sliced through his suit coat as he got out of the car, ducking his head against the stinging ice pellets. Shit, it was cold! Using his remote he popped the trunk lid, remembering too late that a light in the trunk automatically came on whenever it was opened.

Swearing under his breath, he hurried around and leaned in to wrestle Amber's body out of the trunk. He'd rolled her in a blanket, which made her easier to handle, but dead weight was still dead weight. He swore under his breath as he pulled and tugged, bracing his feet and using his own weight to lug the bundle upward and over the lip of the trunk.

Finally, breathing hard, he had her out. He bent down and let the bundle fold over his shoulder, then fought to straighten his knees. Damn it, he was a politician, not a gym rat; he'd never counted on having to haul a body around on his shoulder.

He looked around; there still wasn't any sign of traffic, and without the headlights on he couldn't see shit. Should he risk turning them on? He couldn't just leave her here—though he wanted to. He had to conceal the body well enough that she wouldn't be found right away. He needed time, time for evidence to erode, time to find that little shit Elijah, time to make plans and take precautions.

The pattering of the sleet slowed, and a strange hush fell over the night. Snowflakes began drifting down, soft and fat. His sense of urgency surged even higher. Snow in the south was a disaster, with roads turning to skating rinks in no time. He had to get Amber's body dumped and get home before he was stranded. He still had to think of some tale that would satisfy his wife, but a screaming fight with her was the least of his worries right now.

He'd have to risk turning the headlights on, otherwise he couldn't see where he was going and this job would take more time than he could spare. The falling snow would help hide his actions.

Cursing with every step, keeping the bundle that was Amber balanced over his shoulder because that was less effort than putting her down and having to pick her back up would be, he opened the driver's door and awkwardly maneuvered himself so he could reach the knob that turned on the headlights. The twin beams shot across the rough landscape, illuminating the dancing, swirling snow. Hurrying now, he carried Amber across the littered pavement and stepped up at the curb onto the grass, past the overflowing trash can. The darkness of some woods beyond the little park offered the best chance of concealment; he'd like to take her farther away from the road, but with the snow coming down and already accumulating on the winter-dead leaves, he couldn't take the time.

He was about thirty feet past the trash can when he stepped in a shallow hole hidden by the leaves, lurched off balance, and dropped the blanket-wrapped body.

"Shit!" Breathing hard, sweat slicking his face despite the icy wind, he stared down at her. There was no way he could heft her back onto his shoulder, not from the ground; he'd barely managed getting her out of the trunk.

After only a moment's hesitation, he bent down, grabbed the end of the bundle, and began dragging it. If he left a trail on the frozen ground, the damn snow would soon cover it.

He made it to the woods and stopped to rest, his breath huffing out in white clouds. The car's headlights didn't make much difference here; he was off to the side rather than directly in front. Looking around, he saw that what he'd thought was a nice section of woods was instead fairly thin, maybe twenty yards deep. Maybe dumping her on the far side would be better. Forcing himself to make the effort, grunting now with the exertion, he dragged her to the far edge of the woods and found himself standing on the edge of a rough ravine, a raw, uneven cut in the earth.

Perfect.

He tried pushing her with his foot, but even rolled in a blanket moving a dead person wasn't that easy. Bending down, he gave the bundle a hard push and finally it rolled over the edge of the ravine and down, over brush and rocks, until he lost sight of her in the deep night shadows and the thickening snow.

It was done—all except for the asshole's cell phone.

He pulled it out of his pocket and started to place it in the dirt, as if it had been accidentally dropped, but then he hesitated. He'd deleted the damnable video, and the texts that mentioned him, but what if they weren't really deleted? What if the cops could still pull everything up somehow? One of his senate colleagues had been caught in an embarrassing situation because he thought he'd deleted something incriminating, only to find that the photo was still accessible to the right program.

Shit, shit, shit.

As much as he wanted to point the finger toward the asshole, he couldn't take the risk.

Fumbling in the dark, he tried to remove the battery, but found that he couldn't get the iPhone open. Hell, he couldn't even get it out of the damn case, especially not in the dark and going mostly by feel. He'd take it . . . somewhere. Maybe throw it out the window as he crossed over a bridge. Yeah, that was a good idea, toss it in a river, a lake, get it out of his possession. It would be gone, likely never found.

But even when the asshole's phone was gone, the asshole himself would still exist. He knew Amber had been seeing someone else, an older man. Did he know who Robert was? Could he point the police in this direction? Robert knew forensics in real life weren't nearly as impressive as they were on television, but would a cleaning of his trunk remove all traces of Amber, or would a search turn up a hair, a fiber, a skin cell . . . ?

Robert wanted to dump ungrateful Amber's body, walk away, and forget it. But he couldn't. There was the asshole, and the kid.

He'd killed Amber in a fit of rage, but he wasn't a stone-cold killer.

Fortunately, he knew someone who was.

Elijah woke with a strangled cry, shaking in terror. Uncle Bobby had his hands around his throat, choking him, and was looking at him with dead eyes. The dream—the memory—was so fresh and real he flailed his skinny arms, fighting the horror that wasn't there. His fists tangled in fabric, fabric that seemed to dance away from him, then swing back and try to trap him. He sobbed, trying to scream again, fighting and kicking the invisible threat.

"Help me!" The words scraped from his throat as he threw himself to the side. He landed on something kind of hard and lumpy, but the darkness was so thick he couldn't see anything. He heard his own sobs, and instinctively tried to control his panic. Where was he? What had happened? Had he dreamed everything about Uncle Bobby and Mom, or was it real?

The sense of panic, temporarily pushed back, surged over him again. "Help me!" he screamed, begging for someone, anyone, to come to his aid. His left arm hit something soft, something that fell over, and in the utter darkness he thought the thing and the sound was Uncle Bobby. He shrieked, over and over, scrambling backward as he tried desperately to get away from Uncle Bobby.

He slammed against some obstacle and in his terror he tried his best to simply go through it, anything he had to do to get away. But whatever it was also fell over, this time with a heavy thud. Something fluttered around him, like a bunch of birds in the darkness, touching his face, his arms. There was a kind of swishing sound, then . . . a hush. Silence. Elijah whimpered, almost as afraid of birds being after him as he was of Uncle Bobby. Birds? How could there be birds?

He couldn't hear anything that sounded like Uncle Bobby. Uncle Bobby always breathed as if his nose was stuffy. Elijah couldn't hear any breathing. Cautiously he reached out, felt nothing. Closet—he was in the closet. He remembered now. He wanted out, but where was the door? He couldn't see anything. Maybe he could crawl around and find the crack under the door. He put his hand down and instead of carpet he felt some kind of paper, something thicker than normal, and slick.

He suddenly felt a little weird, as if he couldn't quite catch his breath.

Because he was just seven, because he was terrified and alone, he said, "Help me," again. This time he whispered the words. He was so tired, so scared and alone, he just couldn't yell anymore.

No sooner had the words left his mouth than a bright light hit his eyes, and he squeaked in terror as he cowered down and covered his head with both arms, squeezing his eyes as tightly shut as he could. A flashlight, he thought. It was a flashlight. It was Uncle Bobby, with a flashlight. He'd called for help and had instead showed Uncle Bobby where he was hiding. Whimpering, he scooted back as far as he could and waited for whatever was going to happen.

A few seconds ticked by. Nothing. He couldn't hear anything. Slowly, Elijah raised his head and peeked, just a little.

It wasn't a flashlight.

No one was there.

The box he'd knocked over lay open on its side, and the light was coming from the box, spreading over a bunch of slick, funny-looking cards that had paintings on them. Most of the paintings were of people, though there was one cool picture of a sun that looked like it might be the sun in one of the *Transformer* movies. One card lay on top of the scattered spill, a card with a painting of a pretty woman and a lion. There was a word at the top, but it didn't make any sense to him. It was a word he didn't know, and the letters were crooked and funny; it didn't even look like a word. It looked like some drawings.

Then they blurred and changed, the lines rearranging themselves. He blinked, because words weren't supposed to change. Slowly he spelled it out. S.T.R.E.N.G.T.H. Strength. That was a word he knew, a word he had seen in a book he was reading for extra credit. Iron Man's suit gave him superstrength. Maybe the lion gave the pretty woman strength. Maybe it was her pet.

He reached out and touched the card, tracing the image. It was warm, as if the woman painted on it was alive. She was so pretty, prettier even than his mom. Thinking of Mom made a huge sense of sadness well up inside of him, so huge he didn't think he could breathe. "Help me," he said again, his voice small and strained, so small the words were just a thread of sound.

The picture on the card shimmered. Elijah jumped, peddling backward until he hit the opposite side of the closet, where he squashed himself into the smallest ball he could manage. Wildly he looked around, wondering what was happening. The funny light was still coming from the box and now he could see that he'd knocked over a bunch of stuff: shoes, purses, a box of old jewelry, some sweaters and scarves. The cards from the light box lay all over everything else.

The card he'd touched . . . moved.

He sucked in a breath, his eyes growing enormous as he stared at the Strength card. It grew. It stretched. It got kind of wavy, and floated up into the air. Elijah opened his mouth and tried to yell, but no sound came out. His lips moved, his throat strained, but he couldn't speak at all.

The card slowly floated higher, twisting, getting bigger and bigger and spreading out. Unable to look away, Elijah sat frozen as the card began to look like . . . a door? Yes, a strange-looking door, but not like the closet door; it wasn't solid, but he couldn't see through it. There was some kind of weird fog filling it, but not spilling out.

Suddenly a hand—a real, living hand—poked out of the card/door into the closet. Elijah jerked back, banged his head on the wall because he was already as far back as he could get, then dived sideways beneath the skirts of the dresses hanging on the rack above him. Frantically he pulled the skirts around him, trying his best to hide from the undead hand. It was a zombie hand! But he grabbed one of Zack's mom's dresses and moved it just a tiny bit to the side, so he could see, because he felt as if he couldn't not see. The hand . . . it was kind of pretty, like Mom's, with painted fingernails and rings and stuff.

There was more movement in the foggy doorway: the hand, a foot—more painted nails and jewelry—followed by a leg, and a scrap of white fabric that moved around like it was caught in a wind. He gasped, but didn't cover his eyes. He had to see; he had to.

Then she was there.

She stepped out of that card doorway and into the closet as if this was her closet and she wanted to get a dress. Snow and ice formed everywhere, on the floor and in the air, outlining where the doorway had been, glistening and shimmering like the 3-D fireworks he'd seen in a movie.

And then the snow and the ice and the card were gone.

The woman . . . the woman with the long blond hair and the white dress was still there.

Chapter 3

S omething slammed into Lenna, something that had force but no substance. A bright light blinded her, and searing cold enveloped her. She'd known cold before, but not like this. This was piercing, as if it went all the way to the bone. She heard words whispering in her ear, words that were sound without meaning. Her lungs seized, costing her the ability to call out in alarm, in plea.

She had the sensation of spinning, of being weightless, of not existing. *What was happening?* She wasn't given to panic, but if panic would stop this madness she would gladly begin shrieking.

She was lost in nothingness in which nothing existed except the cold and the light and the sense of not *being*.

Then, gradually, the spinning slowed. She tried to reach out, to grasp something solid, but her hands closed on emptiness. There was a silent but definite *snap!* that she felt against her skin, and her surroundings once more clicked into welcome solidity. She felt ice beneath her bare feet, but it was quickly melting. She stood there gasping for breath, fighting to right herself because while everything around her had stopped spinning, she felt as if she herself hadn't. She wasn't accustomed to being out of control, and she didn't like it. *At. All.*

She was in a tiny room, a room completely unlike her own regal apartments. A bit annoyed, a bit curious, Lenna studied her surroundings. There were unimpressive garments of some sort hanging from bent tubes, piles of shoes on the floor—and she saw some that she admired—a crumpled blanket pushed against a far wall, and finally, a pair of small bare feet. The bright light illuminated all, including the small shivering person clutching some of the garments over itself as it tried, unsuccessfully, to hide from her.

The bright light began fading as she looked around, trying to decipher what had happened. One moment she'd been in her home, studying a long ago war that had taken place in another realm, and then without warning she'd been—

What? Jerked from her home, certainly. Transported? Possibly, maybe even probably. Such things had happened, she'd heard, though not to those of her class.

Had she been kidnapped? But who would dare? Certainly not the small being whose feet she could see.

In the dimming light she saw, at her feet, brightly painted tarot cards spread across the floor. The images were ornate but oddly that wasn't what most caught her attention. Power throbbed from them, a power so strong it caused a slight glow around the cards. She had seen many manifestations of the Arcane, but none like this.

Her own card, Strength, lay on top. It was almost glittering, perhaps in reaction to her nearness.

A shock of recognition went through her. This wasn't just any deck; it was the Alexandria Deck, supposedly destroyed in the fires that devastated the Alexandria Library. The Alexandria Deck was unique in the world of the Arcane, capable of imparting powers beyond those designated to each card by the One. She had never seen the deck before but she knew it, knew it by the power that radiated from the cards.

There had been rumors that the magical deck had survived the fires, but she had never really believed—no one in the Arcane had—that the rumors were true.

Yet here it was, and the implications meant her situation was now far more complicated than she had initially imagined. She had not been simply taken from her home, but had been removed from her very *world*, from Aeonia to . . . She went still, a chill running down her back. If that was truly the Alexandria Deck, she was in Seven—Three in the modern times, but Seven in the initial creation, the one that mattered. There were many worlds, but Seven was the one in which the deck had been created, and supposedly destroyed. Instead, the deck had survived.

Being brought here was complicated, and potentially catastrophic.

The light that had accompanied her from Aeonia into this world finally faded entirely. The small person who was trying to hide gave a piteous whimper as the darkness enveloped them.

That, at least, was easily alleviated; Lenna simply lifted her hand, spread her fingers, and a ball of light appeared on her palm. It wasn't as bright as the other, but it would suffice. She started to order the small human who had apparently called her here to come forth and send her home, when a memory of the words that had accompanied her trip to this place stopped her.

Help me.

Had the plea come from this small person? It must have, for it was the only other being here, with the cards.

She could see part of a face that wasn't hidden by the tumble of garments. She bent closer to more carefully study the partial features, and a measure of surprise lifted her brows. Ah! Unless she was mistaken, this was a child. There were no children in Aeonia, because there was no need for them. Aeonia was home to the twenty-two Major Arcana—not actual tarot cards, as they were known in most worlds, but living representations of those cards. They had existed for much longer than the cards some used for guidance and divination, since the One created all.

Two warring concerns filled her. She knew she shouldn't be here. She couldn't stay. Returning to Aeonia was an imperative, one she couldn't ignore. And yet—this child needed aid. Before she returned home, perhaps she could provide some sort of help, even if it was only to soothe and encourage. So many times that was all the support humans asked for, or needed.

The clothing parted a little, and a large brown eye peeked out, growing even larger at the sight of the light in Lenna's hand.

"Hello, child," she said easily. "What assistance do you require?"

The brown eye blinked, but the child didn't respond.

Perhaps it didn't hear well. She raised her voice and tried again. "Child. What sort of help is it you need?"

After a moment the clothing shifted more, and the child mostly emerged from hiding. It was a boy child, she saw. Hesitantly he pointed at her hand. "Is that magic?"

It was a simple question, but the answer was complicated. She supposed that to a being who didn't have certain abilities, those abilities might be called magic. "Yes, I suppose it is."

"Cool, but why didn't you just turn on the light?"

Confused, she looked from him to her hand, back to him. She moved her hand up and down, making the light dance. "I did."

"No, the real light."

"This is a real light."

He gave her a cautious look, then scrambled from his hiding place and pointed behind her at the wall. Lenna turned and saw a white rectangle with a switch in it. "There," he said. "I didn't turn it on before because I didn't want anyone to see me." His little voice quavered.

Mentally shrugging, wondering what difference it made which light she used, and then wondering why the child thought someone might see him in this small space whether there was light or not, Lenna use a fingertip to nudge the switch upward, and a harsh light appeared overhead.

She closed her fingers and extinguished the ball of light. In the glaring light she got her first good look at the child who had somehow pulled her from her world into his, a feat made possible by the Alexandria Deck. Had he known what he was doing? Was he perhaps an Arcane prodigy, capable of things others couldn't accomplish?

She reminded herself that she needed to be both cautious and calm. She was Strength, but right now she would almost rather be the High Priestess, because wisdom was what was more needed.

The child brought forth a softening inside, and made a smile curve her lips. He looked delicious, in a strangely joyous way. He had flawless skin, like velvet, that invited her touch. The curve of his plump cheeks would just fit in her palm, and his deep brown eyes were full of both innocence and pain. His thick dark hair was mussed, his clothing loose and rumpled. He wore no shoes, but then, neither did she.

"You called me here for a purpose," she said, trying yet again to extract from him the reason why she was here. "What is that purpose?"

A look of intense unhappiness crossed that cherubic face, but all he said was, "I'm hungry," then he opened the door and cautiously looked around before leaving the small dressing room.

Lenna followed, stepping into a bedchamber that was gently lit by an early-morning sun beginning to share its glow through large windows. She didn't take the time to examine her surroundings, though normally her curiosity would be high. "Your hunger can wait, child," she said. "Tell me—"

"My name is Elijah," he said without looking back as he left the room. Lenna fell into step behind him. "Elijah Tilley. What's your name?"

"Lenna Frost. Strength of the Major Arcana. You know who I am," she continued, puzzled. "You called me, you brought me here."

"No, you just showed up." This time he did glance over his shoulder at her, and his brow wrinkled. "You're wearing your nightgown. I didn't mean to wake you up. Sorry," he added in a small voice.

Nightgown? Lenna looked down at herself. She was *not* wearing nightclothes. When she did sleep, it was without any clothing at all. Her dress was made of the finest white Nilean silkine available in Aeonia or any other world. She had been immersed in some interesting studies, so the dress had been chosen with comfort in mind; it hung loosely, in lustrous folds that never wrinkled. She doubted the child cared about her fashion choices, though, so she merely reassured him.

"No apology is needed. You did not wake me."

She followed him down the stairs, through another room, into a room that was—as the bed chamber upstairs had been—lit by the soft, faint light of dawn coming through the windows, a dawn that showed a world of white. "Now, what sort of help do you require?"

He stopped in the middle of the room—a kitchen, if she was correct—and turned to look up at her with wide eyes that held an overbright sheen. Tears spilled down his little cheeks.

Somewhat bewildered, she stared at him. What had she said to cause this reaction? How could she make him stop? "Cease," she ordered.

Rather than stopping, his lips quivered and he began to sob, his slight shoulders heaving. Ordering him to stop didn't work.

"It wasn't a dream," he said, the words shuddering out between sobs. "I thought I'd come downstairs and be in my house and everything would be the same, but it's *not*! I'm not home, my mom is dead—he killed her." He sat down on the floor and the sobs turned to wails.

Finally, a fact to work with! Not a good fact, but still something substantial. Now she had a direction. She crouched beside him and put her arm around his shoulders, touched by his slightness. "Where is this man who killed your mother?"

"I don't know. Maybe he's still at my house, but he doesn't usually stay all night so he might've gone home." Her touch seemed to comfort him because the tears began to subside. He turned his liquid deep brown eyes up to her. "He knows I saw. He'll want to kill me, too."

Lenna felt a sudden and unexpected wave of protectiveness. "Not if I kill him first." She wasn't Justice, but she knew how to mete it out, for what was Justice without Strength?

Elijah blinked hard. "You're going to kill Uncle Bobby?" The idea seemed to astonish him.

"Isn't that why I'm here?" Why else had he called her? She would do what was needed.

He managed to look surprised, terrified, and pleased all at once. "I just wanted a cell phone to call 9–1–1."

That made her pause. What was a cell phone? Who was this 9–1–1? From what she knew of life on Seven, people were not named with numbers. Granted, she had been preoccupied this last little while with her studies, and time was irrelevant on Aeonia, but she normally made an effort to stay abreast of life in all the worlds. What had happened on Seven while she was distracted, that she wouldn't know what Elijah was talking about? But if he had a friend, that was good. She would focus on that. "Who is 9–1–1?"

"The police. They can put Uncle Bobby in jail, when I tell them what he did." The tears threatened to start up again, but he fought them back to ask, "Do you have a cell phone?"

The cell phone again. Whatever it was, she didn't have one, because she had come into this world empty-handed. "No, I have no cell phone."

The negative answer was too much for the child, because he dissolved into sobs again, crying until he was almost choking, his almost unintelligible cries of "Mom!" telling Lenna he grieved for his mother. Without warning Elijah threw himself at her; driven by instinct, she stretched out her arms and caught him. Her action was as much pragmatic as it was sympathetic; it was either catch him, or allow him to knock her to the floor. She went to her knees and tightly wrapped her arms around him, cuddling him to her, offering the comfort of her nearness.

He was warm and soft, his bones thin and fragile under her hands. The smallness of him bemused her; the beings of Aeonia had neither childhood nor old age; they simply *were*. The humans of Seven, on the other hand, grew from tiny infants to full adulthood, then began growing smaller again as they aged. From afar, whenever she turned her curiosity to the other worlds of other planes, she had been interested in the tiny infants, who seemed so pliable and incomplete yet adorable. Elijah wasn't *that* tiny; he seemed to be fully formed, though not yet at his full size. He would be helpless against an adult, she thought, and felt anger grow that someone would hurt this little person.

His tears damped the sleeve and shoulder of her dress, and she patted his back, as she had often observed Seven females doing through the ages. "I will find your 9–1–1," she said, doing her best to comfort the child. "I will see that Uncle Bobby is, as you have requested, in jail." And if that was not possible, she'd kill the murderer herself. "When that is done, you must send me home."

Elijah pulled away, a puzzled look on his little face. He hunched his shoulders up around his ears and asked, "How do I do that?"

He didn't know? Oh, dear. "The same way you called me here, I imagine." Surely he remembered; it hadn't been that long ago, she didn't think, though as an Aeonian she experienced time as a theory rather than something that had an effect on her.

He hunched his shoulders again. "I don't know how I did that. You just appeared. In the closet. Dressed in your nightgown."

Lenna went still as she absorbed an unwelcome truth. This situation might be more serious than she'd first imagined. Elijah was the cause of her appearance here, but he had no idea how to return her where she belonged.

It wasn't just that she wanted to go home; it wasn't that she didn't fit in here—at all—an immortal being who had no idea how to navigate a world as tumultuous as Seven.

Five days.

If she wasn't home in five days, Aeonia would crumble.

Aeonia and all the Major Arcana—including Strength—would cease to exist, and there would be no structure in the universe.

Lenna spent some time studying the clock—or rather, clocks. This kitchen had several, and it was the oddest thing, but they each showed a different time. That small detail was irritating, simply because it displayed a lack of order in this household. For the concept of time to be efficient, it had to be regulated and be the same in each designated area. In this one kitchen, however, time varied from one appliance to the other. These were unlike the timepieces she recalled from her earlier studies of Seven, but surely they could be properly set just as the older clocks and watches could be.

Elijah had patiently answered her questions about each appliance that displayed time—the stove, the coffeemaker, the microwave, the wall clock that had numbers in a circle, which made her wonder if time perhaps ran in a circle instead of linearly, as she had assumed. At least he had stopped crying, and she was glad for that.

Now he sat at the counter eating a meal of what he called "cereal," which consisted of flat pellets in colors that did not exist in nature, as well as a "juice box," the contents of which he sucked up through a narrow tube. She thought that was interesting, so he'd given her one, too, and she sucked the too-sweet beverage while she thought about the disturbing inconsistencies of time.

For instance: time on Aeonia was not the same as time here, but because she paid no attention to it she wasn't certain exactly how it differed. She knew she had five days to return, and by all logic they had to be Seven days. She had studied this world in the past. Even though she was not current in her knowledge, the length of a day would not have changed. Twenty-four of their hours constituted a day. Sunrise to sunset, and then a few hours of darkness before the sun rose again.

Abruptly she noticed that Elijah had stopped eating and was simply sitting there, his head down. His withdrawn state worried her, though she knew she shouldn't be worried about someone who wasn't of her world. That was not how things were ordered. She embodied Strength, which existed for other beings to call on in time of need, to endure, to fight, to support. Why hadn't he called in the Empress? She had strong maternal instincts and would have known what to do to soothe the child.

For whatever reason, he had called forth Lenna. She wasn't particularly maternal, though she was sympathetic. If someone needed willpower, *that* she could offer. She did possess physical strength, as well, but it was mental strength that was her hallmark.

She sighed, and the mental strength that was at the core of her makeup brought her to acceptance—and determination. The Empress might've been best for caring for Elijah, but it was Lenna who would do what he required and see this Uncle Bobby to the authorities—or dead.

She turned that determination to practical matters. Before they left the house, Elijah needed to be functioning at full capacity, and she needed to fit into this world so as not to draw unnecessary attention to herself.

"We must get dressed," she said, pulling him out of his sad thoughts. "Come with me to the upper chambers."

He blinked. "Huh?"

She pointed upward. "Clothing. It is required."

It would also be easy. There was an abundance of it in the dressing room through which she had entered this world. The knowledge she needed would not be as easy. To function here, she had to know how things— all of them—worked. It wasn't just clocks that differed from coffeemaker to microwave; it was understanding the function and operation of each. A coffeemaker made coffee, obviously, but she didn't know how to operate it. A microwave . . . that would be tiny waves, yes? But of what possible use could tiny waves be? And those were just examples. There were many things in this world that hadn't been here the last time she'd paid attention to it.

She loved studying, she loved learning new things, but she liked to do it at her own pace. She couldn't afford leisure in this instance. She needed knowledge. If there were grown humans here she had only to lay her hand upon one and absorb all she needed to know, but there was only her and Elijah. He was too young; he would not suffice.

As she made her way up the stairs, with him close behind her, Lenna constructed a plan. She wanted to see the scene of the murder for herself. Elijah seemed certain that his mother was dead, but perhaps she was merely wounded and had recovered, or would recover with the proper treatment. That was unlikely, but not impossible. When she was convinced that a crime had taken place, she would seek out the authorities—Elijah's 9–1–1—and hand the child and the problem over to them. She had her own problems to solve.

How was she to return home?

It would be easiest if Elijah could return her as he had called her in, but he seemed to have no idea how that might be accomplished. It would be nice to think she might be able to slip back into Aeonia without anyone noticing she'd been gone, but given the importance of her presence there, that was unlikely.

If Elijah couldn't send her back, a Hunter would be sent to collect her. She didn't look forward to that—Hunters had a certain reputation, a ruthlessness that allowed them to operate in all the worlds on all the planes, to keep order as directed. Perhaps one had already been sent, or was on the way. Having never been collected before, she had no certain idea exactly how the Hunters operated. She did hope to finish the job she'd been called here to do, before that happened.

Any Hunter would surely accede to her request if she asked for a bit more time. On occasion the Hunters were hired by the residents of Aeonia to do what they could not: travel. They were not subservient; it was not so simple as that. But they were . . . rarely called upon but valued employees with special skills. It came down to a simple question: Did a Hunter's standing orders supersede her wishes?

She had to assume they did. Therefore, she had to be prepared to either evade the Hunter, or resist. She was not without power, and she would use it if necessary.

But until she knew exactly what she faced, she would do well to concentrate on the present. In the bedchamber, Elijah turned on a bright overhead light. Lenna, who had marched through this room a bit earlier with her eyes on the child, this time studied her surroundings more closely.

While she was not familiar with the culture of the current time, she had studied Seven's history, most particularly its occult history. The residents of this world had always searched for knowledge, for magic, for proof that there was more than met the eye—and for a way to manipulate that more. Evidence of that search was, surprisingly, strongly present in this otherwise ordinary room.

She recognized things, powerful things. A pair of carved animals from the continent of Africa had once belonged to a powerful wizard who swore that he could make them come to life. He had done so, on more than one occasion. Lenna walked to a dresser to more closely study a necklace that contained a stone from a mine in what had once been the Persian Empire. The stones from that mine had magical qualities, in the right hands. She scanned the room. There were other old objects here, some of them imbued with magic, others simply old, but age carried its own power.

It could not be coincidence that these things were in one place.

"Elijah, how well do you know the people who sleep in this room?"

"Zack's mom and dad?" He shrugged his shoulders. "They're nice, I guess. Zack's mom always buys pizza when I spend the night. I like pizza."

"Do either of them dabble in the occult?"

Elijah stared up at her, red-eyed from crying, looking even younger than he had when she'd first arrived. "Huh?"

That word again. Already she knew it signified a lack of understanding; perhaps it was best, with a child, to ask as simply as possible. "Is either of them a magician, or perhaps a witch?"

Those dark eyes widened in shock. "Huh? Zack's mom isn't a witch. She cooks and everything. She's nice."

"What about his father?"

He scratched the side of his nose. "Zack's dad is gone a lot. Zack said he has a job that makes him travel. He brought me back some chocolate last time he went to Ireland. It was awesome. You want me to see if I can find some still here?"

"No, that will be fine. Where does Zack's dad go?"

"All over," he said promptly, unhelpfully. "Zack's mom gets mad, sometimes, because she says she doesn't have room for all the junk he brings home from his trips, but he keeps bringing stuff home, anyway."

Ah. That explained that, then. Was it merely an accident that this man returned from his journeys with powerful objects, or was he collecting them on purpose? At least she now understood how he had come to possess the Alexandria Deck. Well, perhaps not *how*, but definitely *why*. The man was obviously drawn to power, whether or not he understood the nature of the power. After all, if Zack's father had realized what he had in that deck, would he have stored it, open and unguarded, on the floor of a closet? Lenna would think not, but humans were—and had always been—strange and unpredictable.

Lenna walked toward the closet, but a bereft sound from behind her stopped her in her tracks. The child was crying again. Her heart squeezed; he had lost his mother, and he was frightened and alone. Did he have other relatives? A father, or perhaps grandparents? There was only one way to find out.

She turned to face the boy. "Elijah, where is your father?"

He shrugged his shoulders. "I don't have one."

Now was not the time to point out that every human had a father. She understood that Elijah's sire was not a part of his life. It didn't matter if the man was dead or simply elsewhere, not for the purpose of this conversation. "What of your grandparents?"

The child did not react well to that question. There were more tears, and a barely audible, "I don't have any. I just had Mom, and now she's gone and I don't have anybody."

Lenna knelt down so she was face-to-face with Elijah. Her heart broke for him. No child should be alone. Gently she cupped his face.

"You must be strong now," she said.

He sniffled. "But Mom . . ."

"I know. Loss hurts, whenever it strikes. No one is immune from it, or from the hurt." She paused, wondering if a child would care about that. Probably not. Abandoning that avenue, she sought to distract him. "Where I come from, we have soldiers who are called Hunters. They are the fiercest of the fierce. They deliver justice to those who have committed a wrong." And sometimes to those who had made the mistake of crossing a being more powerful than they, but that was not necessary information for the child, nor was it all that the Hunters were or did. For Elijah, she would focus on the positive. "Today you and I will be Hunters."

Elijah's chin came up slightly. His eyes suggested that he was, at least, interested in this new concept.

"Hunters are strong and dedicated," Lenna continued. "They commit themselves to the job at hand. You and I will be no less committed. We will deliver justice for your mother. We will avenge her."

"We'll be . . . Avengers?"

Ah, that word had meant something to him. "Yes, that is what I said. We will be avengers."

The child's eyes glowed with tears again, and Lenna added, "Hunters do not cry. It interferes with their ability to do the job well."

Elijah's lip trembled momentarily, then it stopped, and he squared his little shoulders. "I want to be a Hunter."

"And so you shall."

Lenna had allowed Elijah to help choose an outfit for her to wear. The activity seemed to calm him, and truth be told she had no idea which of the myriad outfits—which included everything from two long flowing gowns to soft plaid shirts with frayed hems and holes in the pockets—would be appropriate for her short time in Seven. It was winter here, and so the clothes they decided upon were warm. There were pants he called blue jeans, and a long-sleeved shirt with an emblem of a weapon on the front, and the word Braves. She thought that an appropriate choice. There was also a warm coat, though as Lenna was accustomed to the cold she might not need it.

Elijah didn't want to be alone, so he simply turned his back while she changed.

Dressed in clothes that were not nearly as comfortable as her own, Lenna chose as her shoes fur-lined boots that were only a bit too large.

There was an extensive collection of bags in the closet. The one Lenna picked out was made of a soft red fabric, and had a long strap. A bag of some sort was a necessity. She would eventually have a weapon to conceal, and the long strap could be used to bind or strangle. These ideas she kept to herself. She also folded her dress as tightly as she could and put it in the bottom of the bag. She didn't want to leave it behind, not only because the fabric could prove useful, but because Nilean silkine didn't exist in this world and leaving it behind could create a dangerous anomaly. She didn't know for certain, so better to be too cautious than too reckless. She also removed her rings and bracelet and dropped them in the bag. They were not of this world, and it was always possible that someone would notice.

After she was dressed she paused, staring at the tarot cards scattered across the closet floor. Should she leave the deck here? It was just large enough to be troublesome, especially if she returned the cards to the box that had housed them. But the cards were incredibly powerful, too powerful to simply leave. She tried to remember everything she'd read about the Alexandria Deck, but the deck had been thought destroyed, legend rather than fact, so she hadn't completely exercised her superb memory. She did know that the deck had to be complete for its powers to work.

If she left the deck here and someone else found it, seized it, Elijah definitely wouldn't be able to find a way to get her home. Neither would whatever Hunter had been—or would soon be—sent to collect her. On the other hand, she didn't want to take the complete deck with her. Some instinct warned her that would be too dangerous, that it would draw to her those who sought power.

Rendering the deck useless was the best she could do. Swiftly she leaned down and plucked her card from the closet floor, and tucked it in a side pocket of the bag. It was just a single card, but it made the bag seem suddenly heavy.

And, as a safeguard, not enough. Without looking she grabbed another card and stowed it in a different compartment of the bag. She would hide it in a safe place, a place only she knew. Then she gathered the remaining scattered cards and neatly placed them in their box, and restored the box to what she thought must be its accustomed place. She hoped no one noticed the closet had been disturbed, or checked that the deck was complete.

Elijah still didn't want to be alone so she followed him to his friend Zack's room, where he put on some blue jeans and a shirt that sported yet another emblem, this one a hawk. He sat on the floor to pull some socks on his bare feet, then put on a pair of Zack's shoes, which were too big and slipped up and down when he walked. There was no help for it; they weren't likely to find any smaller shoes. She pulled a coat out of Zack's closet and bundled Elijah into it.

"When we study the scene of—" she stopped before she said *your mother's murder* and instead finished with "—your home, we will collect your own shoes."

"I don't want to go in there, not ever again," he said, sounding small and weak. Of course he did, because he was both. He was a child.

"Be a Hunter," she whispered.

Elijah shook his head.

The poor child. Lenna held out a small hope that Elijah was wrong and his mother wasn't dead. She could lay her hands on him and see what he had seen, but as she understood it, children were different. Their brains were more fragile. If she learned directly from an adult human by the laying on of hands, the knowledge was shared, not stolen. No damage would be done. She couldn't be sure the same was true of a child, so she wouldn't risk him; instead, she would go to see for herself.

"I will collect your shoes for you," Lenna said, standing and slipping the strap of her bag over her shoulder.

"Okay."

Lenna was surprised when Elijah took her hand and held on. He seemed to take comfort from the connection, and his hand was so small and helpless, the child himself so trusting. If his mother was dead, it was a catastrophe that could destroy his life. She could encourage him to be strong, to pretend he was a Hunter, but reality was much different.

His little hand squeezed hers, and in that moment Lenna was more determined than ever to see that justice was dealt to Uncle Bobby.

When they reached the kitchen, Elijah released her hand and ran to the corner of the room, where he opened a drawer and reached inside. That little hand came out clutching a small wad of green paper.

"Zack's mom's pizza money," he said as he stuffed the paper into his pocket. "We might need it."

They walked along the sidewalk, making the first footprints in the pristine snow. Elijah seemed both amazed and delighted by the snow, in those moments when he wasn't thinking about his mother. He stomped up and down, and once he bent down to scoop up a handful and shape it into a rough ball, which he then threw at a bush. The day was young, so early that no one else was out and about, and the silence had a hushed, waiting quality to it.

The houses were too close together, to Lenna's way of thinking. She was accustomed to more space. In Aeonia each Major Arcana had what these humans would consider their own kingdom, with castles, if that was what they chose, or cabins, if that was their choice, or—like her—a fine house four or five times as large as any of these homes. She'd never wanted a castle or a cabin. Her home fell somewhere in between. Her lands, though, were extensive.

Elijah grabbed her hand again, his little fingers cold from the snow. She continued to survey her surroundings, acquainting herself with his world.

The houses themselves weren't impressive, at least not to her, but many of them sported colorful lights as decoration. She did like those.

"The lights on that house are pretty," she said, lifting the hand Elijah held and pointing.

"They're Christmas lights," the boy said.

Her knowledge of modern Seven was limited, but she did know Christmas.

"I've never seen a white tattoo before," he said, looking cautiously from one house to another. "Why do you have a sideways eight on your back?"

She lifted her brows. "You saw my sign?" She had of necessity bared her body when she changed, but the child was supposed to have kept his back turned to her.

"Sorry. I just peeked a little!"

She wasn't an exhibitionist; the thought of a child seeing her bare made her uneasy, but she would not blush. The sign was one of power, and certainly nothing to be ashamed of.

"It is not a sideways eight—it's an infinity symbol."

"What does that mean?"

"Infinity means forever. Without end." Like her life, though the child wouldn't grasp that concept at all.

His own house, the one he led her to, didn't have any Christmas lights. The front door was locked, the house quiet. A chill walked up Lenna's spine. If Elijah's mother lived, she was badly wounded. The house would be in chaos if the mother was searching for her child, but there was only an eerie silence. They walked through the snow, the going harder now that they'd left the street, and around the house to the back door, which was also locked. Lenna lifted her foot to kick it in, but Elijah said, "Wait!" His expression was alarmed.

"Wait for what?"

"I'll get the key." He released her hand and dug around in the snow, making her wonder if there was a hidden tunnel to the house, which in turn made her wonder what manner of neighborhood this was. But the result was nothing so exotic; after a moment, Elijah stood with a rock in his hand.

"It's a hidden key," he solemnly explained. "Look." He turned the rock over and slid open a compartment in the bottom of it, revealing a key. Elijah looked up at her. "In case I get home from school and Mom's not here."

He handed her the key. "My shoes are in my room. It's upstairs. I want my new Nike shoes, the ones I got for Christmas. They're black." Then he retreated back against the wall and shrank in on himself, as if he could hold the world at bay.

Lenna bent down and hugged him, then unlocked the door and stepped inside.

And smelled death.

Chapter 4

When Caine teleported into the castle, even though the Emperor was there waiting for him he took a moment to look around. He was admittedly curious, having never been in the Emperor's castle before. There was seldom need for a Hunter here. The Arcana stayed where they were, and it wasn't as if a coup could be staged in Aeonia. Changes in this world were rare, so rare there had been none at all for more than two thousand years. When the beings had been able to leave their posts there had been more upheaval, but over the millennia they had lost the ability to travel across all the planes. Truth be told, only Hunters were able to go to *all* the planes. That was the reason for their creation. Some beings on other worlds could go to some planes, but not all. Only those who hunted them had been granted that ability.

He stood with his booted feet apart, his muscled body perfectly balanced like the Hunter he was, ready to attack or be attacked at all times—even here. His coal-dark eyes took in his luxurious surroundings, not in envy, but to assess such things as cover, possible weapons, placement of exits. He didn't *expect* anything to happen in the Emperor's castle, but he took nothing for granted.

He was fully armed, a sword at his back, fighting and throwing knives in his belt and tucked into his boots, a liquid laser blaster slung over one shoulder, and a sawed-off shotgun in a holster strapped to his right thigh. He never knew where he would be sent, so he tried to always have at least one weapon that would work in any world, under any circumstances.

The Emperor had been sitting on an ornate, richly upholstered couch with ram heads carved into the scarlet wood of the arms; at Caine's sudden appearance in the chamber he rose to his feet, not in the least alarmed. After all, when Hunters were summoned they didn't start out on horseback, and ride up to the castle gates. Hunters teleported anywhere they wanted; that was one of the several unique characteristics that made them Hunters. He waited in silence as Caine's watchful gaze took in the unfamiliar surroundings.

The Emperor's name was Jerrick; as befitted his card he was wise, protective, steady, authoritative, and was capable of doing whatever had to be done. No one looking at him would ever think him weak, in any way. His long hair and beard were dark, but the wealth of experience in his face and gaze meant no one would ever think of him as *young*, not that "age" applied to the Arcana. They hadn't developed, they simply *were*. All of the Major Arcana had power, but under his strong guidance all of those egos and all that power stayed mostly stable.

Mostly.

If there were no exceptions, Caine wouldn't be here right now.

After allowing that moment of assessment, the Emperor inclined his head in a brief nod. "Hunter," he said calmly. "Thank you for coming."

"I answer your summons." There was no subservience in Caine's demeanor; Hunters were hired, not commanded. No other beings in the created universe could do what the Hunters did; if they were arrogant, and admittedly they were, it was an earned arrogance. No other beings with physical bodies were completely unlimited in their ability to travel between worlds and planes. Their cost was high, but their results were priceless.

The Emperor's gaze was troubled. "Strength has disappeared," he said.

Caine was taken aback. The Arcane were confined to Aeonia, and had been for thousands of years. But if the Emperor said that Strength had disappeared, he didn't mean that she'd gone visiting without leaving a note for her attendants. The Arcane were linked; they sensed each other, worked together, their very existence dependent on the balance provided by all of them. "How is that possible?"

"We don't know. I have my suspicions, but they are suspicions only, with no facts as yet to support them."

"If you have the thought, it's more than suspicion."

Jerrick inclined his dark head. "The Alexandria Deck must have been found. I can think of no other explanation."

The Alexandria Deck, reputed to hold greater power than any other tarot deck ever created, had vanished in the great fire that destroyed the Alexandria Library and was presumed destroyed. It hadn't been seen in more than two thousand years, nor had there been even a wisp of its power revealed anywhere in the universe.

But it had held the power that allowed the Major Arcana beings to travel to other planes and worlds, much as the Hunters could. If Strength was gone from Aeonia, then the Alexandria Deck must somehow be involved. And if the Alexandria Deck was involved, that meant Strength was on Seven, the planet the humans had named Earth, and where the Alexandria Deck had been created by a great wizard who had taken the secrets of its creation to the grave with him.

Slowly Caine smiled; in the course of his career—and also for entertainment purposes—he'd been to Seven many times. It was one of his favorite places, if only for the sheer lunacy of the populace. All the vices and virtues of the universe, stirred together in a forever shifting mixture, made for some good times. This wouldn't be a pleasure trip, though; retrieving a Major Arcana was a serious, potentially difficult job. For one thing, he didn't know if Strength had bolted or if her disappearance was an accident. When humans were involved, anything was possible.

With that in mind, he asked, "Were there witnesses to her disappearance?"

"No. She was alone in her library, studying. She has always been greatly interested in the histories of other worlds, their wars and politics. When she left—or was taken—we all of course felt the disruption. I sent her attendants to investigate, and they report her cup of tea had been spilled, the cup lying on the floor, her books scattered. All indications are her departure is not something she anticipated."

So, she had been taken, either by accident or by purpose. That truly made no difference to Caine's mission; he had to retrieve her. The existence of the Major Arcana depended on *all* of them being in place, representing the qualities that defined them. They were like critical organs in a body; remove any one of them, and they all ceased to exist.

There was some leeway; he had five days to fetch her back before everything collapsed. Given that time didn't really exist on Aeonia, the length of a "day" depended on the world to which the missing Arcana had gone. In Strength's case, that was Seven; it was a fairly small world, so their days were correspondingly short.

"Show me her image, please," he said, and the Emperor waved his hand. The three dimensional image of a woman formed in the air. Dispassionately Caine studied her, the male in him noting and appreciating the female curves and beauty, while the Hunter in him committed her features to memory. She would be difficult to miss, with that wealth of pale blond hair and skin with a pearly glow. Her eyes were a clear blue, her gaze direct. She was Strength, a being of willpower and endurance, constancy and determination. For the first time in a long while, his interest was piqued in a way he didn't welcome.

"You will need the deck in order to transport her," Jerrick said.

"Of course."

The Emperor's expression was one of determination. Caine saw no worry, no concern for the outcome. "When Lenna has been returned to her place, you will deliver the Alexandria Deck to me."

For destruction or safekeeping? It didn't matter.

Caine gave a curt nod of assent.

"Bring them back," the Emperor said softly.

"I will."

Veton, the Tower, hadn't been this excited in a very long time. He was positively giddy with joy.

For far too many years he'd been trapped in Aeonia, unable to travel to other worlds. His influence was felt in all realms, of course, but that wasn't enough to satisfy him. He got to *cause* chaos from a maddening distance, but he didn't get to experience what he'd wrought. After a while, even destruction became boring.

They were all trapped here, of course, but he seemed to be the only one who cared. The rest of his card mates were perfectly content, living here where all their desires and needs were met. It was a fine enough place, if you didn't mind being bored. He minded.

What did it matter that there were servants to see to

every need, vast libraries where all the knowledge of all the realms had been collected, every entertainment one might wish for? If he knew nothing else that might have been enough, but if they so desired they could see into all the other worlds anytime. All he had to do was close his eyes and wish to see. He did so often, more often than any of the others, and he longed to be there to *see* those civilizations collapse, to experience the small triumph of a single life in total upheaval. It was all so entertaining.

If not for the occasional orgy, he didn't know what he would've done with himself.

He was the Tower. He was chaos. Most thought that was a bad thing, but Veton knew better. Chaos was necessary. It was a part of life, as much as love, death, and happiness. Without chaos, one would not appreciate the more pleasant things in life. If life were pleasant from birth to death, how boring would that be? No one appreciated happiness unless it was occasionally disrupted.

From the rubble left by his influence, new and better things could and would rise.

He'd been trapped here, as they all had, since the fires of Alexandria. Now, that had been great chaos. The destruction of knowledge, the flames that licked from and consumed fragile books . . . beautiful. He hadn't known the Alexandria Deck was in the library, but even if he had, he didn't know that he'd have acted differently. Yes, the chaos had affected *him* also, but chaos was lovely in its own right.

His work had not been appreciated. Some of his card mates had been downright hostile. He still felt sulky whenever he remembered their reaction; what had they *thought* he'd do? Cause a bit of rain?

Silly beings.

They had all been so annoyed because the fire had supposedly destroyed the Alexandria Deck, the means with which they could take short vacations and travel between the worlds. Without the deck, they were all confined to Aeonia. How ironic that they had quickly seemed to adjust and become content with their existence here, while *he*, the one who had wrought the fire and destruction that cost them the use of the deck, was the one who felt most restless and confined. If that wasn't chaos, he didn't know what was.

Then Lenna had disappeared, and the realization of what must have happened had almost sent him to his knees, so great had been his joy. The deck still existed! Someone had found it, and knew how to use it! Now all he had to do was get it under his control, so those silly humans couldn't lose track of it again.

While the Emperor was making certain of the

circumstances of Lenna's disappearance, Veton acted. He *knew* what had happened; why worry about the how of it?

He could barely wait to visit Seven again. Some worlds weren't worth the effort, but Seven—Seven was special. It teemed with humans who were influenced by the Major Arcana each and every day. The One had created the Arcana to embody all the vices and virtues that resulted from the smallest decision; some of the humans believed the cards could be used to foretell the future, but what did humans know? They were wrong about so many things; that was what made them so deliciously unpredictable. Whether or not they believed didn't matter, because they were all touched by the power the cards represented. In love, in fortune, in health, the influence of the vices and virtues held in the Major Arcana existed in all the realms.

Like a child, Veton whirled in happiness, his long white hair flying around him. Then he sobered and quickly summoned three Hunters. While Jerrick was still "investigating," Veton was acting. How delicious was it that he was one step—perhaps even two—ahead of the Emperor?

The Hunters appeared almost immediately. Two of them, Stroud and Nevan, had worked for him before. The female, Esma, was new to him. Interested, Veton surveyed her. Stroud and Nevan were very alike, both about six foot two, muscled, brown hair cut very short. Esma was muscular, too, for a woman, but she had not lost her femininity in her pursuit of physical strength—far from it. He liked how she wore her long dark hair in a tidy bun. Her equally dark eyes were fierce and carried in them a hunger he found attractive. She didn't look away, but boldly met his gaze. Interesting. He knew the picture he presented, a man so handsome it bordered on eerie, with long white hair and pale blue eyes; he carried the image even further by normally dressing all in white, or silver. In some moods he went with all black, but that was almost like a warning so he wore the black only when he was happy. Why be predictable?

How he had envied the Hunters all these millennia; they could travel through the realms at will, experience things he could only observe.

Soon he would once again be able to do the same.

"The Alexandria Deck," Veton said, his voice smooth. "It has been uncovered in Seven, and I want it."

Stroud asked, "How are we to locate it?"

"Strength has been pulled from this plane to that of Seven. Only the deck could have accomplished that. Find Strength, and you find the deck." He looked at each of them in turn. He had been told his icy blue eyes were disturbing to some. How could anything about him be disturbing? He didn't understand it.

"Do you expect her to hand it over without a fuss?" Esma asked, her tone less than deferential.

Oooh, how exciting: insolence! It had been so long since he'd experienced anything except the obedience of his attendants.

"I don't know if she somehow discovered the deck and engineered her travel, or if she was taken unawares," he replied. "It doesn't matter. Retrieve the deck." He thought, intrigued, that Lenna might not be inclined to hand over to him the power to control travel between the worlds. What if she fought? She was Strength; taking the easy path wasn't part of her being. If she knew he'd sent the Hunters for the Alexandria Deck, would she fight? Yes, she definitely would.

With relish, he voiced the unthinkable. "Kill her, if there is no other way."

Nevan gasped. Esma's eyes widened. Only Stroud seemed unaffected, but then Stroud was the most experienced at working with Veton, and knew how his mind worked.

"I know it is unheard of for a Hunter to assassinate one of the Major Arcana," Veton said with a dismissive wave of his hand. "To be honest, I don't know what will happen if one of the Arcane dies. I don't know if we *can* die." Talk about magnificent chaos! "It has never happened, not in all the years of our existence, but that doesn't mean it is impossible."

"You are all as you have been since creation," Esma said. She was not so insolent now, he noticed. Finally, there was a touch of respect in her voice.

"We are, but everything changes. Perhaps when Strength is killed, *if* she is killed, another will take her place." He looked pointedly at Esma. "The One might replace her with a wave of His hand, but I suppose it is possible someone from another world might be assigned to take her place. There must always be Strength. As far as I know, Strength doesn't necessarily have to be Lenna." He looked deep into Esma's eyes as he spoke, knowing the inference she would draw. The Hunter would never suffice for the hallowed position, but now was not the time to tell her so. If she thought she might be elevated, she'd fight all the harder.

Truth be told, if Lenna had voluntarily left Aeonia and didn't want to return, that brought up another problem entirely. If it was indeed possible that she could be killed, a replacement would likely be provided, in one way or another. That was logical, to his way of thinking. If she didn't return to her proper place, Aeonia and all the Major Arcana would cease to exist; that little wrinkle had been thrown in to keep them under control. The *only* solution then might be to attempt to kill Lenna so perhaps another could take her place.

Only the One knew for certain if it was possible.

He lightly clapped his hands to get their attention. There were specifics, important details his Hunters had to know before they left. "Bring me the entire deck. Every card, each one more beautiful than the last." Veton closed his eyes and reached deep, fleetingly, into the world he could not yet touch. Seeing the world in a general way was easy; finding one particular entity in that teeming mass was more of a challenge. Because he knew Lenna he was able to briefly see her, and was surprised by her companion. A child.

And then she was gone.

The deck had to be where Lenna was, because it had brought her over. He wanted his Hunters to find her before she had a chance to hide the cards. He would not allow this opportunity to slip by.

Stroud was the strongest of the trio of hunters, so Veton looked to him. "The Emperor will soon send a Hunter to collect Lenna. She can't be gone from Aeonia long. She must return or be replaced within five days." Or else this world would crumble. Much as he enjoyed destruction, he didn't care to see it here, outside and even within his own home. Would Lenna's death be the same? If she was killed by his Hunters would Aeonia be no more, as it would be if she simply did not return? Possible, but who was to know? Even when his own existence was at risk, Veton loved uncertainty.

He was looking at Stroud but he asked them all, "If this Hunter interferes with your mission to recover the cards, do you have an aversion to killing one of your own?"

None of them did. He was always careful to choose Hunters who were not burdened with scruples. Hunters were as long-lived as the Major Arcana, though their job added a level of danger that had made it evident that while they were virtually immortal, immune to normal death, they were not invincible. They were tough to kill, but they could, and did, die.

With relish, he said, "I've heard the Emperor requested Caine." Gleefully he watched their expressions tighten. For three Hunters to handle one was nothing unexpected; *Caine*, however, was a different proposition. Even for Hunters, he was known for both his ferocity and his tenacity. Had they really thought the Emperor would send an ordinary Hunter— assuming any Hunter was ordinary—on so important a mission?

It was Esma who lifted her chin and asked, "What if he reaches Strength before we do?"

Veton smiled, intrigued by her valor. "I have the power to cause a delay. You will reach her before he does. Go, go now."

They each nodded in agreement, then disappeared without ceremony. Without effort, damn them. Veton set aside his flare of resentment. He wouldn't be imprisoned here much longer. It had begun.

To give his Hunters even more time before Jerrick's Hunter could begin looking for Lenna, he concentrated hard; interfering with time was the most demanding thing he could do, something that required a lot of energy for not much result. Teleporting was almost instantaneous, with *almost* being the important word. There was a time lapse, however small, between the beginning of teleport and the end; a journey had to have a beginning and an end. That small lapse gave him an opening. Creating a wrinkle that would cause the Emperor's Hunter an even greater delay was a matter of agonizing precision, one that was at the very limit of his power. When it was done he collapsed on the luxurious golden rug, breathing hard and barely conscious. Then he began to giggle.

Soon, he would be able to personally witness the chaos he created. It was long past time for the people of Seven to remember what an apocalypse felt like; he'd have to think up something special for them.

"**I don't** want to go in," Elijah whispered. He remained behind Lenna as she stood in the open door surveying the kitchen, and she understood. He'd been traumatized here. He had seen things no child should see.

But she was barely inside before he slipped in, closing the door behind him. He stood very close, too close, and while she needed to continue on she did not immediately move away.

She turned and looked down at him, and he ducked his head. "It's too cold to wait outside," he said in a small voice.

It wasn't the weather that had made him come inside, she knew, but the fear of being alone. She put her hand on his shoulder, giving it a gentle squeeze. She had no experience with young beings, but the child elicited a strong sense of protection in her. He was so small and helpless, so sad, that he touched her heart.

She hated to distress him, but she had to ask: "Where did you last see your mother?"

His little face tightened, and silently he pointed.

"Wait for me here," she said, knowing the instruction was unnecessary. The child had no desire to see what lay beyond this room.

She looked around, orienting herself. This house was much like the other, she thought; it was small by her standards, but more than sufficient for two humans. Leaving Elijah in the kitchen, she moved into a hallway. Pictures hung on the wall, pictures of Elijah—as he was now and as he had been in years past—with a young woman who faintly resembled him. She didn't have Elijah's expressive and impossibly deep eyes, but there was a sameness to their mouths and chins.

The pictures depicted a normal, ordinary woman, but Elijah loved her, and surely she had loved him. That alone was enough to make her special.

She stood quietly for a moment, reading the energies of the house. Though Elijah's pointing finger could have sent her anywhere in the house, she was not drawn up the stairs. Her senses told her where the violence had taken place; she walked toward the front door and turned right, into a room furnished with a sofa and chairs, a large screen, lamps, and tables. The last time she had observed life on Seven, this would have been called a parlor.

The lights on a decorated tree shone, eye-catching and pretty in an otherwise unremarkable room.

There was no sign that a physical struggle had taken place here. No body lay on the rug; there was nothing out of place, at least not to an eye that had never seen this room before. Still, she felt a disturbing maelstrom of anger, and struggle, and death.

Too clearly, Lenna could read the energies. In her final moments, Elijah's mother had fought with all her might. She had not wanted to die. At the very end her only thought had been for her son, for the child she loved. It had always been just the two of them against the world. She'd made mistakes, many mistakes, but she loved her child. She worked hard to make sure he had a good life.

She had possessed a will that even Lenna could admire.

And now she was dead, and Elijah was alone.

Lenna walked the room, studying it, touching the furnishings as she passed them. This room had known love and passion and laughter. It had also known fear, and pain, and death.

But there was no body, nothing to take to the authorities. All she had was the word of a child. She supposed it was only logical that Uncle Bobby would take steps to conceal his crime, but that left her with an even bigger dilemma: If she turned him over, what would they do with Elijah?

It didn't matter. She had to find a way home, that should be her only concern—*should* be, had been, until Elijah had touched her heart.

Lenna stopped in the middle of the room, thinking hard.

Why was she so intent on getting home as soon as possible? Returning was necessary, but returning *now* wasn't. Her time was limited but she had enough, surely, to do what she could for the child. She was also honest enough with herself to admit that she was curious about Seven; it had changed greatly since the last time she'd bothered to "see" it. Technology, clothing, speech—nothing was as it had been. Even more, for more than two thousand years the Major Arcana had been isolated in Aeonia. To be a part of another world, even for a few days, would be an adventure. She could learn so much, and knowledge was always useful.

Why not embrace the adventure?

And in the meantime, she'd find justice for Elijah—as well as a new home.

Elijah waited by the door, but when he didn't hear Lenna say anything his attention wandered, and after a few minutes he realized he was hungry. He hesitated, then went to the small pantry. Mom never let him have sweets for breakfast, but he was hungry, and he knew she had a box of cookies hidden behind the oatmeal. He opened the pantry door, reached up as high as he possibly could, and pushed the box of oatmeal aside. He grabbed the edge of the box of cookies with his fingertips and pulled it forward, then slipped it beyond the edge and caught the box as it fell.

Chocolate chip. His favorite.

Mom's favorite, too. He tried not to think about the last time he'd seen his mom, but it was hard to get that picture out of his head. His lower lip trembled.

When Bosco had been killed, Mom had told him to remember the good times. She said that would ease the pain. It had been hard, but he'd done it. He'd remembered playing with Bosco at the park, and how the dog had loved to lie in Elijah's lap, even though he was really too big to fit. Mom had been right, remembering the good times had helped, though he still wished Bosco hadn't died.

He tried to do the same now with his mom. He didn't want to remember her the way she'd looked when Uncle Bobby had killed her, so instead he remembered how she'd laughed at that last movie they'd seen. Even though it was really a kid movie, she'd laughed a lot. He remembered how she'd hugged him, how she cooked his favorite meal—macaroni and cheese and fish sticks—once a week, even though she didn't like it at all. He didn't think he wanted macaroni and cheese and fish sticks ever again.

He started to cry. Tears stung his eyes and he felt like there was no way he could *not* cry. But then he remembered that he was a Hunter, and Hunters didn't cry. Lenna said so. Hunters were like Avengers. He'd always wanted to be a superhero.

He would be a superhero for Mom.

Lenna looked through every room, downstairs and up, making certain Elijah's mother's body hadn't simply been moved to another room, though why anyone would have done that was completely illogical. She looked because, from what she remembered, that description definitely fit some humans. One could never tell.

Identifying Elijah's room was easy, given all the toys and clutter. She retrieved the shoes he had requested, then paused. The weight of the two cards in her bag was a palpable thing, reminding her of the deck's power. *Better to separate them.* She took out the cards and looked at the other she had picked up; it was the Moon. First she slipped her own card back into the bag, then she tucked the Moon card high on a shelf where it couldn't easily be seen. That done, she returned downstairs. When she entered the kitchen, she blinked. Elijah was eating. Again. He'd eaten at the other house, before they'd left. How could he possibly be hungry?

Then again, he was a small human. Perhaps they needed more food than the fully grown.

"Your shoes," she said, placing them on the floor beside him.

He placed the box he'd been cradling in his arms on the table and sat down in a chair to kick off his friend's ill-fitting shoes. He didn't ask about his mother. He took his time putting on his shoes and tying them, and then he grabbed the box from which he'd been eating and offered it to her.

"Cookie?"

"No."

"They're really good," he said, lifting the box so it was a bit closer to her.

His brown eyes looked hopeful, as if it was somehow important to him that she take the cookie he'd offered. She reached inside the box and took one, examining it with a bit of curiosity. It was brown, with pieces of something darker inside. Tentatively she took a bite, a bit uncertain about eating something brown. There were no drab foods on Aeonia. Hmm, not bad. The texture was crumbly, and the taste very sweet. It wasn't as delicious as the small lemon sweet cakes her cook made for special occasions, but she could see the appeal.

Elijah sighed and put the box on the table. He seemed to have lost his appetite. Finally he looked up at her and asked, "Is she still in there?"

Lenna shook her head. "No."

Elijah's eyes lit up. "Maybe she wasn't really dead! Maybe she's at the hospital!" He slipped off the chair and turned to take the same path Lenna had taken earlier, but she stopped him with a hand on his shoulder.

"I'm sorry, Elijah. You were right. Your mother is gone."

He didn't turn to face her. "Where is she, then?"

"I don't know."

His thin shoulders shook as he began crying again. She wanted to comfort him, but didn't know how. How did one go about soothing a child who had lost his mother? She understood emotion, but after so many years of living distant from the worlds which were like Seven—uncertain, dangerous, and populated with humans who were short-lived—she found she couldn't truly empathize. She had never lost someone she loved, much less a mother. The beings of the Major Arcana had been created, not born. She could, however, see where the mother/child bond would be strong.

As helpless and inexperienced as she felt, she wanted to comfort this child. She wanted to take away the pain, but that was something she could never do. He would carry this pain for the rest of his life, because she couldn't undo the past.

She was saved from uttering words that might or might not help. A man opened the kitchen door and stepped inside without invitation. Lenna was startled, but she wondered if that was a custom here, if the man was a friend or a neighbor. The large man looked at Elijah and then at Lenna.

Abruptly she stood straight and faced him. The same senses that allowed Lenna to feel pain and death in this house whispered to her . . . *Beware.*

Chapter 5

Derek Wilson had one rule: get the job done. He wasn't picky about the jobs he took— understatement—because money was money, but some jobs he should have charged twice his already hefty fee just for the idiot factor. This was one of them. He'd taken care of some problems for State Senator Robert Markham before, but nothing on this level. It wasn't anything he balked at, but he was aware of the high risk level.

The stupid fuck had killed a woman last night. It was bad enough that the asshole couldn't keep his dick in his pants; he had to lose his shit and kill his sidepiece— with her kid in the house. Now the kid was a witness, one that Markham wanted eliminated.

High risk aside, this was also an opportunity. He shouldn't complain. The ordinary jobs Derek took as a legitimate private investigator made him a living, but that was about it. Retirement, or even modest luxuries? Forget about it. On the other hand, cleaning up the messes of the rich and famous so they didn't have to get their own hands dirty? That was pure gold. That was where the high fees came in.

He was fifty-three, looking at retirement in the next few years. He needed every dime he could get. He didn't want to spend his so-called golden years still taking shitty jobs and worrying about maybe having to eat cat food.

Find the kid, Markham said. Did he have a picture of the kid? That was a big no. How old was the kid? School age, Markham said, but little. Seven, eight, nine; how the hell did he know? Color of hair and eyes? Dark hair, yeah, but Markham had blanked on the eyes. State Senator Robert Markham was, without doubt, the least observant client Derek had. All of his attention was focused on himself and his precious career.

Derek needed a picture of the kid, because he sure as hell didn't want to kill the wrong one. That would be all kinds of messy. Markham said there were a bunch of pictures in the house where the woman and kid lived—drop by and get one. Like that was easy, and without risk.

But here he was, parked as discreetly as possible,

because what choice did he have? None. He'd taken the precaution of smearing mud over his license plate in case people were up early instead of sleeping late while they could.

He sat a minute to scope things out, and damn his luck, here came a woman and a kid walking down the street. He scooted down in his seat, so his head was below the headrest, so maybe they wouldn't notice anyone in the car. In his experience, people were generally unobservant, anyway. Derek cautiously watched them, ready to duck completely out of sight if they looked his way. What were they doing out walking this early on such a cold morning? Who were they visiting? Who else was up this early?

To his alarm, they went up to the front door of the house he was watching. What the hell was going on? Was this maybe the kid, Elijah, and someone he'd gone to for help? That didn't make sense. Too many hours had passed for someone to just now be showing up.

The woman and kid didn't ring the doorbell, or knock. The woman tried the knob, but the door was obviously locked. Then the two headed around the house to the back door. He was parked at an angle, so he was able to see the kid bending down and coming up with what was obviously a key, because the woman took it from him.

The likelihood that the kid was Elijah shot way up, though if the kid was Elijah, who was the woman? Not his mother, obviously, because she'd have known her own house was locked, and where the hidden key was, not to mention that she was dead, which was the reason why he was here in the first place. But if the kid had gone for help, why hadn't the woman called the cops? This place should be swarming with them, but instead it was as quiet as a church on a Monday night. Something didn't add up.

But he wasn't being paid to do math; he was being paid to clean up Markham's mess.

After waiting several minutes to see if anything happened, Derek got out of the car, turned up the collar of his overcoat against the icy wind, and walked toward the house. He kept a sharp eye out as he went, but as far as he could tell no one else on the street was stirring yet. That would change soon, and he needed to be gone before then.

The element of surprise was a good thing. He walked up to the kitchen door, opened it, and went in as if he belonged.

The two of them—the woman and the kid—were there in the kitchen. That kind of surprised *him*; he hadn't exactly expected that, but they had to be more surprised and he could use that to his advantage. He had to make sure he had the right kid. He also wanted to make sure this Elijah could actually cause a problem for Markham. Derek loved a big payday, but he had never hurt a child before. He didn't want to do it now, if there was any other choice.

They both turned toward him, expressions a little shocked at his intrusion. The kid had big brown eyes. The woman was a looker, on the smallish side, with long blond hair and big blue eyes that seemed to see right through him.

He shoved away the chill those blue eyes gave him, and pulled the fake badge from his jacket pocket, flashed it at them. "Detective George Benton," he said as he slipped the badge back in his pocket. The kid would be fooled, but it would be best if the woman didn't look too closely. Judging by the set of her mouth and the spark in her eyes she was suspicious enough.

The boy looked up at the woman and whispered, "9–1–1."

The blonde narrowed her eyes at him, not the reaction he'd expected. "You are a police officer?"

Derek nodded. "One of Lawrenceville's finest."

The kid took a deep breath. His eyes went wide and his hands started to kind of flail. "Uncle Bobby killed Mom! I saw him, and then I ran, but I couldn't find a phone and Zack wasn't home, and . . ."

Well, shit. This was Elijah, after all. He was a cute little kid. Too bad. Derek dropped down on his haunches so he was face-to-face with Elijah. "Can you identify this Uncle Bobby fella?"

It was a perfectly reasonable question, but the woman got all spun up about it. She grabbed Elijah's hand and pulled him away, shoving him behind her. Her gaze locked on Derek and her posture changed subtly. Another man might've missed it. Man or woman, that was a ready-to-fight stance. She was balanced, muscles tensed and ready to move. He looked up at her, caught her eye as he slowly stood. Yes, she was ready to fight, but she was also almost a foot shorter than he was and maybe a hundred pounds lighter.

"I'm really sorry . . ." he said in a calm tone as he reached inside his jacket for his shoulder holster and the gun there.

She pushed Elijah toward the door, then exploded upward and kicked. Derek had good reflexes—this was not his first fight, far from it—but she took him by surprise and she was *fast*. Weird fast. Her foot slammed into his midsection and threw him back with more power than he'd have expected from someone who barely topped five-three, if that. He crashed into the edge of the kitchen counter, hard, the force of impact pushing a loud grunt from him. His hip and side set up a howl of protest, one he ignored as he launched himself at her. He had to take her down, and take her down fast.

She yelled at the boy, "Run!" then whirled back to meet Derek's attack. This time when she kicked he was prepared; he grabbed her ankle and jerked upward, intending to dump her on her ass, but she . . . she did a kind of sideways whirl that jerked her ankle free, and she kicked him again—in the balls.

A guttural howl tore from his throat as paralyzing, nauseating agony shot through him. He collapsed on the floor, rolling around and holding both hands over his nuts. All he could think was that they were ruptured, the pain was so bad. He was only vaguely aware that she shot past him, following the kid out the door.

Derek rolled onto his back, seeing double, trying to get himself up so he could chase that damn blonde and repay her for putting him down. He could barely breathe, much less move. Did the woman's damn boots have steel toes?

He should get up and chase her, but it was all he could do to keep from vomiting. He lay there in a cold sweat, feeling the icy air rushing through the open kitchen door, and wondered what the fuck he was going to do now. The woman and kid would be long gone by the time he could get to his feet, plus he had to allow for the possibility that she had already called the cops.

He needed to get out of here. His chance of catching the kid was small and getting smaller, while his chance of getting caught by the cops was getting bigger by the minute. He'd leave the kid for now, go after the mechanic who'd been screwing the senator's whore. *Make it look like a suicide*, the senator had said, like that was easy. This was a fucking soap opera, and he'd signed on to make it go away.

He'd get right on that . . . as soon as he could walk. As soon as he didn't feel as if he'd puke his guts up if he uncurled from his protective ball. He'd take care of Sammy the mechanic, then he'd come back for the kid—and he'd make the woman pay.

He was already planning on instituting a "busted nuts" surcharge.

The three Hunters stood in the shadows of a child's playhouse and watched as Lenna and a small boy ran away from the house, toward the line of trees set well back from the row of houses that were so much alike. The woods were thick but also narrow, as forests go. Lenna might feel safely concealed there, but she would be wrong.

She had been easy to find. Hunters had many

talents, and one of them was the ability to home in on the energy of the Major Arcana when they were out of their place. It didn't happen often—had not happened in thousands of years—but still, the call was strong. Even if those woods were a hundred miles deep, they would be able to locate her again.

In preparation for this job, all three of the Hunters had dressed as residents of Seven might. Their weapons were concealed. Not that the three of them—especially all three together—would blend into any human crowd. Nevan and Stroud were too tall, too imposing, to be ignored. Hunters were often mistaken for military men, in this or any other world. That was appropriate, Esma supposed. She herself was tall, for a woman, and she had never learned how to put on the mask of serenity, to pretend that she was anything other than what she was: a Hunter.

"Does she have the Alexandria Deck on her?" Nevan asked.

"How the hell are we supposed to know?" Esma snapped. Really, Nevan was strong and he was deadly, but he wasn't all that bright.

She should be hoping that Lenna would gladly hand over the deck. They could return Strength to her place in Aeonia, Tower would be happy, and Esma would move on to the next job. She loved the excitement of being a Hunter, of being feared on all the planes of the universe—by those who knew of them, of course. Some planes, such as this one, still worked in ignorance of how things were really ordered.

Veton had hinted that Esma might take Lenna's place, if the current Strength met a violent end during her time on Seven. For a Major Arcana to die was unprecedented, but if Esma knew one thing, as a Hunter, it was that everyone could and did die. Some were harder to kill than others, but no one was promised true immortality. In truth, Veton didn't have any idea what would happen if Lenna was killed. No one did.

If it was possible for Esma to take Lenna's place, would she? Could she? It was tempting, she'd admit, but there was enormous panache attached to the Hunters. Whenever a Hunter swaggered into a bar, everyone else stepped aside. That was just the way it was. Would she be happy if she gave that up? There were only a few female Hunters, but she had learned to keep up with the strongest of men. She was well known, and well respected.

Esma would not waste her time on "what ifs" and "maybes." She had a job to do.

She said to Nevan, "We need to find the deck, fast, before Caine arrives. Strength might have it in that bag she's carrying, but she might have hidden it somewhere. She had several hours in this world before we arrived."

"How can we find out?"

Stroud, who was smarter than Nevan, had remained silent throughout the exchange, but it was he who said, "We need to separate. One of us will have to confront Strength, overpower her, and search the bag while the others spread out and keep watch for her next move in case she escapes. If the cards are in the bag, our job here will be an easy one." He sighed. "Whoever manages this task will probably be a favorite of Veton's for a long while. If Strength decides to resist . . . she will be formidable. Not every Hunter possesses the ability, or the will, to destroy a Major Arcana. I should be the one to take the risk—"

"I'll do it," Nevan interrupted, holding his head high and winning the argument Stroud had fully intended to lose.

Esma looked doubtful. "I don't know—" She was going to say she didn't know if Nevan could accomplish such a task, but she bit the words off. He would know what she intended to say whether she finished or not, be appropriately insulted, and insist on taking on the task just to prove them wrong.

As Stroud had no doubt planned, Nevan said fiercely, "I am more than capable. Leave it to me." He turned his back and abruptly she realized he was about to teleport; she grabbed his arm.

"Not here!" she said urgently. "Someone might see!" There were too many houses about; Strength hadn't seen them, but that didn't mean someone else wouldn't. The Hunters went to some lengths to keep their powers hidden in the lands that didn't know of them.

Nevan gave a curt nod and began to run toward the tree line; once he was hidden from view, he could safely teleport to Strength's location.

After a few moments, Stroud shook his head. "No matter the outcome of this task, I doubt Nevan will have a long career as a Hunter, as we have."

"No. He's strong enough, he has the physical skill, but he doesn't have the proper mental makeup to embrace this job and succeed." As with any race, some Hunters excelled at their task, and some didn't, but even a weak Hunter was a force to be reckoned with. Others, like the legendary Caine, were practically one-man armies. Nevan was nowhere close to Caine's skill and capabilities.

Lenna, as a Major Arcana, would have special abilities; they all did, in some form or another. There had been no time to study her properly before setting out, in order to arrive before Caine, so they had no idea what those abilities were. She might be able to fight back against the fiercest Hunter, and win. Best to let Nevan test the waters; if he succeeded, that would be excellent. If he failed—better him than her.

"He's far too gullible." Stroud slanted an assessing look at her, raking her from head to foot. "If you are elevated to Strength, I will happily serve as your personal Hunter and consort, if you so desire." One eyebrow quirked.

"Perhaps," she said coolly, though she smiled.

Stroud was handsome, and they had enjoyed one another's company often, in the past. She liked him well enough, and a Hunter who was loyal to her would always be welcome, so long as she never forgot that all Hunters were mercenaries.

Nevan disappeared into the trees, near where Lenna and the child had done the same.

"Who will emerge from those woods, I wonder?" Stroud asked, a touch of humor in his voice.

"We shall see," Esma murmured.

Once they had run far enough into the trees that they were hidden from view, Lenna halted and knelt down to study the child's face. He was pale; his eyes were wide with shock. He had seen too much, was far too traumatized.

"Why did we run from the policeman?" Elijah

asked, breathless. "He could've arrested Uncle Bobby. He could have—"

"No," Lenna said. Her inexperience with children troubled her. She knew of no way to soothe him; she could only offer the truth. "That man, policeman or not, meant to do us harm." She could not explain how she knew that to be true, not to any human, and certainly not to a child. If she had waited for the man to make a move, to draw his weapon or grab Elijah, it might've been too late. Was George Benton—if that was indeed his name, and she had her doubts—truly with the authorities? If he was, then she could not take Elijah to the police. She could not trust them.

Beware.

She had only her instincts to go on, but she never doubted them. The man had not had good intentions toward either her or the child.

She pulled Elijah close to her and wrapped her arms around him, offering him the comfort of her touch, the knowledge that he wasn't alone. In spite of the chill of the day, he was warm, his smallness making him feel soft and fragile to her. She didn't want to let go of him. Poor child, his heart was beating so hard she could feel it under her palms. His distress was palpable.

And in that moment, she knew she would do whatever she needed to do to protect him.

She felt a warning tingle race up her spine a bare second before she heard someone approaching. The fallen, dead leaves on the floor of the forest made a quiet approach impossible. Whoever was headed their way was not the man she'd laid low, she knew that. This was another, someone more dangerous than a crooked policeman.

She stood, spun to face this new danger, and pushed Elijah behind her.

A Hunter was coming toward her. She knew it by his bearing, that erect, alert posture, the predatory sharpness of his gaze. One could always tell a Hunter just by the eyes, something *other* about them, even without the long knife he wore that was of a shape and metal peculiar to the Hunters. She had been expecting one, though truthfully not so soon.

What she had not expected was that he would draw his weapon as he approached her.

Despite her puzzlement, she kept Elijah firmly behind her. "Stop!" she commanded.

He didn't pause. The Hunter knew who she was, and didn't care.

"Do you have the deck?" he asked, finally stopping when he was mere feet away.

Taken aback, she stared at him. He was here for the Alexandria Deck, not for her. That was . . .

immediately relieving, that he didn't mean harm to her or Elijah, followed hard on its heels by alarm because that wasn't what it meant at all. "Who sent you?" she asked sharply. The magical deck was so powerful many of the Major Arcana would desire having it under their control, but who would send a weapon-bearing Hunter after it? There were a few who were capable, but with no more than a flash of thought she knew exactly who had sent this one. "Ah," she said quietly. "Veton." Of course. None of them would want it more than the one who would see the deck as an unending source of entertaining chaos.

The Hunter smiled and tipped his head, without a sound telling Lenna her supposition was correct. She carefully didn't glance at her bag, or make any protective move toward it. Did he realize he needed every card in order for there to be power in the deck? How much did he know?

Still smiling, the Hunter moved closer. "Give me the deck, and I'll gladly take you back to your home."

"And if I don't?"

"I hear you can be replaced."

Replaced? Impossible.

Before she could respond, the Hunter lunged for her, his knife blade gleaming with magic, his face determined. Lenna shoved Elijah to safety and danced to the side, drawing the Hunter and the danger away from the child, rapidly trying to plot a strategy. The Hunter would make a much more fearsome opponent than had the human in Elijah's kitchen.

She spun to meet him and lashed out with a kick, but they were both moving so fast her foot barely grazed the Hunter's back. He rolled away from the force of the kick and sprang back up, not only uninjured but not even stunned. And smiling.

"Tell me where the deck is," he said.

"Lenna?" Elijah whispered, and then he said more loudly, "You leave Lenna alone!" With a cry he rushed toward the Hunter with his hands curled into small fists.

Lenna's heart almost came through her chest. "Elijah!" He didn't have a chance against a normal adult, much less a Hunter! Forsaking her own protection, she threw herself at the child, tackled him, and went rolling with him across the icy ground. Dead leaves rustled beneath their bodies, and the snow and ice that crusted the leaves stung her face and bare hands.

The Hunter laughed, coming toward them as she rolled up onto her feet and faced him again, once more with Elijah behind her.

She had no delusions about her capabilities in a battle. She was fast, yes, with some skill, and she did have an impressive physical strength compared to the humans of this world, but she had no weapon and she couldn't defeat the Hunter with strength alone. She might hold him off for a while, but in a physical match there could be only one end, one that didn't favor her.

"Let the child leave," she bargained. She had to get Elijah out of danger. She could send him to a neighbor, or a friend. That wasn't her plan—she didn't really have a plan—but once he was out of the way she would at least have one less worry to occupy her mind. She didn't have the skill to defeat a Hunter, but perhaps she could outsmart him, if she didn't have to expend energy on protecting Elijah.

"I don't think so," the Hunter said, his eyes gleaming with cunning. "Give me the deck, and I won't hurt him. I will send you home, unharmed. Fight me, and . . ." He shrugged. "In the heat of battle, there are always innocent victims."

He would hurt Elijah to get the deck. She would gladly give him the cards to protect the child . . . if she trusted him. She did not. She had promised to help Elijah, which she couldn't do if the Hunter took her back to Aeonia as soon as he had the deck, not that she trusted him to keep his word on that. He had been sent to retrieve her, yet obviously he was also working for Veton. From all she had seen, he seemed perfectly willing to kill her. At least, he was more than willing to try.

Lenna didn't know what would happen if she actually died. She had no desire to find out.

She squared her shoulders. She had to defeat this Hunter. When he didn't return with her, surely another Hunter would be dispatched to retrieve her. Somehow she had to help Elijah. The two things she needed to do—return to Aeonia, and aid Elijah—were at odds with each other, yet she was determined to do both. She had some time, and she would use every last second of it trying to keep her word to the child. She would do everything she could, and if in the end another Hunter didn't come for her, she would find her own way home.

She was certain the One had a contingency plan, too. Didn't He always? Despite the dire situation, that thought made her smile.

The Hunter was instantly suspicious, and she saw his grip tighten on the supernatural weapon in his hand. If she could be killed, that knife would be the weapon to do the deed. The Hunters had weapons to handle every situation.

Quickly she said, "I don't have the deck, but I know where it is."

"Take me there."

If she had trusted him . . . but she didn't. She turned

as if to start off through the woods, and as he reflexively relaxed at this indication of her obedience, Lenna seized this as her best chance to catch him off guard and threw herself sideways into him as she shouted, "Run!" at Elijah, and hoped he obeyed as willingly as he had before.

Out of the corner of her eye she saw the child dart away, then all of her attention was focused on the battle. It was brief but fierce, and the outcome not unexpected despite her willingness to do the worst she could while the Hunter was logically hampered by his desire to keep her alive until he knew where the deck was.

She managed to snap her head up under his chin and daze him a little, something that made him snarl like an animal. But he was too strong, too fast, and trained in battle, and in short order he had her pushed up against a tree, the cold bark rough against her back. He held her there, both her hands captured in one of his, the blade of his knife resting on the skin of her throat.

Despite being pinned and barely able to move, Lenna lifted her chin as much as she could and coolly met the Hunter's malevolent gaze. "Do your worst, and face the consequences."

"There will be no consequences," he said with a curl of his lip. She felt a bit of satisfaction as she saw some blood on his mouth. Either she'd managed to land a blow or he'd bit his lip when she butted him under the chin. "Not to me, anyway. You, on the other hand . . . Tell me where the Alexandria Deck is or I will cut you up a piece at a time until you give me what I want." His tone was low and menacing.

She faced him calmly, resolutely. She would tell him nothing. If that meant a slow and painful end to her very long life, then so be it. "You will never find the deck, and you will never catch the boy."

The Hunter smiled, and it wasn't a pleasant smile. "The boy is running straight for my companions. And you will talk. Eventually."

The blade bit into her skin.

Chapter 6

E lijah ran. The day was kind of dark, with all the clouds, but there was gray light beyond the trees. He could see the back of his house. The kitchen door was still standing open, the way they'd left it when he and Lenna ran away from the policeman. He slowed, his run turning into a walk. He was breathing hard, trying not to cry again, but he was so scared and didn't know what to do.

What if that bad guy hurt Lenna? Mom was gone, and if Lenna was gone, too—

He couldn't finish the thought.

He stopped.

Lenna had told him to run, but . . . he and Lenna were Hunters, right? She'd said they were. Hunters didn't run; Hunters didn't leave their friends to the bad guys, no matter how scared they were.

He was at the edge of the woods where he and Zack sometimes played superheroes or cowboys. This wasn't playing. He turned around, took a deep breath as he clenched his hands into fists, and began running again, as hard as he could—back toward Lenna. He wasn't sure what he'd do when he got back to her, he just . . .

He just didn't want to leave her, and even if he did, he didn't have anywhere else to go. That was the worst feeling, not having anywhere to go.

He dodged through the trees, his sneakers slipping in the thin coating of snow and ice, his breath heaving in and out, until he hurtled back into the small clearing where he'd left Lenna.

Lenna and the bad guy were fighting. Elijah was so frightened his legs almost went out from under him. She was a good fighter, he thought, but then all of a sudden the bad guy shoved her back against a tree and held his knife to her throat, and at that sight, Elijah's legs went out from under him, after all, just collapsing and dropping him to his knees.

The bad man was going to kill Lenna. She'd be dead, just like Mom.

Elijah's vision started to fade around the edges. Everything was going gray. He couldn't breathe, he couldn't stand up, he couldn't even move. He heard himself screaming in his mind but no sound came out of his mouth. *Noooo!*

Caine teleported into Seven, feeling as if something was wrong. Normally teleporting was effortless, a brief cold but smooth sensation, then he was where he intended to go. This had been different, strangely bumpy, but the feeling was gone before he could analyze it and then he was in a cold, snowy forest, the early-morning light dull and gray, the energies reading as another Hunter, Strength herself, and a human child who was collapsed on the ground.

In the span of a heartbeat, he assessed the situation. The other Hunter had a knife at Strength's throat, about to slash her. "Why" didn't matter, not when his own mission was to take her back to Aeonia. He didn't ask, he acted, exploding with the supernatural speed for which he was famous—or infamous—slamming into the other Hunter from the side and knocking him away from her. She slumped to the ground, but he didn't take the time to check her for injury. His first instinct was to simply kill the man, but he had to allow for the possibility there was something going on he needed to know. Instead of attacking, he drew his own knife and positioned himself between Strength and the other

Hunter, who had staggered but then swiftly regained his balance. He whirled back with a snarl, then he checked, his pupils flaring as he saw Caine.

Nevan. The other Hunter's name was Nevan. Caine recognized him, because the Hunter society was fairly small and extremely exclusive, but knowing someone's identity wasn't the same as knowing someone as a person. The Hunter had been about to kill one of the Major Arcana, something unheard of—not that the Hunters weren't dispatched sometimes as executioners, but never of any of the card entities, not that he knew of. Whether or not he'd known Nevan better wouldn't have made a difference. Strength was his mission; he'd allow nothing to sway him from returning her to her place in Aeonia.

Nevan balanced himself, gripped his knife for an upward slash. "Cease," Caine said softly, offering an out even as he balanced himself for battle.

"Can't," Nevan replied, and charged forward with the inhuman speed of a Hunter. Caine met it with his own speed, parrying the thrust of Nevan's knife and pivoting to land a back kick on the side of Nevan's knee, crushing it sideways and collapsing Nevan to the ground. The other Hunter wasn't without skill; despite what had to be intense pain he rolled and came upright again, facing Caine.

Caine slid sideways, pulling Nevan's attention with him and away from Strength, who had risen to a crouch at the base of the tree. He was acutely aware of her every movement, though he didn't glance at her or in any way indicate that his attention was anywhere other than on his opponent.

He had options. He had his shotgun, and from what he could see, Nevan had no weapon other than the knife. The shotgun was loud, though, and would draw the attention of any humans nearby. Knife it was, then, unless he was forced to use the shotgun. He'd do whatever was necessary to protect Strength and complete his mission.

Unfortunately, "whatever was necessary" was likely to cost a fellow Hunter his life. Nevan wasn't a neophyte, but neither did his experience come near to equaling Caine's. Caine was faster, stronger, and smarter. He would never have let himself be lured away from his target. To give Nevan one more chance, he said, "Go, and live."

"Can't," Nevan replied once more, and attacked. Caine stepped into the charge, and they closed together in the blurred speed of Hunter battle, a ballet of inhuman speed and uncanny accuracy, because no Hunter survived long without both. His movement disrupted Nevan's aim and momentum, and he used his forearm to block the intended lethal stab and force Nevan's arm upward, leaving the midsection exposed.

Caine would have preferred not to kill another Hunter, but Nevan had made his own choice by not quitting the fight. Caine struck upward into the other's vulnerable midsection, his magicus silver blade slicing through bone as if it were water, straight into Nevan's beating heart.

Nevan dropped as if his legs had been severed from his body, straight to the icy ground. He lay there with his eyes open but blank, blood leaking from a body whose heart no longer pumped, his essence already fading.

Caine knew he had only seconds. "Who sent you?" he asked, going down on one knee beside the still-sentient Hunter. Who would want to destroy Strength? Before he'd left Aeonia the Emperor had warned him others might've sent Hunters for Strength, though not as protectors. Others would want the Alexandria Deck for themselves and would do anything to have it—but retrieving the cards was one thing, and killing Strength was another.

Nevan slowly focused on Caine, awareness there for the smallest moment—and then he was gone, faded away as if he had never been, leaving Caine kneeling beside nothing more than dead leaves and patches of snow. The body had ceased to exist on this plane, perhaps on all planes.

Caine mentally shrugged. He would have liked to get some information from the other Hunter, but he could still appreciate the tidiness of not having to dispose of Nevan's body.

He looked over at Strength—Lenna—who was slowly rising from her crouched position, her gaze locked on his face. A faint buzz ran through his veins, a heat and an energy that sent all his senses on high alert. He'd known she was beautiful; many of the Major Arcana were blessed with extraordinary beauty, and she was no exception, which in a strange way made her ordinary. Her harmonious features, though, weren't what first caught his attention. What snared him, held him, was the steadfast determination of that direct gaze. Even knowing she was Strength personified, facing that willpower in person gave him the unwelcome sense of having met his match. He was accustomed to being the most determined being in any situation, his enormous focus and will giving him a power beyond that of the body. Looking at her, seeing her in the flesh, he knew that in *this* situation he couldn't be certain that was true.

She had been injured; a thin slash of blood marked the place where Nevan's blade had touched her. Thank the One it was no more than a scratch, and as a Major

Arcana she would heal quickly. There was no reason for him to even make note of the injury.

Without taking his eyes from her, he gave her a curt but proper bow, one that acknowledged her position but not necessarily her superiority.

She was much more beautiful in the flesh than in the vision the Emperor had shared with him. Vae! She glowed, with a faint but definite luminosity to her skin. He immediately thought of seeing *all* her skin . . . in the dark . . . beneath him. *Vae indeed.*

The electrical charge surged stronger, making his penis thicken. He turned his own force of will on his body, slamming down a mental wall on that avenue of thought and subduing his mating urge. He allowed nothing—*nothing*—to interfere with the mission.

There was sudden movement behind him but his acute senses told him it was made by the human child, who was not a threat to anyone, certainly not to Lenna or to Caine himself. The child ran on unsteady legs to Lenna and threw himself at her, locking his skinny arms around her and burying his face against her side.

A gentle expression crossed her face. Bending her bright head over the child's dark one, she soothed the boy with a hand on his head, with softly murmured words of comfort.

Then she looked back up at Caine, and the gentleness

was gone. To him, she didn't offer softness and caring; in those powerful eyes he saw the willpower she represented, the inner strength she shared with all the worlds, and a gathering storm of anger. He didn't want to see an angry Strength; according to legend, her fury could send armies surging across the land, laying waste to all who angered her. She was normally calm, even serene, but her reverse was a lack of control that could devastate this plane.

"He worked for Veton," she said in a clipped tone, "and he did not come into this world alone."

Ah. So she already knew the answer to the question he had been asking Nevan. She could have spoken before, he thought irritably; then he could have dispatched the other Hunter without hesitation.

He pushed the irritation behind his mental wall to accompany his lust. Neither was useful. Instead, he immediately processed this new information.

The Tower. He wasn't surprised. Chaos was capable of anything, which was the reason for its existence. He was less concerned about Veton's involvement, though, than he was about the news there were other Hunters. They would be able to locate Strength as easily as he had, and he might not be able to protect her from a multipronged attack. "Then we have no time to waste," he said curtly as he sheathed his knife. "I will return

you to Aeonia now. Is the Alexandria Deck nearby?"
Getting her to safety was of paramount importance.

But Lenna shook her head. "Not yet. I need to see
the boy to safety and bring his mother's murderer to
justice."

Her resistance was an unpleasant surprise, one he
hadn't anticipated, and one he couldn't allow to stand.
The other Hunters must be waiting for their fellow to
accomplish his task, but they wouldn't wait long. They
would be able to sense that Strength was still here, and
they'd realize Nevan had failed.

"Not possible," he said, dismissing the problem
of the human child, who simply didn't matter. "The
Emperor has requested your immediate return. We
will collect the deck and—"

She interrupted him with a cold look and an
upraised hand, as if she would stay him. "I forbid you
to transport me until all my tasks here are completed."

Forbid? He was a Hunter. She couldn't *forbid* him
to do anything. There were laws that governed him
and his existence, but servitude to the Major Arcana
wasn't one of them. They could hire him, but they
couldn't rule him. She had to know that, which made
her statement even more annoying.

He hadn't realized until now just *how* annoying such
willfulness, such determination, could be; he could

only thank the One that he wasn't bound to obey her. "I don't work for you. I work for the Emperor. His orders carry more weight than yours," he said as he strode to her.

She drew back, her blue eyes taking on a sharp warning. "The child—"

"I'll see to him," he said briskly, cutting her off. He didn't have time for any of this nonsense. "When you are safe."

The boy held on to Lenna's waist, clasping it with everything he had as he peeked up at Caine with a mixture of awe and fear in his big dark eyes. Caine realized he'd have to forcibly pry the child away from her, presenting him with yet another annoying delay.

"No," she said, her jaw setting. "I want to—"

"It doesn't matter what you want, not this time," he snapped, interrupting her yet again. He stood so close to her he could feel her body heat, even on this cold day. He towered over her, a head taller and twice her size in volume. Major Arcana or not, she didn't have the physical strength to stop him; if he wanted to wrest her away from the child, he *would* succeed.

He had noticed the bag she carried securely across her body. She couldn't have traveled to Seven without the cards; the deck was required for her return to Aeonia, as it had been required for her departure.

Knowing that, would she keep the deck with her? He knew he himself would. Logically, she would have the cards in that bag. There was one easy way to find out.

Teleporting was as effortless for a Hunter as thought. Caine placed a firm hand on her shoulder, and with his other easily moved the child away. He lifted his hand from the boy, and—

Nothing happened.

Their return to Aeonia should've been instantaneous.

The child gave a high-pitched shriek and lunged for Lenna. Hastily, before the child could touch her, Caine tried again.

Nothing.

He swore under his breath, frustration raw in his gut. Obviously she didn't have the deck with her. She could have hidden it anywhere, and given her insistence on staying here, she'd refuse to tell him where it was. She'd resist telling him anything about the deck. He tried again. There should have been a flash of awareness, a burst of energy felt in every cell of his body. Instead, there was . . . nothing.

He said a very pithy Seven expletive.

The child had once again latched on to Lenna, and this time Caine didn't bother moving him away.

He glared at Lenna. No words were needed. She had a maddening expression of satisfaction on her face as she said, "The deck brought me into this world. It is necessary to transport me home again."

He already knew that, and he snarled a frustrated sound. "Take me to it. You must go home."

She smiled, a lovely smile that hit him hard and low. "As soon as I've taken care of Elijah and fulfilled my promise, I will be glad to go with you."

The surly Hunter was unhappy with this turn of events, but she didn't care. While she appreciated that he had saved her life, she had given Elijah her promise of aid; what kind of person would she be if she then simply left the child to fend for himself without trying as hard as she might to stay here? Lenna was glad she hadn't decided to store the complete deck in her bag, that she'd had the forethought to separate the cards; otherwise she'd be back in Aeonia, facing the Emperor.

Her relief when the Hunter had failed in his attempt to teleport her had been so intense she had almost laughed, which he definitely wouldn't have appreciated.

Being happy and relieved was one thing; gloating at a Hunter was something else. They were immensely dangerous beings, rough and violent, and indispensable to the universe, which made them arrogant. On the other hand, because they traveled the universe and all the planes, having the aid of one such as he would be invaluable. He had the option of simply leaving her here, but Hunters were renowned for never walking away from a mission: they accomplished it, or they died.

"I am Lenna," she said, omitting her title because obviously he already knew it. He would also know her name, but proper introductions were still called for. "This is Elijah. What is your name, Hunter?"

"Caine."

Elijah straightened away from her as he gaped up at Caine, and his dark eyes rounded in astonishment. "Hunter?" His voice rose in excitement. "I'm a Hunter, too, and so is Lenna. We fight for justice, like all the other superheroes." He swiped a hand across his tear-streaked cheek. "Sorry. Hunters don't cry."

Caine looked down at the boy. He was so tall the child barely reached his waist; and so close Lenna could feel the heat of his body even on this cold day. "No," he said, the words clipped. "No, we do not."

"Can I have one of your guns? I'll be careful." With a small finger, he poked at an unusual weapon with which Lenna wasn't familiar. "Can I have that one? It looks kind of like a Super Soaker. Is it a Super Soaker?"

"It is not. It's a liquid laser blaster. And no, you may not have one of my weapons." His head swiveled as he alertly surveyed their surroundings, and she knew he was searching for the energy of the other Hunters. "We can't stay here," he said to Lenna. "You aren't safe."

The other Hunters could be on them without warning. She knew that, and in the back of her mind she had been braced for their appearance. Caine would fight, and from what she'd seen he was a superlative warrior, but he'd be outnumbered. She, too, would have to fight, and though she had some skill she wasn't a Hunter. "They can find me anywhere," she pointed out.

"Not necessarily." He looked down at her with his inscrutable coal-dark eyes. "I can shield my energy from other Hunters. If you are close to me, the shield will enclose you, too. But you will have to stay within the shield."

"How close?" She meant the question in the most prosaic of ways, literally asking for a measurement of space. She dealt better with absolutes, in knowing exactly what was expected of her, rather than risking her life on differing definitions of close.

"Very," he said, and clamped his arm around her waist as he pulled Elijah to him with his other hand. She felt a rush, a sharp zing of energy, and a dizzying sense of enormous speed that was nothing like when Elijah had called her here through the Alexandria Deck. In what was less than the blink of an eye, their surroundings coalesced around her; they were still in the wooded area—or *a* wooded area, as she had no idea if it was the same one—but the trees crowded more thickly around them. While the Hunter could not teleport her between worlds without the Alexandria Deck, he could—apparently—teleport her within this world.

At some point during that flash of time, she had placed her hand on Caine's shoulder to anchor herself. She could feel the thick pad of muscle, the heat and sense of coiled strength seeping through his clothing to her fingers. Every nerve ending in her body was awake and tingling in reaction to the energy he was using to both shield and teleport them.

Her stomach clenched and her knees went weak. The sensation was so similar to that of sexual desire that heat pooled between her legs, and she reflexively tightened her pelvic muscles as if he had pushed his penis inside her.

Oh, this would not do.

He had dropped his arm from around her waist as soon as they teleported, and now she removed her hand from his shoulder. She immediately felt more grounded, more in control, as if touching him interfered with her ability to concentrate. How odd; she had known Hunters had an energy field, but she hadn't realized it was so strong. But then, she'd never actually touched a Hunter before, so her knowledge had been incomplete.

She must remember this. It could be one of the Hunters' secret weapons, the ability to confuse thought with a touch.

Or it could be because he was so very . . . male. She had noticed, of course. She wasn't just a card entity; she was a living woman. But because she was Strength, in one instant she realized all this, and in the next instant she gave him a calm look and said, "Elijah is—"

The child himself interrupted her. "*Whoa!* That was *awesome!* Can you teach me how? Poof! Nobody ever told me grown-ups could do that! It's a secret, isn't it? Grown-ups keep lots of secrets. *Poof!*" he said again, waving his skinny arms in excitement. "That's even better than Iron Man, because he has to have his suit or he can't do anything."

Caine looked as if he were in pain, but instead of deflating the child, he said, "You aren't old enough to . . . ah . . . *poof.* One must be old enough to drive before he can poof."

"Oh." Elijah looked severely disappointed, but also faintly suspicious, as if he didn't necessarily believe that time restriction. She suspected this wouldn't be his last attempt to find out Caine's secrets.

Lenna waited a beat, then directed the conversation

back to her desired subject. "I'm sure you are anxious to have this task done and move on. Our first objective is to see to Elijah's safety, and to the apprehension or elimination of this . . . Uncle Bobby, the man who murdered his mother. I believe he has cohorts—another man accosted us in Elijah's house, but we escaped."

"How?"

"I kicked him," she replied with a slight lift of her eyebrows, leaving it to him to decipher her exact meaning.

He grunted, then moved on to what he obviously saw as a more important topic. "*My* first objective is to keep you safe from the other Hunters. They can't find us now, but obviously we can't simply stand in the forest all day. It's cold. We'll need shelter and food. The boy is shaking with cold already."

Concerned, Lenna looked down at Elijah and saw the truth of that statement. She herself withstood the cold very well, but Elijah was small. "Very well. What do you suggest?"

He gave her a slightly exaggerated expression of astonishment, just enough for her to catch his sarcastic response to her cooperativeness. She shrugged; whether or not he liked her stance on staying to protect Elijah wasn't something that concerned her. The child needed her help, and she had promised it.

"We'll take the child to a safe place—" he began.

"No," she snapped, not losing her temper but barking out the word with the authority she was accustomed to displaying. "We can leave him nowhere. I told you, the man who tracked us in Elijah's home had ill-intent against him. He witnessed a murder," she added in a lowered voice, hoping the boy would not hear. Her eyes flashed, hard and angry. "Elijah called me into this world to help, and I will not abandon him."

Caine's already grim mouth pressed into a straight line. "I can take you anywhere on this plane and leave him behind," he said in a cold, flat tone. "Never forget that."

"And never forget that you need the deck to take me back," she shot in return. "I give you my word I'll cooperate when we have stopped the people who mean harm to him." Not *if—when.*

Caine had seldom been more annoyed in his life than he was right now, but he didn't have much choice. If she had been *anyone* else—meaning someone with a softer will and less determination—he could have overridden her protests and done his job. He couldn't do that with her, because she was Strength. She had set her course, and damned if he could see a means to sway her from it. If she changed her mind, it would be because of her own reasons, not his.

He would have to keep her safe on Seven, where she was as noticeable as the blazing sun. At the moment she was at least appropriately dressed like any ordinary human woman of this world, but her bearing was anything but ordinary. Her looks weren't ordinary. She *glowed*. Not brightly, but anyone who wasn't an idiot would eventually notice the glow wasn't a trick of the light. She was attempting to blend in, but she never would.

He wanted to be rid of her more than he'd ever wanted anything, but instead he had to keep her within arm's-length for what promised to feel like an eternity. He'd have to bathe with her, sleep with her—

Bet she hadn't thought of that.

The perverse satisfaction he got from that thought helped ease his frustration, but he couldn't stop himself from muttering, "My damn bad luck you have to be Strength."

She gave him a cool look. "You prefer weak women?"

He kept his answer simple. "Yes." It was a lie, but what difference did it make to her what kind of woman he preferred? "They do what I tell them to do. I like that." He showed his teeth in something that only pretended to be a smile.

"Then you do have a problem, but your problem isn't mine."

He glanced down and saw Elijah staring up at them with round, worried eyes. The boy had no one now except Lenna, and though he was young he wasn't so young that he didn't understand most of what they were talking about. Faced with those apprehensive dark eyes, and seeing how the kid was shivering, Caine elected to leave their disagreement for now.

"Enough of this. I'll take both of you somewhere safe, and warm." First things first. He put his arm around Lenna again, pulling her in close to him. She *felt* disturbingly small and frail to him, but that was deceptive. She wasn't tall, her bones were small, but her muscles were smooth and likely more powerful than people would expect. Her skin was surprisingly warm, her body supple against him.

Every muscle in his body tightened, and hot wave of sheer lust surged through him.

Just what he needed. He clenched his teeth and swore long and viciously to himself. He wasn't a man who dealt in self-deception, though. He wanted her. He admitted it. Lenna was gorgeous and tempting; he'd have to be dead not to respond to her, and he was far from dead.

Tough shit. That was a phrase often used here on Seven, and it was remarkably appropriate. Their worlds and positions were so different they had almost nothing in common other than being carbon-based life forms. She was of the Arcane. He was a mercenary, and he intended to remain one.

She distracted him by putting her hand on Elijah's shoulder. "Is Elijah protected by your shield, too?"

"No," he said, clipping off the words because he was still so damned annoyed. "The other Hunters can track you and me by our energy, which is not of this world, but they can't track the child." The child could be under their noses or miles away, and no Hunter would be able to find him.

Lenna nodded, satisfied with that answer. "You are more familiar with Seven than I am, Hunter. What do we do next?"

He gave the only answer he could. "I'll take you to a safe place first. Then we find Uncle Bobby."

Chapter 7

Too much time had passed. Esma was beginning to feel on edge. Judging by the expression on Stroud's face, he felt it, too. She reached out with her senses, dismayed by what she felt—or rather, what she *didn't* feel.

"Nevan is gone," Stroud said. He took a few steps toward the woods but stopped, because there was no point in investigating. They both sensed the same thing. "Teleported out of this world or dead. So is she."

They had known that the Emperor would send Caine after Strength, but they had hoped the wrinkle Veton had provided would slow Caine down for at least a day, or two. Instead, the time difference in their arrival and Caine's had been minutes, which could be catastrophic. Damn Veton, for overestimating his power. On the other hand—he was chaos, after all, so nothing he touched would mean there were no problems. His reason for being was to *compound* the problem. She should have remembered that.

So now they had Caine to deal with. They had both felt him, and now they didn't. She could feel nothing—not Nevan, not Caine, not Strength.

She had no idea what that meant, because the options were so varied. Hunters weren't easy to kill, but they could be taken out. It would be next to impossible for a human to kill a Hunter, but Lenna might've, if her powers here were strong enough. Another Hunter could do the job, too, especially if that other Hunter was Caine.

It was the way of things. The Hunters were long-lived, and they served a vital purpose. But it wouldn't do for mercenaries who could travel between worlds to be *invincible*. That would give them far too much power.

Nevan wouldn't have deserted. No, he was either dead, or he'd taken the deck and teleported to Aeonia, perhaps to steal any credit and favor for himself. But where was Strength?

If Lenna had remained in this world, they'd feel her. They'd be able to locate her. Esma searched for the energy of a Major Arcana in Seven, which should be easy. Nothing. She tried again, knowing she hadn't been mistaken, but feeling bound to make the effort, anyway.

So . . . had Nevan killed her, or possibly taken her back to Aeonia?

Or had Caine killed Nevan, and teleported with her and the deck?

Stroud—who had surely been thinking along the same lines—turned to look at her. He knew as well as she did that returning to Veton empty-handed would be disastrous for their health and well-being.

Before they could discuss their next step, a man stumbled out of the house Lenna and the child had run from a short while ago. He glanced in their direction, grumbled something nonsensical, and studied the tracks in the snow that led to the woods. When he muttered, "Fuck it," and turned away, she understood him very well. Something was not to his liking, and he was disgusted.

The man limped around the house and disappeared from view. Esma opened her mouth but before she could say anything, an older woman with white hair stepped out onto the porch of the house next to the one where Strength had been. She looked at them, waved, and asked, "Can you believe it? Snow! Too bad it didn't come on Christmas. I'd like to see a white Christmas." Then she squinted. "Oh, I don't know you. Who are you? Are you Amber's friends?"

Esma had no idea who this Amber was, but nodded her head.

The woman smiled. "I expect Elijah and his little friend will be out here before too much longer, building a snowman and throwing snowballs. Tell him I'll make them some hot chocolate when they get too cold!" The woman hugged herself, shivered, and went back inside her house.

Interaction with the local inhabitants was best avoided. Esma and Stroud exchanged a glance, then of one accord they began walking toward the woods and whatever they might find there.

"This 'Elijah' must be the child who was with her," Stroud commented.

"My interpretation of the events, with the man entering the house and then Strength and the child running from it, is that for some reason she's protecting the child. Perhaps if we find him we will have a way to her."

"But we have no way of locating a Seven native," he pointed out, frowning.

"We know what he looks like, we know his name, we know he lives here. We can't sense his energy, but we can use our other faculties." *Such as our brains*, she thought somewhat caustically, but left the words unsaid. She liked Stroud well enough; there was no gain in antagonizing him.

On the other hand . . . why ignore the most obvious explanation of what had happened, and why they could no longer sense *anyone*. "Caine must have taken her back to Aeonia," she said with a sigh. "She couldn't have returned unless she had the deck with her. It must've been in that bag she wore." The bag she'd carried hadn't seemed large enough, or special enough, for such important contents, but what other explanation was there? The most valuable artifacts were often in the most modest containers. "If Elijah is in those woods, we can grab him, return to Aeonia, and find out exactly how attached Lenna is to him. Maybe she'll give us the deck in exchange for his safety. The main thing we need to do is retrieve the deck and give it to Veton. Everything else is secondary."

There were far too many uncertainties in that scenario, but even a hundred uncertainties were preferable to returning to Veton with nothing.

Lenna suffered the Hunter's half-embrace as he held both her and Elijah, and in an instant they were elsewhere. She barely had time to register the sharp sting of energy on her skin, the heat and speed, before it was over. She fought off the dizziness—which didn't seem to affect him at all—and realized that in the flashing moment she had instinctively grabbed Caine's shirt, her fingers fisted in the cloth. She swiftly released him, wanting some distance from the disturbing physical contact with the Hunter. She had to stay close to him; she did *not* have to touch him. Unfortunately, he didn't drop his arm from around her waist but continued to hold her close.

Another split second let her realize he was holding her until both of them were able to take stock of their surroundings. It wouldn't do for her to lurch away from him in surprise, or do anything else that would bring unwanted attention to their abrupt appearance out of thin air.

They were no longer in the woods, but she doubted they had traveled any great distance. There was snow on the ground here, too, and the atmosphere felt the same. Instead of being surrounded by trees and well-kept homes, they stood near a large blue metal box filled with refuse, with tall buildings rising around them. She wrinkled her nose at the smell, thankful for the cold weather because how noxious would this smell during the summer?

"Wow!" Elijah shouted. "That was so cool!" He

started jumping up and down. "Do it again! Do it again!"

Caine sighed. "Later." He searched the area, looking into the big blue box, digging around within it, and coming out with a long, tattered brown canvas bag with a broken strap. He unzipped the bag and, one after another, removed his weapons and stored them inside. He did keep one sheathed knife tucked at his spine. She doubted he was ever without at least one weapon of some sort on his person, and usually more.

He slipped the canvas bag beneath the blue box, giving it a push so it was well hidden, then he took Lenna's hand, put his other hand on Elijah's shoulder, and steered both of them between the buildings toward a broad avenue where loud vehicles on wheels swished back and forth. She stifled her resentment of being pulled along as if she were a pet. She wasn't stupid; she understood the importance of staying close enough to him that he could shield her energy from the other Hunters.

"Where are we?" she asked, not letting him see her annoyance because that would give him a power over her, knowing how to prickle her composure.

"We need somewhere to stay while we work everything out. This is a hotel," he said, indicating the building beside them. "It's as good a place as any."

She looked up at the hotel, which was constructed of an unimpressive pale brick; many windows lined the building, marching upward in perfect rows that struck her as boring but efficient. They reached the avenue, and she got a better look at the vehicles. There had been nothing like this here the last time she had bothered to study Seven, but evidently what felt like a year or so on Aeonia was a much longer time elsewhere.

"What are these conveyances called?" she asked, indicating them with a slight movement of her hand.

"Automobiles," Caine replied. "There are different types, such as cars, different sizes of trucks, vans, SUVs."

His knowledge told her that he'd visited this world often. She herself valued knowledge so much that she wasn't hesitant at all to ask him questions. "How does one operate them? Do you give them commands? Do they decipher thoughts?"

Elijah blinked up at her as if she was speaking a different language entirely, his mouth falling open.

"No," Caine said. "They are physically steered, using a small wheel inside, and pedals that increase or decrease the speed."

"Hmm." She thought the steering wouldn't be difficult, but operating different pedals at the same time could be troublesome. Teleporting was much more efficient.

Caine turned them toward the hotel, and she saw a set of large glass doors . . . which opened as they approached.

Neither Caine nor Elijah seemed concerned or impressed by this fact, so Lenna remained silent. Omniscient doors were a convenience she hadn't considered before.

Inside the air was warm and had an odd but pleasing mixture of faint scents, both chemical and floral. Enormous lights hung from a very high ceiling, the floors were both carpeted and tile, and a long desk was situated by one wall. Caine approached the desk, which was manned by an unhappy-looking person in a dark suit. His "May I help you?" was delivered without enthusiasm.

"I know it's early," Caine said, his voice much friendlier than it had been anytime he addressed her. He even smiled, which took her aback before she admitted how absurd it was to be surprised. Of course Hunters would smile, and even laugh, though she doubted Caine did either very often. "Do you by chance have a room? Preferably a suite. We've been traveling all night and there are so many slick spots on the road I'd like to wait it out. We might even decide to stay a few days and explore Atlanta."

The man at the desk didn't seem impressed by Caine's well-delivered story. He began to tap his fingers on something in front of him, something Lenna couldn't see without standing on her tiptoes and leaning over the high desk, which she refrained from doing. As much as she loved knowledge, she knew they shouldn't attract undue attention.

The tapping fingers made a distinctive clicking noise. After a few long moments, the man stopped and looked up at Caine. "We do have one suite available. It's so early, I'm afraid I'll have to charge you for last night."

"Not a problem." Caine reached into his back pocket, pulled out a leather wallet, and withdrew a rectangular piece of plastic. He handed the card over to the man, who nodded, called Caine "Mr. Smith," and again began to tap away on the device at his station.

Lenna took the opportunity to more closely survey the area. Some things were familiar to her: the furnishings with groups of chairs and sofas and tables, the paintings on the walls, the flowers. Other things were completely foreign. She needed to place her hands on an adult human so she could absorb some of the knowledge of this world. It was annoying to see things and not know what they were called. If she had known she'd be pulled to Seven, she would have studied the recent history and their current technology, though how she could possibly have anticipated her present situation? She couldn't have.

Caine and the man at the desk—he wore a name tag that read "Franklin"—continued with their ritual. Another plastic rectangle from Caine's wallet was passed to the man. Papers were signed. Caine asked if the hotel offered something called "room service" and seemed relieved with the affirmative answer. The plastic rectangles were returned to Caine.

Franklin—not unhappy, Lenna decided, just bored—placed yet another plastic rectangle in a paper holder and handed it to Caine. She was beginning to think nothing in this place was accomplished without plastic. "Do you have luggage?" he asked.

"I'll collect it from the car later," Caine said. "I wasn't sure you'd have an availability."

Franklin looked down at Elijah, who was pressed against Caine's side and closely observing every move they made. "Cute kid. He looks like you."

Caine gave another smile, though this one seemed a bit tight, and steered both her and Elijah to a large, metal square. He punched a button and the metal door slid apart in two equal pieces, much as the glass doors had operated. Instead of admitting them to a large room, however, the metal doors opened into a box. The three of them stepped inside, Caine punched another button, and the doors closed. There was a slight jolt and the box began moving upward. Briefly alarmed, Lenna braced her hand on a metal bar that ran around the inside the box, then released it because the ascent seemed smooth and uneventful.

Caine scowled and muttered, "The child does not look like me. How could he?"

"Perhaps his coloring swayed the man's judgment," Lenna offered, because she herself saw nothing alike in their features. Elijah's face wore the softness of innocence, while she doubted Caine had an innocent bone in his body.

The customs and manners on Seven concerned her, because she didn't know what to expect or how she should act. She asked, "Why were you so much nicer to Franklin than you are to Elijah and me?"

He slanted a brief glance down at her. "I was being pleasant in order to get what I wanted, which was a room in this hotel."

"A pretense?"

She saw a muscle twitch in his jaw. "I can be pleasant."

Perhaps it wasn't polite to express doubt, but she didn't hold back the doubtful noise that formed in her throat. "Indeed? Perhaps you should pretend to be pleasant more often."

"Perhaps you should stop interfering with my job."

The doors opened and the three of them stepped into a carpeted hallway that was lined with doors, one after another, each door identical but for the number upon it. Elijah said something beneath his breath. Lenna stopped and leaned down so she could see his face.

"What was that? I couldn't hear you."

He looked up at her. His lower lip quivered, and his dark eyes were filled with tears. "I said, don't argue. It makes me sad."

Lenna saw more than sadness in his eyes; she saw worry, the kind of worry no child should ever suffer. She suspected his mother and Uncle Bobby had argued before her death. How much had he heard, and seen?

Caine towered over them all, obviously impatient, but at least he wasn't towing them down the hall. Lenna looked up at him, gave him a warning look, and said, speaking for them both, "We're sorry. We won't argue again."

Caine laughed.

Chapter 8

The two room suite—a bedroom with a king-sized bed and a parlor with a couch and two chairs, plus a kitchenette with a small table, and a full bathroom in each area—was more than sufficient for their needs. The hotel, an independent rather than a chain, was older than some of the others in the area, but it was hardly a rat trap. It would do; he hoped they wouldn't be here very long.

Lenna remained close to his side, so she could stay shielded, but Elijah immediately began wandering around to investigate his new surroundings.

"Come here," Caine said briefly to the child, and when he obediently returned, Caine once more pulled both of them close and teleported to the back lot to retrieve his weapons from underneath the big blue trash bin. The complication of taking them everywhere annoyed him; retrieving the bag should have been as simple as thought. Instead, he had to take Lenna with him in order to keep her shielded, and she wouldn't leave the kid alone even for a couple of minutes—not that the kid *wanted* to be left alone; he'd probably panic if they both disappeared without him—so by necessity it was a group effort. Caine wasn't a fan of group efforts. He especially wasn't a fan of group efforts that included a kid who was overawed by the experience and kept up a never ending rush of questions.

"How do you *do* that? You don't have a magic suit! Who taught you how? Can you teach me?"

"No," Caine said briefly. He thought they'd already covered this ground. "You're too young." Plus he wasn't a Hunter, but getting into specifics would likely only invite further questions. He knelt down beside the Dumpster and reached far beneath it so he could snag the bag containing his weapons.

Further questions evidently didn't need an invitation.

Elijah squatted beside him, so close his skinny knees actually bumped Caine's head. "Do you have to hold your breath?"

"No."

"Do you have to think really hard?"

"No." Caine tugged the bag free and tied the ends

of the broken strap in a knot so he could more easily carry it.

Elijah was determined to worm the secret of "poofing" out of him. "Can you take us along without touching us? Do you have to eat spinach? Were you generally altered?"

That last made Caine pause. "Altered?" The only kind of altering that came to mind was castration, and he suppressed a shudder.

"Like Captain America. He was generally altered and made strong and fast, but he's got a magic shield, too." Elijah pointed at the bag. "You've got magic weapons, right?"

Captain America. Right. Caine remembered seeing the movie on television in a hotel one time when he'd been visiting Seven.

He got to his feet. "That's *genetically* altered, and no, I wasn't. Put your arms around me," he said to Lenna, while he pulled the kid close with his free hand.

She had been standing there looking amused while he deflected Elijah's questions, something that he found vaguely surprising—that she had a sense of humor—but at his direction she slid her arm around his waist and hooked her thumb inside his belt. His muscles involuntarily tightened at her touch; he'd been ignoring, with varying degrees of success, how lithe and warm she felt when he put his arm around her. Having *her* arm around *him* was an entirely different sensation, reminding him of how it felt when a female responded to him. He knew he was intimidating to most beings but particularly to females, so he'd learned to appreciate the level of trust signified by a soft arm going around his neck.

There were first times for everything. This was the first time he'd ever teleported with an erection.

Then they were back in the hotel room, and the kid immediately started running in circles while emitting high-pitched whooping sounds.

Caine eased the bag containing his weapons down to the carpeted floor. "Is he always like this?" he muttered to Lenna as he warily watched the boy.

"It's better than crying all the time," she replied, keeping her tone low to match his.

He stowed the weapons in the back of the closet in the bedroom, though they had no luggage or clothing to hide them from view. It was still the best he could do on short order. He hoped they wouldn't be here long enough to need extra clothing, but right now he wasn't feeling optimistic. How was he—they—supposed to find "Uncle Bobby"? They didn't even know the man's last name. They knew *nothing*, had no trail to follow.

Regardless of the complicated disaster this mission had become, he still functioned better when he was well-fed, and teleporting used an inordinate amount of bodily fuel. "I'm hungry," he said, looking around for the room service menu, which he picked up and showed to Lenna. "What do you want?"

She had been staying right with him, shadowing his every movement, and never getting more than a step away from him. She took the menu and looked through it, then gave it back to him. "I'm unfamiliar with these foods," she said. "Choose for me."

"Pancakes!" Elijah shouted. "And French toast! And bacon. I want lots of bacon. And chocolate milk. Where are we going? Can we go to IHOP? I *love* IHOP."

Lenna put her hand on his arm, calming him down from what looked like a fit of ecstasy. "Perhaps you shouldn't hop in here," she suggested. "We don't want to disturb anyone."

Elijah gave her a bewildered look. "I wasn't hopping."

Rather than go into any explanation, Caine said, "We aren't going anywhere. I'm going to order room service." Delirious. He'd been injured during his last mission and was now delirious, and none of this existed except in his fevered imagination. That was the only explanation.

Except his growing hunger was very real, robbing him of the mild comfort of his musings.

Two pairs of eyes turned toward him. "What is this room service?" Lenna asked in interest.

"We aren't going to IHOP?" Elijah asked, beginning to pout.

Caine narrowed his eyes at the kid. "Hunters don't pout. Hunters make the best of every situation, turning it to their advantage." To Lenna he said, "Room service means our food will be brought to us here."

"Ah. Food is always brought to me, though I've never heard it called this."

Of course food was always brought to her. She was a Major Arcana, waited on hand and foot for the entirety of her existence. The differences in their lives were starkly drawn. He couldn't say he'd never been waited on; he had a couple of delicious memories of lying naked with a woman and feeding each other, but that wasn't in the same category as being treated like royalty every day of his life. He wasn't afforded service; he was afforded fear.

All in all, he thought he preferred fear; having everything done for him, everything provided to him, wasn't at all appealing. He liked the rough, adventurous life of a Hunter.

Sighing, he called room service and ordered pretty

much everything: pancakes, French toast, bacon, eggs, regular toast, fruit, juice, chocolate milk, and coffee—service for three. The à la carte orders would cost a small fortune, but maybe the kid would be happy, eat, and be quiet for a while.

Delivery of the food took half an hour; when the room service waiter wheeled in the cart loaded with dishes, Elijah stared wide-eyed for all of about two seconds, then he began bombarding the waiter with questions: how many people ordered their food that way, did he always have to wear a suit, what were those round things—"Domes to cover the food and keep it warm," Caine interjected, because the waiter was looking around for round things—what time did he come to work, did he have any kids, and had he watched Captain America?

The waiter was a champ. "Lots, yes, six a.m., no, and yes," he rattled off with a grin. "Is Captain America your favorite?"

"Almost," Elijah said. "But I like Iron Man, too. He's got a magic suit and can zoom around. Hunters don't need magic suits, though—"

Lenna put her hand on Elijah's arm, interrupting him before he could start talking about poofing, and earning Caine's gratitude because he'd been thinking about clamping his hand over the kid's mouth. "Would you like to begin with pancakes?" she asked, diverting him to the food.

Caine signed the ticket and added a hefty tip. As soon as the door had closed behind the waiter he said to Elijah, "You must be careful not to tell other people about what Hunters can do."

The big brown eyes blinked solemnly. "Is it a secret?"

"Yes. An important one." It wasn't, but not being noticed made navigating this plane less complicated.

Lenna having to stay close to Caine complicated matters; they had to move together to the table, and she couldn't separate from him to get Elijah settled. Luckily, when it came to food, the kid didn't need shepherding. He climbed into a chair, curling one leg beneath him so he was sitting higher, and surveyed the array of dome-covered plates. "Which one is mine?"

"Almost all of them," Caine replied.

Lenna briefly hesitated, then distributed the three plates and silverware. Probably that was the first time in her life she'd ever served anyone else; reluctantly Caine admitted that she was handling herself with more grace than he'd have anticipated, considering how long it had been since the Major Arcana had been able to visit other worlds.

She picked up the carton of chocolate milk, studied

it with interest, then murmured, "Open here," and with only one false start popped open the spout. As she was pouring the milk into a glass for Elijah, Caine took care of the coffee, filling cups for both him and Lenna.

They all sat down, and Lenna somewhat cautiously tried the coffee. She didn't exactly grimace, but Caine could tell she didn't care for the beverage. "Try putting milk and sugar in it," he suggested, pushing the two items toward her. "It won't be so bitter then. Or try the orange juice instead." He indicated the small carafe of juice; he knew from the Emperor that she enjoyed studying other worlds, but he didn't know how extensive her knowledge of minutiae was.

She shook her head, and waited as Caine filled Elijah's plate with his requested items and drenched them with syrup, then added a couple slices of bacon. The kid began eating as if he were starving, and Caine turned his attention to Lenna. He didn't want to serve her, but found himself offering her each plate and explaining what every item was, as well as the seasonings or toppings she should try. She willingly tried them all, though she took only a small amount of each.

No one went hungry, though. The kid ate more than he and Lenna combined, a fact which seemed to amuse her.

When they were all fed, Elijah turned on the

television and stretched out on the couch to watch. Caine lingered over a second cup of coffee, turning the current situation over in his mind and examining all angles. No matter how he turned it, though, he kept coming back to one unwelcome fact: Lenna wasn't willing to leave the boy, and he couldn't teleport her without the Alexandria Deck, the location of which she refused to tell him until she'd done what she could for Elijah. Therefore, Caine had to join in that effort, and turn his not inconsiderable talents toward resolving the problem.

He set down the empty cup and got to his feet. Lenna immediately rose, too, mindful of his order to stay close to him. He'd much prefer sending her to the other room so he could handle the kid without her interference, but that wasn't an option.

Great. Another group effort.

Caine leaned down, took the remote from Elijah, and turned off the television. The cartoon the kid had been watching was annoying, anyway. The high-pitched voices, the bright colors and unnatural movements of the characters . . . It was maddening to a Hunter for whom no sight or noise was ever entirely in the background.

"Hey!" Elijah said, jumping up off the couch. "You turned off the TV!"

A Hunter used whatever weapon was available, so . . . "Hunters don't watch that crap," Caine said. If the kid thought he was a Hunter-in-training, maybe he'd give up the cartoon without much protest.

"Crap is a bad word," Elijah said, but he perched on the edge of the couch and worked up a serious expression.

Lenna murmured a slightly amused, "Yes, it is." She stood right behind Caine, so close he could feel the heat from her body. Her constant nearness, the scent and warmth—and damn, even the *air* felt softer around her—were chaffing at him, making him feel as if his clothing had tiny spikes embedded in the cloth. He could not get this done soon enough.

"We have work to do." Caine planted himself in front of the kid, crossed his arms over his chest, and looked down. Elijah craned his head to look up, narrowing one eye. If he was intimidated, it didn't show.

"Where can I find Uncle Bobby?"

Elijah shrugged his shoulders.

"What is his full name?"

"Uncle Bobby."

"Caine, this is . . ."

He held up a hand to silence Lenna, and—will wonders never cease—she was silenced.

Frustration flared hotter within him, snaking its way through his body like a physical invasion. "Bob something?" he prodded. "Or perhaps Robert? This man must have a last name. Surely you heard it at some point. Think back."

"Nope." The child seemed supremely unconcerned by his lack of knowledge.

So, Elijah didn't know the man's last name. That was a problem, but it wasn't the worst problem Caine had ever encountered. "Where does he work? Where does he live?"

Again, the answer was a maddening shrug of little shoulders.

Caine turned to glare at Lenna. "In a metropolitan area that's home to five million or more humans, how can you expect me to find a man with the name 'Bobby' and nothing else?" he snapped.

"*Uncle* Bobby," Elijah corrected from behind him. "His car is gray, does that help?"

"No." Caine shoved his hand through his hair. How many tens of thousands of gray or silver cars were in the Atlanta metro area?

"There's no need to interrogate the child as if he were the criminal," Lenna said in a soft voice, but her gaze was accusing.

"Uncle Bobby isn't a Maj—he isn't like you. I can't find him just by focusing on energy. Do you have any other ideas?"

"No," she admitted.

He wanted to believe that the kid was spinning a tale, that there was no Uncle Bobby, or if there was, his mother had run away with him and left the kid behind. It was an ugly truth that kids were left behind all the time, in this world and in others.

But Elijah and Lenna had been threatened, and that wasn't a coincidence. Lenna herself seemed sure of the child's tale, and while he might not necessarily believe a kid as young as Elijah, he did believe her.

"The man downstairs said I look like you," Elijah said, drawing Caine's attention away from Lenna. "Do I?"

The kid's attention jumped around like a rabbit. Caine looked over his shoulder at him. "No."

The kid didn't give up. "My hair and eyes look like yours, don't they? A lot of my friends look like their dads—some of them, anyway. I don't have a dad. Is there any more chocolate milk?"

Caine was speechless. Where to begin? What did he address first, the chocolate milk issue or genetics or—

Lenna saved him, moving around him to sit beside Elijah on the couch. She took the little boy's hand and held on. "It's important that you tell Caine everything you remember about Uncle Bobby. How else are we to find and punish him?"

"All I know is he's old and ugly and mean and he killed my mom. I always called him Uncle Bobby, but sometimes Mom called him Robert. He gave me a Christmas present, but I don't want it anymore. It's . . . it's crap!" He shot Caine a defiant look as he forcefully uttered the so-called bad word. Then he wrinkled his nose, said, "I have to pee!" and jumped up from the couch to run to the bathroom.

Caine sighed and sat beside Lenna. He rubbed his head; he never had headaches, but damn if the kid wasn't giving him a major one. No, to be fair, it wasn't just the kid; it was the entire situation. He studied her with narrowed eyes, both angry and aroused. He needed some space from her, but he couldn't have it, not if he wanted to continue to shield her. And he did; not only was he committed to a successful end to his mission, he didn't want to see her dead by a Hunter's knife.

"Now what?" he asked, scowling.

She placed a hand on his knee. "Be gentle with Elijah. He's been traumatized, and he's so young he doesn't know much of the world."

"We can leave him—"

"No," she said sharply, lifting her hand. "We can't

leave him, anywhere. He can't identify Uncle Bobby, not without seeing him face-to-face, but Uncle Bobby can identify him. We make Elijah an easy target if we abandon him."

Caine growled. You'd think Elijah was her own kid, the way she looked out for him. Why? His life, the life of any human, was no more than a blink of an eye to any one of the Major Arcana. They touched this world, they influenced the people here, but it was unheard of for them to develop emotional attachments. That's exactly what this was: emotion.

Emotion wasn't rational, but still he tried to appeal to her common sense—assuming she had any. No, that was unfair. The truth was that he was annoyed by her opposition, and by the knowledge that, being who she was, she wasn't likely to change her mind. "There are ways to keep him hidden. I'm not proposing that we leave him alone, to fend for himself. Take me to the deck. Let me return you to Aeonia where you'll be safe, and I swear, I'll return and see to the boy. You have my word."

She completely ignored that proposition. "A few days, that is all I ask," she said, her voice calm and deceptively reasonable. "I know I have to go home. I understand the importance of my presence in Aeonia. But Elijah pulled me into this world with his plea for help, and I can't simply hand him over to someone else. Not even to you. I don't doubt your capabilities." Her chin jutted out a bit and her gaze went cool. "I do, however, doubt your commitment to Elijah."

The expression on Caine's face mirrored what Lenna herself felt. Frustration, anger, worry. Neither of them were desperate—not yet, anyway.

She had to return to Aeonia; there was no other option. Moreover, she *wanted* to go home. If the Hunter couldn't transport her there within the allotted time frame, her world would cease to exist. She wouldn't allow that to happen. As much as she cared for Elijah, she couldn't sacrifice an entire world to personally see to his well-being. In a few days, if they didn't make progress, she would have no choice but to reassemble the Alexandria Deck and allow Caine to take her home. She wasn't about to tell Caine that, though; he'd immediately conclude all he had to do was keep her shielded until she was forced to go home. She wanted him actively trying to solve Elijah's problem, because no one in the universe was more ferocious in achieving their ends than a Hunter.

She wondered if the Emperor would be satisfied with that plan. And what about the Tower? Her time here was unprecedented, and she had no way of communicating with the others. Perhaps they could look in on her, perhaps they could see, but she was blind. She didn't know if or when they might be watching, and she didn't know if they could hear. Even if they were—Caine was shielding her. Could they see through that power? Did the Emperor know what Veton had done?

The Hunter who had tried to kill her had said she could be replaced. Was that possible? The Major Arcana was as it had always been, complete and powerful. There had been a time when they'd traveled to other worlds, before the deck had been lost, and while a few had been slightly injured during their adventures, none had ever died.

If she died, how would another Strength be chosen? What effect would there be on the worlds touched by the power of the Major Arcana? Would her death be as disastrous as if her time here went beyond the allowed five days?

She had so many questions, and no clear answers.

The door to the bathroom opened, and Elijah shot out, headed for the couch. He stopped halfway, braced himself, squatted slightly, made two fists, closed his eyes, and grunted.

"No!" Caine said explosively, surging to his feet. "Go back to the bathroom! Don't—you're too old. You're not wearing diapers!"

Lenna stared up at him, her mouth falling open. What? What was wrong? She didn't understand.

Elijah opened his eyes and made a sound of disgust. "I'm not pooping in my pants! I'm not a little baby. I was trying to disappear and then appear somewhere else, like you did. No one ever taught me how. I didn't even know it was something grown-ups could do! I thought I'd just, you know, try it and see what happened."

Caine sat back down, rubbed his face, pinched between his eyes. "You can't teleport. You are hu—"

Lenna interrupted. "You're much too young." When she and Caine left this world, Elijah would necessarily be left behind. The less he knew of who they were and what they could do, the easier his new life would be. Eventually he would forget some of what he'd seen, and the rest, the rest he would relegate to the back of his mind as a faulty remembrance or perhaps even a dream. The less specific they were, the better.

Elijah accepted her explanation, and with a burst of speed rushed at the couch—and launched himself into Caine's lap.

He landed with force and flying arms and legs. A startled Caine grunted, then looked at her with an easy to read "help me" expression on his hard face.

Hunters didn't deal with children. Lenna knew little of the Hunter species; she wasn't even sure Caine had once been a child, though she suspected he had been, a very long time ago. She was somewhat bemused that he expected her to have more experience than he; he *did* remember that she was Major Arcana, didn't he?

Elijah leaned backward and looked upside down at Lenna. "If I can't poof, will you at least teach me how to make the magic light?"

"I'm afraid you are too young for that, as well."

The boy frowned, frustrated in all his efforts to learn a power but determined not to give up. "Will you teach me, when I'm not too young?"

"If I can."

With a sigh, Elijah rested his head on Caine's chest. The Hunter lifted both his big, hard hands in a helpless movement, then he sighed and placed one hand on the boy's back.

Elijah yawned. "I'm kind of tired," he said. "I'm too old for naps, but sometimes I get sleepy, anyway." His eyes drifted shut, then he jerked awake and turned his head to look pleadingly at Lenna. "Don't leave me while I'm asleep."

"I won't," she said gently.

He tipped his head back to look at Caine. "You don't go anywhere, either."

All manner of expressions flashed over the Hunter's face, none of which Lenna hoped Elijah could read.

After a short pause, Caine said, "I'll be right here when you wake." He glanced at Lenna as Elijah burrowed in and closed his eyes again. "Where else would I be?"

Derek had almost stopped hurting, but he was pretty sure his balls wouldn't be anywhere near normal for days to come. Sitting behind the wheel of his car, down the street from the garage where Sammy worked, he adjusted his aching equipment. It didn't help. He was in a very bad mood and looked forward to killing someone today.

He was furious with the blonde for kicking him, but at the same time, he was impressed that she'd managed to take him down. If he had a daughter, he'd want her to do the same, in that situation. Not that he had a daughter . . . that he knew of. Even though he was impressed with the blonde's abilities in the self-defense department, that didn't mean he wouldn't deliver a little payback when the time came. Still, at the moment he felt a mixture of anger and admiration, as well as a lingering pain.

The auto shop where Sammy worked was north of Atlanta and well out of Lawrenceville and the other major satellite cites. The place was open until two on Saturday afternoon, thank God, otherwise Derek would have had to wait until Monday to take care of the man Markham wanted snuffed out. He'd put off taking care of the kid for now, though he wouldn't let the job drag on too long, but this could happen today. Derek had no reservations about killing a grown man who had obviously stepped into something he shouldn't have.

Making Sammy's death look like a suicide was possible, but it did complicate matters—not that Markham hadn't paid extra for the trouble. The police force in the small town might be easier to fool than the Atlanta PD. He could hope so, anyway.

Any grown man who let people call him Sammy deserved to die. Okay, that was a little harsh. What about Sammy Davis, Jr.? But show business was different, right?

Derek entertained himself trying to think of other famous people named Sammy while he watched the front entrance. It was possible—likely—that there was a rear entrance, as well, but there were too many people around for him to check it out for himself. So far, everyone seemed to come and go from that front entrance, but he hadn't yet seen any employees leaving.

Markham had shown Derek a picture on a cell phone—a god-awful selfie—and then he'd taken that phone with the intention of dismantling it and tossing it in the river. Derek was curious about what an auto mechanic might have on his phone that would cause the senator to go to such lengths. He was a bit surprised that Markham hadn't asked his all-purpose PI to get rid of it, but it didn't matter. He was just curious.

The phone was likely gone by now, but Derek had seen Sammy's face and that was all he needed.

It was a good thing he hadn't decided to wait until closing time to check out the shop. It was just before noon when a man who might be Sammy walked out of the shop. The man had a long, cocky stride, but he was too far away for Derek to be certain this was his target. Grasping the wheel he leaned slightly forward, focusing his attention on the man, waiting for him to turn his head so he could be sure. Soon enough, he did. *Bingo!*

Sammy walked past two rows of cars, those waiting for service and other employee cars, before stopping and pulling keys from the pocket of his overalls. He slid into the driver's seat of an old, rusted embarrassment of a car, and pulled out of the parking lot.

Derek followed.

Chapter 9

Strength had not returned to Aeonia, after all. So now what?

After confirming that Lenna hadn't been returned to her proper place, Esma and Stroud checked every other world she might've traveled to, in case she'd possessed the Alexandria Deck and—for some reason Esma could not comprehend—had decided not to return to Aeonia. There were a handful of livable worlds; Strength had been on none of them. While it was possible that Lenna had been moving from world to world herself, and they had simply never been on the same world at the same time, that scenario was highly improbable. Strength was not a skilled traveler. Even if she did possess the deck, she didn't possess the necessary skills to use it so deftly.

"Where *is* she?" Esma wondered aloud, her voice

soft so no one could overhear. She and Stroud had once again checked on Aeonia—just to be certain—but there was still no sign of Strength. She kept her tone low so no one would report to Veton that two Hunters were searching on Aeonia for the missing Major Arcana.

"We need to go back to Seven," Stroud replied in the same low tone. They hadn't wasted a lot of time, not with their teleporting capabilities, but the fact remained that the minutes were passing and they hadn't completed their mission. With a quick glance between them, the two Hunters returned to Seven to resume the hunt. Neither of them wanted to face Veton empty-handed.

Veton couldn't hurt them, not in the conventional sense. But he could—and would—touch them with his essence. Worst case, nothing would ever succeed for them again; everything they touched, every relationship, every mission, could be a disaster. If that happened they might as well be dead.

When they returned, darkness had fallen. Time passed quickly on Seven; the days here were short. In the time they'd been gone, the day had passed, and at this time of the year night came especially early. Esma rarely noted the fluid movement of time from one world to another, but here, for this job, time was an important element.

Not much more than four days remained before Strength had to be returned to Aeonia. And if she couldn't be returned, then killed, in the hopes that there was some kind of cosmic contingency plan.

It seemed an unnecessary risk to Esma.

"The Alexandria Deck is the thing," she said as she and Stroud studied the dark house from which Lenna and the boy had run, earlier that day. "I don't know how Strength has hidden herself from us, if she is running from Caine as well as from us or if he's helping her, but the how doesn't really matter." She had her suspicions. While it was possible Lenna possessed the power to shield herself, it was more likely that Caine was protecting her.

That in itself was unlikely; Caine let nothing sway him from the mission. Yet Strength hadn't been returned, and neither could they sense her—or Caine—on this world. As unlikely as the probability was, Caine *had* to be shielding her.

The problems with that were so obvious she could only shake her head in disbelief. Caine and Strength would have to remain physically close at all times. If one of them stepped away, even for a moment, she would be outside the protective blanketing and they would immediately sense her. How could they possibly function? What was the purpose of all this?

Nevertheless, Esma would be waiting and watching for Strength to slip, because *if* there was a mistake of that nature it would be Strength who made it. Caine would not; his focus was too intense.

She would wait, all her senses alert.

Until then, she and Stroud could search for the deck. The logical place to start was this house.

Snow started to fall again, light and icy, the drifting flakes illuminated by lights from the houses on either side of the one they watched. The night would be considered cold, by some, but Hunters felt neither heat nor cold as intensely as humans did. She thought the snow was actually pretty, an unnecessary observation she didn't share with Stroud.

Instead, she turned to business. "If Lenna has the deck on her, Caine would have returned her to Aeonia. He would've insisted. On the other hand, if she managed to escape—for whatever reason—and went to another world, we would have found her. There are two possibilities. Either the deck is damaged and isn't working properly, or for some reason Lenna isn't ready to leave Seven."

"The deck managed to bring her here. It's unlikely it would've been damaged so soon, after surviving for more than two thousand years. As for Strength choosing to stay . . . Why?" Stroud asked, his own frustration clear.

"Who knows? We don't need to know why. We just need to do what we were sent here to do." Which was retrieve the deck and kill or save Lenna. Esma knew what her preference was. "Let's assume she has chosen to stay. If that's the case, she must have hidden the deck. If she has it with her, Caine would have teleported her regardless of what she wanted."

Her companion nodded, mulling over the most likely circumstances. He looked at the house directly before them. While lights shone from the homes all around, this one remained lifeless and dark. "There?"

"Maybe." It was probably too much to hope for that the deck was hidden in the ordinary house, but it wouldn't hurt to take a look around. From there they would fan out. Lenna hadn't been here long before Esma and Stroud—and poor Nevan—had arrived. She didn't have the power to teleport, and she didn't know how to operate the vehicles—she had come here with no method of speedy travel.

There was only one logical conclusion. The deck had to be nearby.

In spite of his long nap earlier in the day, by nine that night Elijah was soundly asleep on the couch in the parlor. It pulled out into a bed, but Elijah had insisted he could just sleep on the couch with a pillow and blanket. It was a small thing to ask, and Lenna hadn't seen any reason to deny him.

She wasn't blind to the circumstances she and Caine were in. She wasn't happy about it, but the situation was of her own design and she accepted that she'd simply have to make the best of it.

In order for the shield to hold, she and Caine would be forced to sleep close together. The bed was wide, but it wasn't nearly large enough when she considered that she'd be sharing it with a man like the Hunter.

"Shower," he said, taking her arm and leading her toward the bathroom. What was it about his touch that made her feel as if a current of energy was running from his hand to her? Was it something peculiar to the Hunters? But when that other Hunter, the one who had tried to kill her, had touched her she'd felt nothing like this. She'd felt fear, and anger, and determination, but not this surge of tingling heat. Hunters were peculiar beings, beyond a doubt. She would assign that as the cause.

She had studied the large walk-in shower more than once during the day, and had even longed to stand beneath the spray—alone, of course. She wanted to let hot water wash away the events of the day, stand there until she had her thoughts sorted and her emotions settled. At the moment, her usually ordered mind was a muddle.

In the bathroom, Caine released her and immediately began to strip out of his clothes. Lenna did the same, but far more slowly. She wasn't shy; why would she be? But for some reason being naked before Caine disturbed her a little—more than a little. She felt vulnerable. The emotion was so alien to her that she stopped a moment to examine it. Was it the situation, being here on Seven and out of her element, or was it Caine? He hadn't done anything that she found threatening, but . . . but he wasn't an ordinary man. He was adapting to the circumstances she had forced on him, holding himself in check because for the moment she had the upper hand. Every so often, though, she caught a hard gleam in his eyes that told her he was simply waiting— waiting for a split second of opportunity to seize control from her, ready to exploit any weakness he could find. Hunters were notoriously focused on completing the mission, and Caine was notorious among the Hunters, which said more than enough about him.

At the moment he seemed not to even notice her; she had to admit his concentration was superior to hers, at least in this matter. She was acutely aware of the breadth of his bare shoulders as he shrugged out of his shirt, the way his skin gleamed over the stretch and bulge of solid muscle. His arms were thick and sinewy, testifying to a physical strength she could only imagine.

He removed his boots and socks, then shoved his pants down and stepped out of them. Completely naked, he turned on the spray in the shower, then threw her an inscrutable look. "Are you showering with your clothes on?"

Lenna steeled herself to be nude in front of him, and silently finished removing her clothing. She might as well have been a piece of furniture, though, for all the attention he paid her. He stepped under the spray of water and she didn't allow herself to hesitate again, following him into the enclosure that would have been spacious for just her, but with him in there with her it felt much, much too small. It was, in fact, too small for both of them to bathe at once.

He turned his back to her and began to apply soap to his body. He washed himself briskly and efficiently. Lenna wondered if he was ever . . . inefficient—in anything. The thought made her a little breathless. She had to stand so close behind him that just a bit of the spray hit her bare body, and as any female would have, she looked. She admired. She very badly wanted to touch, but she disciplined herself to stillness and did not.

Taking her time, pleasure filling her with a warm rush, she looked him up and down. He was so hard and sculpted he could have been a statue come to life. She studied the powerful lines of his back, the furrow of his spine running through pads of muscle, his hard round buttocks, his powerful thighs. Up her gaze went to once more linger on his impressive arms, and it occurred to her that he was as much machine as man, a weapon, more than anything else.

He opened a small bottle of liquid and put a drop in his palm, then lathered his hair with the same quick efficiency with which he'd bathed. Lenna continued to watch, to admire the sheen of his wet muscles and the way he moved. *No touching*, she reminded herself, though her fingers did twitch a bit as she fought to resist the urge.

When he was finished bathing, he turned and lifted an eyebrow at her stillness. "Why are you just standing there? Bathe, if you're going to. We don't have all night."

"There is room for only one of us beneath the spray," she pointed out reasonably. "And, actually, we do. Have all night, that is." He turned to the side and she twisted her back to maneuver past him, the tight confines necessarily meaning her bottom brushed against him, and she felt the bulges of his genitals on her bare skin as she slid past. She ignored him and angled her face up to the spray of warm water. It was as pleasurable as she had dreamed it would be; normally she soaked in deep, jeweled tubs made of valuable stone, in perfumed, silken water, but the spray was invigorating. She resumed what she'd been saying. "Elijah needs rest, and we can't leave him alone. Morning will be soon enough for us to resume our work, so we do have all night. Do Hunters sleep?"

"On occasion. You?"

Lenna plucked a washcloth from a neat stack sitting just beyond the spray, and also took the soap Caine had used from a dish sticking from the wall. "Now and then. It's pleasant to relax, to dream." She began rubbing the lather over her body.

She kept her back to him as she bathed, and couldn't help but wonder if he admired anything about her, as she had admired him. She wondered if he was tempted to reach out a hand and almost touch her, as she had almost touched him. It was possible he was completely unaffected by her closeness. She was a job to him, nothing more. He was irritated with her, annoyed that she wouldn't obey his commands.

Weapon. Not man. She would do well to remember that.

She leaned over to wash her legs with the soapy washcloth. For some reason, Caine growled, the sound low and rough in his throat. Startled, Lenna straightened.

"Would you hurry?" he snapped.

Annoyed, she turned to face him, to snap that she hadn't rushed him and he could allow her the same consideration. The words dried in her throat as the water ran down her back.

It was very clear from this vantage point that he was not as unaffected by her as she had believed him to be. He *was* a man, after all.

This could get complicated.

Caine dried his body with a towel, as Lenna turned her back to him and did the same. It didn't matter. Looking at her slim, lithe back and smooth round ass did nothing to ease the heavy strain of his erection. Her skin glowed. A litany of curses rolled through his mind. He cursed her for being so stubborn; he cursed her for being beautiful. He cursed himself for watching her bathe and getting as hard as a young Hunter who had no control over his own body.

Still naked, she combed her wet hair and began blotting the dripping ends with a towel. The action reminded him of the things they needed and didn't have, and gratefully he seized on that as a means of distracting himself.

"When the boy wakes, we'll go shopping."

"Why?" Lenna asked. "Shopping seems a waste of precious time."

"You need things of this world, and so does he."
The hotel had sent up toothbrushes and combs at his
request, but they needed more. "You'll need a change
of clothes, and you and the boy both need pajamas if
we are to be here more than a day."

"Pajamas," she repeated. "That is nightwear,
correct?"

"Yes."

She shrugged. "I don't wear them. When I do sleep,
I find it preferable to do so naked."

Impossibly, he got harder. He took a minute to swear
some more to himself. "Maybe we can do all that needs
to be done tomorrow, and you'll be home by tomorrow
night." Please. By the One, please let that be so.

She sighed. "I wish I thought that was possible, but
I have no idea how to proceed, nor how long it will take
to find Uncle Bobby."

"You could let me—"

"No." She didn't even let him finish, but then,
she knew what he'd been about to say because they'd
already covered this ground. She would *not* go home
until this problem with Elijah was settled.

That was an argument he would never win. Not
with her. Not until another four days had passed.

Four days. Four days was nothing, not in the
extraordinarily long lives of a Hunter, and certainly not

to a Major Arcana. It was the blink of an eye to them, and yet, if he had to spend it in close proximity with her—an eternity.

"I don't know this world well enough to navigate it without difficulty," she said.

Caine wrapped his towel around his waist—for all the good it did—and turned to face her. He would be wasting his breath to ask her, again, to let him handle this situation while she waited in Aeonia. At least she admitted she was out of her depth; that was an advantage to him, if he could get her to negotiate.

She hadn't bothered to wrap the towel around herself, using it instead to continue wiping over her hair . . . slowly. Maddeningly slowly. Her body was bare, fair and smooth and shapely. Frustrated, he had to admit she knew exactly what she was doing to him, and that she was as ruthless in her own way as he was.

"You can help me with that issue, if you will consent," she said.

"Help you how?" he asked between clenched teeth.

Her hair mostly dry, she shook her head and rubbed the edge of the towel against the place on her neck where one last drop of water trailed down. Down and down, until she stopped it. "I can lay my hands on a being and absorb their knowledge. You have great knowledge of this world. If you allowed me to—"

"No." Lenna, Strength, poking around in his head? Reading him like a book? Absorbing not just his knowledge of this world, but all his secrets? Not that he had any secrets to speak of, but still . . . "No."

She looked peeved. Not angry, just annoyed. She still didn't cover herself with the towel. "Then I will choose another tomorrow, someone from this world. Perhaps while we are shopping."

It wasn't his imagination that she sounded disappointed.

One corner of his mouth lifted in a quirk. After all, negotiation was the name of the game, and he had something she wanted. "What concession will you make if I allow you to read me?"

She stiffened, her blue eyes flashing. "There is no knowledge you could give me that would cause me to turn my back on Elijah."

No, of course not; she was called Strength for a reason—damn it. She continued in a frosty tone. "If, however, you require sex before you will agree to help him, that is nothing to me and you may relieve yourself with my body."

He could have her. His penis surged even harder and thicker, urging him to say, Hell, yes, but then, it wasn't a thinking organ. He liked living on the knife edge of danger and tangling with her in the sheets would be that, and yes, he wanted her, but he didn't want her as payment. He didn't want having her to mean nothing to her. Being near her all this interminably long day had worn on his nerves, and this almost made him snap. He was savagely angry that she would even suggest such a thing.

"Thank you, but no," he said as coldly as she had, and turned his back on her to go into the bedroom, leaving it to her to follow or risk losing the protection of his shielding.

He had turned on one bedside lamp before going into the bathroom, illuminating the bed but casting shadows all around. Lenna dropped her towel on the floor and slipped into bed, making herself comfortable.

Caine ground his teeth. She had insulted him, and he returned the strike. "If I sleep, will you take what you want from me, even though I refused?"

"No." She looked more than a little pissed by his question; she looked as enraged as he felt. *Good.* "Don't be insulting. I would never invade your mind without your permission. That would be rude."

Caine dropped his towel, walked around the bed, and slid under the covers on the other side. "As insulting as thinking you could buy my cooperation with sex?"

She didn't reply, and he turned off the lamp.

The darkness was worse than the light. It was more

intimate, wrapping them together in night's cocoon. Darkness was when bodies came together, when barriers were let down. He was in bed with a beautiful woman who obviously didn't mind being there, who didn't mind being naked in front of him—but a woman who hadn't given his erection much more than a glance. What was he thinking? She wasn't a woman; she was Strength.

But he wanted her. Bad idea.

More than that, for him to succeed in his mission he needed her to function as efficiently as possible in this world she didn't understand. For that, she needed knowledge. She needed not to be so obviously out of place. She could get that knowledge from someone else. Tomorrow would be soon enough.

"Can you read the kid's mind?" he asked. "Maybe he knows something about the man who killed his mother that he just doesn't remember. You could at least figure out what this Uncle Bobby looks like."

"Elijah is too young, his brain far too fragile."

Too bad, but . . . they'd find another way. He turned toward her and moved closer. She was warm, as warm as he was. The comfort of animal warmth shared in the night wasn't lost on him. Somehow she glowed a little, as if she drew more light to her body than ordinary beings did.

"What else can you do?" he asked. "You never know what might be helpful."

She lifted a hand, which made the covers fall back from her just enough to reveal her breasts, and created a ball of light that danced on her palm—a light as soft as stars, rather than glaring like sunlight. A soft light. This had to be the magic light Elijah had mentioned earlier.

"Great. You're a walking flashlight and you can read fully formed minds with a touch. What else?"

The light on her palm died. "My purpose is strength of will and determination. I represent, and share across the worlds, patience and courage. I would think a Hunter would appreciate all of those, though I suspect patience is not one of your personal virtues."

"No, not really." He turned the focus back on her. "What about this great temper I've heard of? Can you truly wreak havoc when it's roused? Can you control it?" *That* would come in handy.

"It's been thousands of years since I've lost my temper," she said, obviously uncomfortable with the turn in the conversation. "And it's not something I can control, any more than other beings can control their tempers. It is, as I recall . . . unpredictable."

Now it was she who moved closer, turning on her side to face him. Her smallish, exquisitely shaped breasts were just inches from his hand. Perhaps she didn't notice, but he did; his fingers twitched, and he moved them away from temptation. She said, "Once I was called Fortitude, but over many years that changed, and I became Strength. Even though I was not in the worlds where that shift took place, I, too, was changed. Who I am, what I am, has not faltered."

"So, you don't shoot lasers out of your eyeballs." He barely knew what he was saying, but he was intensely aware of every word she said, every movement she made.

She smiled. "Not to my knowledge. I have never tried to do so."

"Well, don't try now."

She laughed, the sound low so as not to disturb the sleeping child in the next room. He liked laughter on her, better than the annoyance and stubbornness. Vae, he didn't need to like anything about her.

"It seems that I'm a little faster than the humans of Seven, and a little stronger, too," she added. "It's been so long since I've ventured beyond my home . . . so much is uncertain."

Caine considered all the variables and options, cutting through his innate dislike of leaving himself open to anyone. Nothing she had said swayed him, but he did find himself swayed by what she hadn't said.

Here they were, lying naked in bed together—talking. She was silently offering him more trust than anyone else ever had, in all his travels across the universe. He'd been pissed off at her all day long, and yet now . . . now he felt the strong impulse to show his trust to her.

Silently he said one of the most pungent curses used on Seven. Ah, well. Might as well get it over with.

"You have my permission." His voice was low, but the words were clear and laced with steel.

She had evidently dozed off in the few moments that had passed; at least, her eyes had closed. Even a Major Arcana got tired after such a tumultuous day, being jerked from Aeonia into this world, nearly being killed, fighting and running and dealing with being responsible for a child. "What?" she murmured, opening her eyes.

He said roughly, "Touch me."

Chapter 10

He'd given his permission, but now Lenna hesitated. She knew she needed to read him to acquire crucial information about Seven, but . . . touching him while they were both naked and in bed was infinitely different from touching him when they were fully clothed and in Elijah's company. He was very male and, at least where he was concerned, she was more female than she'd quite realized before. Liking the male sex in general was not the same as being intensely interested in one particular male. She couldn't remember ever before being aroused by just looking at a man's body.

Regardless of how uncharacteristically hesitant she felt, she knew she had to do it. Gently she placed one hand on the side of his head, then slid the other to his neck. Her fingers conformed to his shape. Her eyes closed as she cradled him.

He was hotter than she'd expected him to be, turning his hair to warm silk under her hand. His strong neck was hard and corded; she could feel the vibrant rush of blood pulsing deep within. This wasn't like before. She'd touched him; he'd touched her—but not like this, leisurely, without haste or direction. She liked the sensation of his flesh against her palms, the sound of his breath, the beat of his heart.

Though he had given his permission, finding her way into his mind wasn't as effortless as reading someone usually was. Everything about him was tough, body and mind. Mentally she pushed, and felt his instinctive resistance.

She took her hands away. "If you hate the idea this much, it won't work."

"Shit," he muttered, a Seven expletive with which she was familiar, having heard it before when she'd looked in on this world. Back then the major mode of transportation had been horses, so even though much time had passed on Seven while she'd been distracted, evidently the expletive was an enduring one.

"Shit," she repeated, pleased that she both remembered and agreed with the application.

Surprised, he laughed. It was a rusty, stifled sound, one he obviously didn't make very often. "Making myself mentally available isn't something I've ever done before. Let's try this." Before she could ask what "this" was, and agree or disagree, he slid one muscular arm beneath her and rolled her on top of him.

Luckily a fold of the covers got caught between them, or the situation would have been far more intimate than it already was. His big body was hard and vibrant beneath her, her tender nipples nestled against his hairy chest. She took a quick, startled breath, distracted by the rush of pleasure that made her bones turn liquid. She wanted to melt over him, absorb all that strength and intensity inside her, learn about another kind of strength.

He kept that one arm around her, and slipped his other hand up her back to clasp the nape of her neck. "Try again," he said, his tone so low she could barely hear him.

Once again she cupped the back of his head in her hand, and lightly laid her other hand along his jaw. The roughness of his whiskers scraped her palm. She felt the strong beat of his heart against her breast, his breath against her temple. She closed her eyes, concentrated. She still felt resistance, but this time instead of pushing, she merely let him feel her presence, and after a moment he mentally relaxed and she slipped inside him, to touch not just his thoughts, but his very essence.

Instantly she felt the strength in him. She had known it, of course, but now she *felt* it.

She hadn't been certain about Hunters—they were different—but Caine had indeed been a child, long, long ago. He had been born on a world similar to Seven and yet unique, as all the worlds were. As a child Caine had been chosen, he'd been favored, thanks to a genetic quirk a small number of beings from his world possessed. He'd been taken from his family and trained to become what he'd literally been born to be: a Hunter, a mercenary, a weapon.

He was a weapon *and* a man. Not one or the other, but both.

His fellow Hunters both admired and feared him, and he knew that to be true. His reputation had been honestly earned, with fierceness and his exceptional ability in a race of exceptional soldiers.

Caine was familiar with the details of many worlds, but she pushed past those memories to focus on his vast knowledge of Seven. He had been in and out of the world so many times he didn't know the precise number of his visits. Over hundreds of years he had seen Seven grow and change. He'd watched, he'd learned, and though he hadn't been trained to do so, he had enjoyed many of the pleasures here: food, sex, music.

And, oddly enough, thunderstorms. He loved them, as he loved the mountains and the oceans. As he loved to watch the sun rise and set. Through his memories she saw the majestic storms, heard the boom, and felt the power of the wind.

Words flowed into her, as did songs from every age of Seven. Music beautiful and harsh, haunting and exhilarating, soothing and disturbing. Numbers. Science. Languages. He knew them all, and now, so did she. She learned the advances in technology, the customs and manners, the intricacies of everyday life here.

Then the knowledge of Seven passed, and she was elsewhere within his soul.

A small part of her realized that she had everything she needed in order to function in this world and she should immediately end the link and withdraw, but she didn't. To be inside Caine's mind was unexpectedly delicious, and she wanted more.

She stilled her body and her own mind. She didn't probe; she simply waited, and slowly he opened even more to her. This was more intimate than any other connection she had ever experienced. The Hunter was smarter, savvier, more wonderfully layered than he appeared to be at first glance. And still, Elijah befuddled him because, like her, Caine didn't deal with children, not ever. He barely remembered being a child himself, and as he had been taken from his family so young his childhood and Elijah's could hardly be compared. Caine hadn't been coddled; he hadn't been loved as Elijah had been. No, he had been forged, as any other weapon would be.

Mingled with his irritation and uncustomary confusion, she caught an unexpected—unexpected by her *and* by him—bit of caring for the child he now protected, as he protected her. Though he put on a show of being gruff and unconcerned, Caine did care.

He cared about doing what was right. He was a man of his word.

If it came to it, she could—and would—leave Elijah in the Hunter's hands.

She should pull away, end the connection. She knew she should. But now it was as if *he* held *her*, as if his mind held hers captive. No, not captive—willingly melded.

She saw that Elijah wasn't the only one who befuddled Caine. He liked *her.* He wanted her, so much that feeling the intensity of his need made her tremble. Lying in bed with her was torture for him, and yet because it was his duty to protect her, to shield her from the other Hunters, he remained close. He had studied her in the shower much as she had studied him. He wanted to touch her now, so intensely that his hands ached to stroke her skin. She sensed in great and breathtaking detail what he wanted to do to her.

What she wanted him to do to her.

Her eyes flared open and she found herself drowning in the darkness of his gaze, so close to her, so focused, that she knew he was aware of what she'd been reading and was feeding her more. He shifted beneath her, and the hard rod of his penis pushed upward. She could pull aside the fold of sheet that was between them, open her legs, and he'd be inside her. He wanted it. *She* wanted it.

And yet . . . something held her back. He was too much, too male, too alpha, for their personalities to be a comfortable fit. Part of being who she was, was that she could resist temptation.

She severed the mental connection.

She'd gone too far, seen too much. She shook a little as she withdrew her hands and rolled to the side, away from him. Immediately she felt the absence of his heat, wanted anew the feel of his steely body against her. Never before had she delved so deeply into another's mind; she hadn't known she could, and likely wouldn't have if he hadn't actively pulled her in. He had taken an action of surrender and turned it into a strategic victory for himself.

She had always maintained strict control when reading someone, wary of doing damage with her enormous will. Her invasion into Caine's essence had taken only a few seconds—hadn't it?—yet it had seemed much longer. It seemed as if they had lain together like this through the long dark hours of the night. She knew him now. She knew him more intimately than any other being did, or ever had. For a short time, she had been a part of him.

She felt humbled, an unusual emotion for a Major Arcana. Caine was not simply a Hunter; he was a good man. Unlike Nevan, he would never kill an innocent for gain or sport. He experienced emotion in a way she had not, not for a very long time. Pain and joy were as much a part of him as duty.

He wanted her; she wanted him. Those moments when she'd been in his mind had been foreplay, bringing sensations to life as surely as if he'd been kissing and stroking her. They weren't bound by the human moral restrictions of Seven—restrictions she understood now, as Caine did—so there was no reason for them not to take what they wanted. Just the thought of sex with him caused a tremor, a fire, deep inside her where he would be if she acted on her desire.

"Is everything all right?" he asked.

He knew what he'd done, yet his voice was as impersonal as if they had done no more than shake hands.

Somehow it was important that she meet his strength with her own. Did he think to influence her with sex?

"Yes," she said, her voice purposely cool. "I'll be able to function more capably in this world now. Thank you."

"You're welcome."

Had all that been a strategic move to undermine her determination to stay with Elijah? If so, then he would be disappointed. She had touched his soul, but he barely knew her. They were strangers; she was an assignment to him, a mission to be completed.

She didn't need much sleep, but tonight she would try. She hoped Caine would, too. Sleep would make the night pass more quickly. But first—

"I intend to fulfill my promise to Elijah," she said into the darkness, "but if I can't accomplish the task in the days I am allowed in this world, I will trust you to take me home and then return here to see the job done."

The only hint that the offer surprised him was a very slight lift of one eyebrow. "You trust me."

"I do."

She could almost see his mind working as she looked into those mesmerizing dark eyes. "Then tell me where the deck is," he said. "We'll both feel better when it is safe in our hands."

There was some truth to that argument. The majority of the deck was where Elijah had found it, in the corner of a closet in Zack's house where anyone could stumble across it. The Moon, on a shelf in Elijah's bedroom, was all but out in the open. The only card she could be positive was safe and well-guarded was the one in her bag.

But if she reunited the cards, Caine would take her home without further delay. He was an honorable man, she knew that, but his first duty was to the Emperor, not to her or Elijah.

"Not yet," she said.

He made a sound that was just short of a growl.

"Don't worry," she said. "I do believe that if it is necessary you will keep your word and see to Elijah, as you said you would. I'm not being purposely difficult—I do understand the importance of my return to Aeonia and I give you *my* word I'll allow you to take me home when time dictates."

"I'm glad to hear it." He didn't sound glad. He sounded distinctly grumpy.

She smiled at him, though she didn't know whether

or not he could see in the dark as well as she could. "You could argue with me a little and tell me that in the short time you've known me I haven't been at all difficult."

He did not smile, not exactly, but there was a small crook at the corner of his mouth as he said, "I would never lie to you."

It was truth and a tease; she felt something relax inside her, and didn't take offense.

She nestled more deeply into her pillow. "We could return," she mused. "After my time here has passed, you could take me home briefly and we could come back, if necessary."

"You can't travel without the deck, and the Emperor has hired me to hand it over to him. My mission is to return you, and take the Alexandria Deck to him. I'm obligated to fulfill my mission. If I take you back to Aeonia, do you think the Emperor would then immediately turn the Alexandria Deck back over to you—or me—so we could return here and start the dilemma all over again?"

He could've lied to her, made promises he couldn't keep, but he hadn't. That only made her trust him more. The truth, no matter how unpalatable, was solid ground on which one could depend.

Still, she was disappointed. If he could bring her

back to Seven as often as was necessary, then she wouldn't be under the stress of a time limit for taking care of Elijah's problem.

She sighed. "Good night," she said, turning away and presenting her back to him, not because she was annoyed but because if she was to get any sleep she had to turn so she couldn't see him. She must be content with the knowledge he had shared; she had all she needed.

But, oh, she wondered what he was thinking now . . .

Caine lay awake, his arms folded behind his head. For a minute there, he'd thought he might be able to convince her to tell him where the deck was, to let him take her home. If she had, he'd have acted immediately, taken her back, and then returned here before Elijah even knew he was missing. The kid wouldn't be happy that Lenna was gone, but Caine figured he'd be able to settle the little guy down. How long it would take to find this Uncle Bobby was anyone's guess, so he wanted Lenna back on Aeonia where she belonged.

No such luck.

He could have lied to her. A Hunter had no problem lying, if that would help complete the mission. But a Hunter was by default always strategic, and he knew that if he lied to her she would never forget, never forgive. In the future . . . well, in the future, trust could become indispensable for them, and he didn't want to squander that.

But she'd said no, and he knew better than to try to make her change her mind. If there were a Major Arcana card with the name "Stubborn" scrolled across the top, her picture would be on it.

He finally slept some, and so did she. Luckily neither of them needed much sleep, because if he had to spend every night—naked—in the same bed with her, the results would be—

Damn satisfying.

Finally it was morning, and he could hear Elijah stirring in the living room. Caine was glad enough to leave the bed that was nothing short of a torture chamber.

Silently he left the bed, but not silently enough, because Lenna opened her eyes and got out from under the covers to pull on her clothes. Caine dressed with angry jerks, trying not to look at her and failing, because, vae, he was a man and she was a woman and she'd been made with more than a passing nod to temptation.

It was with relief that he finished dressing first, then as he was about to go into the living room, he remembered he couldn't get very far from her and paused to wait until she was ready. He stood with his back to her, and when she said, "I'm dressed," he simply opened the door and went into the living room.

"I'm hungry," Elijah said, pouncing on the couch and turning on the television.

"Good morning to you, too," Caine replied drily.

Elijah rubbed his nose. "I didn't say good morning."

"I know."

"Oh. I get it." He giggled. "I *should* have said it, right?"

"Yes."

"Good! Morning!" Elijah pronounced each word with enthusiastic emphasis. "I'm! Hungry!"

Caine chuckled a little to himself. Children were quite a bit of trouble, but at the same time, they were often interesting and entertaining. He would much rather Elijah be mischievous than crying the way he had yesterday. There would be more tears, he had no doubt, but for now the novelty of being in the hotel, of being with Hunters, was taking his mind off the tragedy of losing his mother. He slept, ate, and watched cartoons. For now, that was good enough.

Life continued.

"What do you want for breakfast today?" he asked.

"Everything," Elijah said blissfully. "Like yesterday."

Caine got on the phone to order another huge room service breakfast, and eyed Lenna as he talked, gauging her mood. She looked as calm as always; if she was in any way disturbed, about anything, it didn't show on the surface.

He'd thought she would put back on the clothes she'd been wearing yesterday, but instead she had on a white dress that she must have been wearing when she'd been brought to this world. Caine clenched his jaw. The woman was trying to kill him; he knew that for certain now. The dress was some soft material that floated about her body as if it were her own personal slinky cloud, and he went from half-mast to hard as a rock in what felt like a single heartbeat. There was nothing about her that was normal, nothing about her that blended in.

"You'll need to change clothes before we go shopping," he said, keeping his tone neutral.

She looked down at her dress, a faint frown wrinkling her brow. "Why? I'll be getting new clothes then, won't I?"

"You attract too much attention in that dress," he said. Not only was it too flimsy for cold weather clothing, it exposed too much of her glowing skin.

She had looked inside his brain, and when she stopped to consider how she would appear to the citizens of Seven, she understood and gave him a brief nod.

After they ate he shooed Elijah into the bathroom to take a shower, then he and Lenna went back into the bedroom so she could change clothes. The constraints of shielding her were going to be the death of him, because there was no way he could have even a moment away from her, without risking her safety. He watched her strip out of the dress and step into the jeans she'd been wearing yesterday, and despite himself he had the traitorous thought that maybe they could wait until the last possible moment to finish this job.

She turned, her hair swayed to the side, and he saw the white tattoo on her back. Infinity. Forever. His fingers twitched from the temptation to reach out and trace that symbol with the tip of one finger. He wanted, more than he'd ever wanted anything else, to spend another night or two or three right here in this room . . . with her.

Dangerous thoughts.

Chapter 11

After breakfast, Lenna and Caine had a whispered but heated exchange in the bedroom. Elijah was once again watching cartoons, with the sound on the television turned up so loud they could probably have spoken in normal voices without him being able to hear, but they didn't take any chances.

"Why buy the boy clothes when all we have to do is go to his house to get whatever he needs?" Caine asked, not unreasonably.

"Because Uncle Bobby might be there! If he's hunting for Elijah—and he has to be—the most logical place would be at the house."

"I'd welcome an encounter with Uncle Bobby," Caine said, smiling a smile that wasn't in the least humorous.

"So would I, if Elijah wasn't present, but we can't

leave him here alone. He's a child—when he noticed we're gone, he'd panic. He might run, he might do anything. If he runs, how would we find him again? What if he gets hurt? Killed?"

Caine gave her a cool look. "If Uncle Bobby was indeed there, he wouldn't have the opportunity to hurt Elijah." Because Caine would immediately take care of Uncle Bobby, the way he'd taken care of Nevan. Caine had no compunction against taking a life, if such an action was warranted.

"But what if the police are there, instead of Uncle Bobby? How would we explain suddenly appearing in the middle of a crime scene?" She now had a much more secure idea on how things worked here on Seven, not to mention she had been paying attention during the morning television news shows. Crime took up a lot of the programs. "If Elijah's mother has been found, the police will definitely be there, which is a problem in itself. What if the man who assaulted us yesterday is there? He was a law officer—he showed us his badge. The other policemen would listen to him, rather than us. One or both of us would be arrested, which means we'd be separated."

"No, we wouldn't. Even cuffed, I can still teleport. They couldn't hold me, and I wouldn't leave you behind."

"You want to disappear with dozens of police officers as witness?" she asked incredulously. The Hunters didn't bring attention to themselves, and generally all the beings on other planes were very cautious when visiting a different world.

In truth, she didn't want Caine in Elijah's bedroom, not with the one card hidden there. Elijah knew where the majority of the deck was, but even he didn't know about the Moon, which sat on a shelf along with some of his toys. What *she* didn't know, however, was whether or not Caine might take the time to thoroughly search Elijah's room.

"We can't take him there," she pressed, concentrating on that one reason because it was the one most likely to convince Caine not to go to the house. "He was . . . upset when I took him back there to look for his mother's body. He didn't want to go in." That was the truth; all that she'd said was the truth, though some truths were less important than others. "Whatever his new clothing costs, I will reimburse you."

Caine's face darkened with more than annoyance. "I have funds here on Seven. I don't need your aid to buy his clothing."

Men and their pride, she thought, mentally shaking her head. At least she had successfully deflected him, for now—she thought.

Caine opened the hotel room door and placed a Do
Not Disturb sign on the outside handle and closed the
door again, with them still on the inside. From his
pocket he pulled a small device unlike anything Lenna
had ever seen before. Running the device around the
outline of the door, he "sealed" it against any intruder
who might be tempted to ignore the sign. That was
wise, as he had an impressive cache of weapons hidden in the closet, and the simple request for privacy
might not be honored. It occurred to Lenna that she
could hide her own card in this protected room, but
instincts warned her to keep it close. As long as it was
in the red bag that hung on a strap across her body,
she knew where it was and could guard it.

The suite secured, Caine gathered her and Elijah
close. Lenna thought by now she would be accustomed
to the rush and burn of energy as he transported them,
but she still found herself breathless, still found herself
clinging to his broad shoulder. Elijah was as ecstatic as
usual, and scholar that she was, she wondered if teleportation affected her differently than it did a human. She
must remember to ask—no, she immediately thought.
She didn't want Caine to know how he made her feel,
didn't want him to know that she was particularly vulnerable immediately after being teleported.

When they traveled in the manner of a Hunter, the three of them in a close huddle, Caine was always careful to land in a private area so no one would witness their arrival. Like her, he had to take care to remain unnoticed in this world. This time he took them to the back corner of a . . . garden, or at least a place where garden things were sold, though at this time of the year there wasn't much gardening going on. She looked around and saw a large overhead sign that said Garden Center, though she wondered why its purpose needed announcing.

Inside, she could see a line of artificial trees displayed in a group. Since Christmas was past, she was surprised so many people were checking out the trees. Then she noticed that all the trees bore sale tags, so that mystery was solved. Outside, where they were, were a few straggly real trees.

"What is the name of this place?" she asked politely.

"Walmart."

"Yay!" Elijah said, jumping in excitement. "Can I go to the toy section? Please, huh, can I?"

"After we find clothing," Caine said firmly, taking Elijah's hand. The little boy clung to him, his small hand disappearing in Caine's much larger one. He looked down at Lenna. "We'll find all that you need here. It isn't as fine as what you're used to, but we won't have to go to several different stores to get everything."

"Shopping" was an exciting concept to her, though she wisely kept that observation to herself. Thanks to reading his memories she knew what shopping was; on Aeonia, everything she wished for had simply been brought to her. Gazing around the huge store, she thought that this must be like hunting, and the fastest shopper got the best items.

They walked past the straggly trees, which looked nothing like the cheery example she had seen where Elijah lived. There were no twinkling lights, no decorations hanging from the branches to make the trees merry. Two of the trees even leaned crookedly to one side. She wanted to straighten them, place decorations on them, make them pretty.

They entered the store and Caine grabbed a shopping cart, which he pushed before him as if he had—oddly enough—done this before. Warm air replaced the cold; harsh artificial lighting replaced sunlight.

Elijah jumped on the front of the cart like a monkey, holding on and chattering nonstop about toys, something called an Xbox, food, and basically everything other than the clothing they were there to buy. Lenna's head was on a swivel as she tried to absorb everything about this huge store, and the intricacies of "shopping." How did people find anything? How did they know where it was? How did they even know what they wanted?

Caine glanced down at Lenna; his mouth twisted wryly, and he turned the cart into a section called Health and Beauty. "Look around and see if there's anything you'd like to have," he said. "I'll stay close to you."

"Aww," Elijah said, pouting. "I want to—"

"Hush," Caine said sternly. "Lenna needs things. Your turn will come, unless you keep whining, in which case you will *not* be getting a toy."

Elijah opened his mouth to complain, but the expression on Caine's face made him rethink the situation.

Lenna wanted to say that they should concentrate on clothing—their reason for being here—but Caine would say so if they were spending too much time looking so she allowed herself a bit of indulgence. She *was* curious about this Health and Beauty designation. How did one buy health, or beauty?

She wandered down the aisle, not picking up anything but trailing her finger across products that the advertising said were waterproof, would make her eyelashes incredibly voluminous—fat lashes?—small boxes of color to put on the eyes or cheeks. She stopped at a picture of lips, incredibly red and shiny pouting lips; they looked as if they had been painted. *Lipstick,* she read. Because of Caine's knowledge she knew what this was, though his brain had been incredibly deficient on the fat lashes product. Lipstick, a stick for lips. She studied the packaging, and thought the name was appropriate. Then she saw one that said lip balm, and she liked the sound of that better. Balm was good. The color was a soft pink, and the flavor was bubble gum. She picked up the package, sniffed at it because she wanted to know what bubble gum smelled like. To her disappointment, no scent came through the hard shell of the packaging.

"Get it," Caine said, a little amusement leaking into his tone. "Put it in the cart."

She did so. Nothing else on the aisle caught her attention, but a couple of aisles over she found a lotion that she liked the smell of—Baby Powder Fresh, an alarming thought but she didn't think they actually turned babies into powder, so she put the lotion in the cart. Then there was "bath gel," and shampoo for her hair. Those four items were enough; she could think of nothing else she needed, other than clothing.

The detour into the Health and Beauty section took all of five minutes.

When they left there, Caine took over with the skill of a battlefield general. He'd allowed that five minutes, but after that he was ruthlessly efficient in this shopping arena. Lenna didn't complain, because she understood why. They had so much to do, and so little time to get it all done. Under any other circumstances she would have loved to browse, to more closely examine the eclectic collection of goods that were for sale in this massive store. Housewares! Automotive! Electronics! She wanted to explore it all.

Instead, Caine wheeled the cart to the area of clothing, and she remained close at his side and watched the people they passed. The citizens of Seven were fascinating. Some were relaxed and smiling as they shopped, while others were as rushed as Caine, perhaps even more so. She caught snippets of conversation as they walked quickly down the aisles. Many of the shoppers talked about the snow, which was apparentiy not the norm in this area. They were alternately thrilled and annoyed by the unusual weather.

Lenna peeked into their shopping carts when she could, curious about what the contents might be. Each cart said something about the person who was pushing it. One woman had collected nothing but sweets and makeup. Another had gloves and bananas and laundry detergent and chocolate—a lot of chocolate—in her cart. Yet another was buying dog food, chew bones, and coffee. Knowing more about Seven thanks to Caine allowing her to read him, she tried to imagine the lives of these women—and the one man who had nothing but potato chips, cookies, and ice cream in his cart. It was a fascinating place, and for the first time she resented not being able to regularly visit and observe this rapidly changing world. Why must the Major Arcana stay on Aeonia? Hunters could freely travel between all worlds, and after a short while in this Walmart place she fiercely envied them that ability. This was just one store. What other marvels did all the worlds hold, that the Major Arcana didn't even know existed?

A red-haired woman wearing a jacket that appeared to be made of pale blue fur, open over a bright yellow top that revealed almost the top half of her breasts, stopped in her tracks and gave Caine a long, lingering look. Lenna understood that; she had noticed several women watching him pass while they pretended—as best they could—that they weren't doing exactly what they were doing. Looking at him was a definite pleasure. She did not, however, understand how the woman got her breasts to stand out like that, as if they were propped on a shelf. She had noticed that on a couple of others, and her curiosity got the best of her.

She leaned close to Caine and whispered, "Is it a secret how some of the women get their breasts to do that?" She demonstrated with her hands, though her much smaller breasts couldn't achieve the same effect, even with her help.

He looked down at her and his gaze lingered on her breasts before flicking briefly to the other woman's bounty. "It's a garment called a bra. Support, and padding," he said succinctly. "You don't need either."

Elijah giggled. "I know what that is. Mom calls them her booby-traps." The words came out without thought, but at the thought of his mother his eyes suddenly filled with tears and his little face began to crumple.

Lenna laid her hand on his shoulder, calming him. "Concentrate, Hunter," she said. "We're on a mission."

Elijah's lower lip still quivered, but he sniffed and nodded. Caine began pushing the cart faster, taking turns a little too hastily, and in no time the little boy was clinging to the cart and giggling as he said, "Go faster, go faster!"

Lenna started to protest, but a look around told her that there were many children who rode in the shopping carts, or skipped alongside them, or clung to the front as Elijah was doing. She watched them, noting that most of the children were so full of joy, so energetic and . . . happy. Elijah should have that happiness. He'd had it in the past, and he would have it again. She swore it, on her standing as Strength.

She barely looked at the things Caine piled into their cart, simply kept pace with him as he moved purposefully through the store, barely slowing down to grab goods before moving on. He knew what was necessary to get them through the next couple of days, and she trusted him to make the proper decisions—in this instance at least.

Because Caine had promised, the last place they stopped was the toy section. Elijah hopped down from the cart and went to stand beside Caine, his expression solemn. The two males had bonded, if reluctantly so on Caine's part. "I don't know," Elijah said, and heaved a sigh. "I got most of what I wanted at Christmas, and there isn't much left." To Lenna's eyes there was still a plethora of toys, but this was Elijah's decision. She wanted him to smile, to run and laugh and ask for silly toys as the other children did, but now that he was here he didn't.

Then something caught his eye, and he wandered over to a section of boxed games. "Magic," he said, sounding out the word slowly. "Hey! This is a magic set! I wonder if it'll teach me how to poof."

"You're too young," Caine said automatically, but he picked up the rectangular box and looked at it. "It has a cape, and a magic wand, and a book of instructions. I

don't know about magic—I believe more in powers—
but you can give it a try if you want."

Elijah nodded eagerly, and Caine placed the box in
the cart.

She half expected them to pop out of Walmart
the same way they'd popped in, taking their chosen
items with them—somehow—but they stood in line
with other shoppers so Caine could pay with the
"Mr. Smith" credit card. The bill, for this trip and for
the hotel, would be paid in the currency of this country,
via computer.

Because she had read him, she could put this in
context. It was only fair, he thought, that the goods and
services he used be properly paid for. To not pay would
leave a small footprint on the world, and that needed to
be avoided at all costs.

Their purchases were stuffed into plastic bags—
toiletries dropped into one bag, clothing into another.
Elijah's magic set went in one bag, then there was yet
another larger one for a box that seemed rather heavy.
She should have paid better attention to the things
Caine had been adding to the cart. She'd been more
interested in the people.

At the last minute, she noticed Elijah studying a
display of chocolate, and though he didn't ask for a treat

she reached out, grabbed a handful of the thin bars, and added them to their purchases just as the cashier was finishing scanning their goods. Caine turned to look at her, his brows lifting.

"Chocolate," she said. "I have a craving."

The look he gave her was one she couldn't quite read. Maybe she shouldn't use the word craving in his presence. After last night, she had to admit that she craved him much more than sweets from this world or any other.

Frustration gnawed at Caine when they were safely back in the hotel suite. He wasn't able to do what needed to be done with both Lenna and Elijah underfoot. He couldn't do anything about Lenna; he had to keep her close by, at least until she could bother herself to tell him where the deck was.

But Elijah—Elijah was a different story.

Lenna was determined to protect the child, but she wasn't battle-trained. He knew beyond doubt that if they had to fight Hunters as well as deal with a murderer, the child would need to be left in someone else's care. There was no other choice.

One of the day's purchases was a small laptop computer, a cheap one, but it would do. Electronics didn't fare well on jaunts between worlds, so he just bought a new one when and if it was needed. It didn't take long to get the new computer set up and running. He'd done this before, many times.

Elijah sat on the couch, eating a chocolate bar from Walmart as he intently watched cartoons. Cartoons seemed to be the child's escape, Caine thought, a way to let reality go for a while.

Lenna stood at Caine's shoulder as he worked. "It's fascinating," she said in a lowered voice. "So much knowledge, right there for the taking with nothing more than a bit of typing."

"And Wi-Fi," he added.

Lenna nodded. Thanks to him, she knew very well what Wi-Fi was.

He pulled up the local news website, and there it was, what he'd been searching for. A woman's body had been found by a young man who'd lost control of his car on the ice and slid into a roadside park. He'd gone into the nearby woods—to take a piss, most likely, though the story didn't get into specifics—and had found the body, which had not yet been identified.

It would be, by fingerprints most likely. As soon as the police had an ID, Caine would be tripping over investigators right and left as everyone attempted to find the murderer. It would make his job—his secondary job, which had to be completed before he could get to his primary job—that much tougher.

It was possible this body was a different murder victim, not Elijah's mother at all, but . . . he didn't think so. He also didn't think the car sliding into that roadside park was coincidence. So little, in this world or any other, truly was.

"We need to get busy," he said.

Lenna, who had been reading over his shoulder, gave a nod.

"We can't do what needs to be done with a child tagging along."

"But—"

"No buts." He spun his chair to face her, and slowly stood so he could look down at her. "I'll be facing a murderer as well as at least two Hunters who are working for Veton. Judging by what happened at Elijah's house, the murderer has the assistance of at least one man. It will be dangerous. I would prefer to leave the boy with friends of mine."

"You have friends? Here?"

"That surprises you?" he asked crisply.

"A little. I didn't—" She stopped and began blushing.

"You didn't see them when you peeked into my head?"

"No," she admitted.

He couldn't say he was sorry to still have a few secrets left. "I'm here on Seven often enough that it makes sense to have useful acquaintances in this world."

She looked up at him, earnestly searching his gaze as if looking for . . . something. "Is that all they are? Useful acquaintances?"

"I trust them. Elijah will be safe."

He would love to leave Lenna with his friends, as well, but if he did, if they separated, she would no longer be shielded from the other Hunters. No, he was stuck with her for the duration of this damnable situation.

Lenna wasn't yet convinced. "How can we be sure Uncle Bobby won't find Elijah, wherever you leave him?"

Caine grinned. "Trust me, no one will find him."

She glanced at the kid and her expression changed. It softened, but at the same time there was a fierce determination in her eyes. She barely knew Elijah, but she did care for him.

"He won't be happy to be left with strangers," she said.

"No, but he'll safe. He can be happy some other time."

For Elijah and for Lenna, happiness would return.

For Caine, happiness was elusive. Unnecessary. Not a part of his job description. He was pleased, on occasion. He could be content, for short periods of time. Happy? Never.

He did get the distinct feeling that he might finally experience happiness of a sort when this damn job was over and he saw the last of Lenna and Elijah.

Chapter 12

Lenna frowned at the purchases that had been placed atop the bed, trying not to feel ungrateful, and failing. She should have paid more attention to the clothes Caine had grabbed for her, rather than eavesdropping on the shoppers around them, because she would certainly have countermanded his choices. He'd apparently gone out of his way to pick the drabbest, plainest clothing possible: pants in brown and black, and the shirts were a drab green and the other gray. Really! There were so many wonderful fashions on Seven, so much color and fine fabrics, why had he chosen these atrocities?

Then she made a wry face. Despite how much she disliked the plainness of the garments, she understood. He wanted her to blend in, to disappear into the background no matter where she might be. Fading into the woodwork wasn't in her nature, but in this case she would try to be as invisible as possible. That, too, was why he'd chosen solid colors instead of shirts with pictures or words on them; she'd seen some that were entertaining, if not exactly pretty, and therefore more likely to stick in an observer's memory. That was what they *didn't* want. Though, really, the underwear he'd picked out wasn't going to be seen, so why had he chosen black for them?

At least he allowed her to keep the boots she had taken from Zack's mom's closet, as well as the red bag that held her own card from the Alexandria Deck, tucked into a back inside pocket. He'd told her to wear the bag *under* her jacket, which she was more than happy to do. She was glad now she hadn't taken the entire deck, because it would have been far too noticeable in that small bag; Caine would have pounced on it at once.

Making an effort to ensure that she wouldn't stand out in a crowd of humans had nothing to do with the atrocious nightgown he'd bought for her to wear. It was long, in a material he called "flannel," and decorated with a thousand tiny pink roses. She didn't know why she cared, since no one other than him would see, but she did. She'd rather sleep naked.

And she would. *He* could wear the damn nightgown if both of them being naked bothered him so much.

She gave a little smile at the realization that she had just sworn using Seven terminology, and hadn't even had to think about it; it had come naturally, which meant Caine had used the term more than once. He was very at home here.

Elijah's new clothes were more colorful, but she'd noticed all the children's clothing was, anyway, with no drab choices available. There were also some short pants and T-shirts, as well as underwear. He seemed to like what Caine had chosen, but then, none of them were made of flannel. He was more taken with the magic set; he'd donned the cape and kept flourishing the magic wand around, though he didn't seem disappointed when nothing happened. Perhaps in his imagination, he was making magic happen all around him.

A child who had lost everything needed a little bit of something he could control.

Caine was standing beside her as she surveyed his purchases, his narrowed gaze on her face as if he waited for her protest. She didn't intend to give him that satisfaction; she didn't like the drab clothing and she didn't like letting Elijah out of her care, but she understood *why* both were necessary.

They hadn't yet told Elijah that they were taking him somewhere to leave him, that he couldn't stay with them while they tried to find out who Uncle Bobby was. She thought he'd take the news better if he met these friends of Caine's first, and got comfortable with them, but if they gave him warning he'd already be resentful when they arrived, which wouldn't be a good situation for any of them.

Caine was evidently still waiting for her to comment about her clothes, so she shrugged. "They're ugly, but they'll do." Except for that nightgown. That thing was in a class all by itself, and it wouldn't do at all. After all, she didn't have to blend in when they were alone at night. But she didn't mention the nightgown because right now they had more important things to deal with—such as Elijah.

Together they packed Elijah's clothes, as well as most of the chocolate, in one of the plastic shopping bags. When that was done they went into the suite's parlor, where Elijah was still whirling around in his cape and performing invisible feats of magic. "Ready to go poof?" Caine asked. "Bring your magic set."

"Yay!" Elijah scrambled to get everything back in the box, then he tucked it under his arm and dashed over to Caine. With his free arm he hugged Caine. "Where are we going this time? Let's do a circus!"

"I don't know where any circuses are," Caine replied. "But I think you'll like this."

Lenna was holding the plastic bag. Caine put his arm around her and his hand on Elijah.

She would never get used to it, she thought, the sensation of electric energy and speed too great to comprehend, the sense of power that was all Caine. If he hadn't been holding her, she'd have fallen to the . . . sand. In the blink of an eye, their surroundings changed from a hotel room to a beach. This was more of a shock than even the first time he'd done it, because the environment was so wildly different.

Instead of cold, there was a balmy warmth that felt like silk on the skin.

Instead of gray sky, there was a vibrantly blue sky, and a deliciously hot sun. The turquoise waves of the ocean flowed endlessly at them, shading into palest green as it reached toward the beach and foamed almost at their feet. The smell was fresh and salty, a little fishy, lush and rich and so different it took her breath away. Was it always that way with travel between and within worlds? Was it always a shock to the system?

She was holding the plastic bag in one hand, with the other clinging to Caine. She didn't immediately release him; she never did. She needed that moment of contact with him to steady herself, to recover from the heated sexual rush and regain her composure. Perhaps touching the man who had caused that sexual rush wasn't the most intelligent choice but it was what it was. In that moment after, she needed his strength— she, who was strength embodied, needed him.

After a moment she lifted her head and looked out at the ocean. The ocean! She had seen the seas of Seven in Caine's memory, and she had glimpsed them from afar—from Aeonia. Long ago in the beginning, when the Major Arcana had been able to travel, she had seen an ocean, had stood upon a shore, but . . . not this one. Her ocean had been gray and rocky and rough. This one was gentle and jewellike, the blues and greens sparkling and clear. The sand was so white it was dazzling.

It was utterly magnificent.

Perhaps being separated from Seven for so long had enhanced her appreciation of its natural beauty. Aeonia was beautiful, of course, but there was no contrast, no sense of adventure or exploration, no *vibrancy*.

"Where are we?" she asked, her voice low and reverent.

"Caribbean island," Caine said. He released her and Elijah and turned, pointed toward a lush-leafed jungle. "We go that way."

She was reluctant to leave the ocean—she wanted to go wading—but the vegetation ahead had its own appeal. It was all shades of green, dotted with the reds and yellows and pinks of flowers. Now that she was looking she could see a sandy trail leading through the jungle.

"Yay!" Elijah jumped up and down, kicked up sand, spun in circles. "This is so cool! I love magic. I can't wait to be a magician! Can you teach me? I know I'm too young, but just one small trick. Anything. Maybe I can disappear. Poof! I saw a guy on TV once. He disappeared. It was so cool! Teach me! Teach me!"

"Not today," Caine said.

Elijah kicked the sand again and made an almost adult-sounding snort of disappointment, but he obediently followed along. Both he and Lenna kept turning their heads to look back at the ocean, lured by the hypnotic power of the endless water.

As soon as they stepped into the shelter of the trees, the shade made them feel cooler, and even the sound of the waves was muted. Musing, Lenna looked around, marveling at the massive differences between here and Atlanta. Some corners of this world were crowded, humans upon humans, nowhere to turn without running into one another. There was a lot of noise, thanks to vehicles and thousands of voices and an abundance of technology. Here, the land remained primal and all but deserted. She had the sense that the three of them were alone, surrounded by the mighty ocean that both isolated and protected. The quiet was deep and complete, until an animal of some sort that was deep in the jungle tittered and another answered. She liked it. She liked it all.

The jungle closed about them, but in a remarkably short time they suddenly stepped into a clearing. A rambling and weathered house sat in the middle of the clearing. A path made of stone and crushed shell led to a wide porch that ran the length of the house. All the windows were open; white curtains danced in the breeze, moving in and out. Any kind of structure should look out of place here, but this one, with the silvery weathered wood, suited the setting. It was civilized, but not completely; comfortable, but not luxurious.

The front door opened and a man holding a shotgun walked onto the porch. Alarmed, she reached for Elijah to pull him behind her, but as soon as the man got a good look at Caine, he began grinning and propped the shotgun against the side of the house.

"Chantel!" he called in a deep voice. "Come on out! It's Caine." The man limped across the porch and down the steps. There was a squeal from inside the house, and in just a few seconds a large, pretty woman wearing a brightly colored loosely fitting dress came running through the open door.

She and the man were both middle-aged, or what Lenna would call middle-aged for the residents of

Seven. They were in their late forties, she supposed. Their faces were tanned and lightly wrinkled. The man's hair was salt-and-pepper gray, the woman's a vivid, unnatural red. They were dressed casually in loose and colorful clothing, a far better choice for the climate than what their visitors were currently wearing.

The man reached Caine and they exchanged a hearty handshake, both of them smiling. Chantel worked her way around her male companion—husband or boyfriend, Lenna assumed—and gave Caine a hug.

Both of them gave off an air of sturdy competency, as well as kindness, the shotgun notwithstanding. An island . . . Caine was right; Elijah was completely safe from Uncle Bobby here. There was no way he could be found.

Elijah pressed close to Caine's legs as he surveyed his surroundings, and the strangers who lived here, with some caution. Instead of dancing around in delight and asking to be taught magic, as he had been moments earlier, he had withdrawn in the presence of these strangers.

Poor child, she thought. If he'd been any older, the things he'd seen in the past two days likely would have made him question his sanity, and that was leaving out the trauma of seeing his mother murdered. Instead, he accepted the impossible things he had seen, designating it all "magic." To a child who spent so much of his time immersed in the worship of fictional superheroes, magic was not such a stretch.

Caine reached out and drew her closer to his side. "Lenna, this is my good friend Wiley and his wife, Chantel."

She made the appropriate human response. "Nice to meet you."

Caine placed a hand on Elijah's head. "And this is Elijah. I thought maybe he'd like to do some fishing, and what better place than this?"

Wiley grinned, his faintly homely face lighting up. He didn't ask a single question about who the child was, or who Lenna was, or why Caine had shown up out of the blue. "Fantastic." He dropped down so he could look Elijah in the eye. "Son, have you been fishing before?"

Elijah shook his head, his big brown eyes still full of wariness.

"Well, have I got a treat for you! I was just about to head out in my boat and see if I could catch some sea bass or maybe some snapper. Chantel cooks up a mean fish fry, and my mouth has been watering all day just thinking about it."

"I certainly do," Chantel said, somehow dislodging Elijah from Caine without being in any way obvious about it, simply replacing Caine with her own body. She draped her arm around Elijah's shoulders, and Wiley bracketed him on the other side. "I made a fresh coconut cake this morning, and when I say fresh, I mean *fresh*. Do you like coconut cake?"

"Yeah!" Elijah said enthusiastically, the lure of cake pulling him out of his instinctive withdrawal.

"Well, come on, and I'll cut you a great big slice of it."

As they walked toward the house, Elijah between Wiley and Chantel, Lenna reached out and caught Caine's arm. When the others were a few yards away, she whispered, "Do you truly trust them enough to leave Elijah in their care?"

"I do." His black eyes glittered down at her.

"You don't just want to be rid of him?"

"I wouldn't risk his safety," he said shortly, and she saw how her question had annoyed him. He could just deal with his annoyance, because protecting Elijah was *her* mission just as she was Caine's.

"How long have you known them? Do they know what you are?"

"A long time, and yes," he said shortly.

She should have stayed connected to him longer; she should have reached deeper. She hadn't seen Wiley and Chantel. There was still so much about him she didn't know, which meant she needed some wariness herself. "I thought the humans of Seven had to be kept in the dark about our existence."

Caine shrugged. "Who says Wiley and Chantel are humans of Seven?"

Lenna shouldn't have been shocked, but she was. There were many worlds, and the beings who populated them had all been created in the same image. There were many differences beyond appearance, of course, in abilities and length of life, some much shorter, some much longer.

She opened her mouth to ask a flood of questions, but Caine seized her, his big hands biting into her waist. "We don't have time for this," he snapped. "Read me. Concentrate on my memories of them."

A little shocked by the directive, Lenna threw an apprehensive look toward the house. She had read beings before without any drama, but reading Caine was different. Somehow, with him, it was an act so intimate it was almost like sex, and she was hesitant to do it where others could see. Still, there was no way she would refuse such an opportunity. Turning so that his back was to the house she pressed close to him, clasped her hands on his head, and let her head rest on his chest. She didn't have to do it exactly that way, but she liked the feel of him under her hands, liked hearing his heartbeat.

The connection was immediate, and as powerful as if they were lying intimately connected. But she wasn't here to get a thrill—she was here for information—so she blocked that and instead concentrated on Wiley and Chantel. Finding those memories was ridiculously easy, so he must have brought them to the forefront for her to access.

Wiley and Chantel were from Two, a world that no longer existed. Both were nearing two hundred years old, though she couldn't tell how those years were measured. Wiley had saved Caine's life in the waning days of the final war on Two. Lenna had a confused impression of a shouted warning, an expert shot, then shelter to rest and heal. Finally, as fire had consumed that once-beautiful world, Caine had transported out. On that occasion, he hadn't traveled alone. He had brought them to Seven; then, when the teeming humanity put too much stress on Chantel, he'd found this island for them and brought them here.

They lived their lives isolated on this island so they wouldn't have to constantly move before friends and neighbors began questioning their longevity. The modern age made even that much more difficult, with birth certificates and identity cards, computers. Living alone suited them. Besides, Chantel was so sensitive to the moods and emotions of others, living among humans was extremely stressful for her. Like many who came from her world, she was a powerful empath; that was how she had so swiftly realized how to ease Elijah's wariness and fears.

"That's enough." Somehow Caine sensed how much she had seen, and broke their connection.

"Yes," she said calmly. "It is." That calmness cost her, but she refused to let anyone see how rattled she was— not from what he had shown her in just a few seconds, but at how being so connected to him aroused her.

Together they walked on to the house and climbed the steps to the porch. They entered a large open space, with the kitchen on the left, a trestle table in the middle, and a seating area off to the right. The interior was bright with sunshine, and cool from the breeze blowing through all the open windows. A ceiling fan turned lazily over the table, where Elijah sat shoveling big bites of coconut cake into his mouth. "It's good!" he said to Caine and Lenna, and returned to eating as if he were starving to death.

She knew they could stay only a short time, that Caine wanted to leave immediately, but Lenna wanted to be certain Elijah was going to be well cared for. She sat at the table and chatted with Chantel, watching as Elijah swiftly became comfortable with the couple. Odd, how attached she was to this child she had only known for a couple of days. It was reassuring that she could almost *see* Chantel also becoming attached. Obviously she'd picked up on Elijah's distress and was touched by it. No matter the species, women always wanted to heal those who were broken.

After finishing his cake, Elijah began peppering Wiley with questions about fishing. He was excited about it, and no wonder. He needed an escape, an activity to take his mind off the tragedy that had set these events into motion, and this place and these people provided it. From fishing he segued to the jungle, and the animals they'd heard, and why Wiley limped. Nothing was off-limits to a seven-year-old.

And then the subject changed. "Do you know magic, too, like Caine and Lenna?" Elijah asked, almost breathless.

Wiley gave a conspiratorial wink, and a slow grin. "I do."

"Will you teach me something?" Elijah whispered, but it wasn't low enough to hide his words from anyone. "They think I'm too young."

"Grown-ups, eh?" Wiley whispered in answer. "What a downer. When they're gone I'll teach you—"

"Wiley!" Chantel snapped, looking alarmed.

"Just a simple trick or two," he finished, slanting a guilty look at his wife, then reaching behind Elijah's ear and pulling out a quarter.

But Elijah wasn't deflected. He'd caught that word—gone—and he whirled on Lenna, magic tricks forgotten. "Gone? Where are you going? Are you leaving me here?" His eyes widened and his face paled. "Are you coming back?"

Chantel placed a hand over her heart, her eyes shining as tears welled. She felt every nuance of Elijah's distress, and would shed his tears for him.

Lenna sat down and beckoned Elijah to her. He darted into her arms, and crawled into her lap. She wrapped her arms around him, began gently rocking. "Caine and I have things to do," she said. "Important things that wouldn't be safe for you. We want you to be safe, and Wiley and Chantel will take care of you for us, until we—"

"Are you going to catch Uncle Bobby?"

"We're going to try," Caine said. He was right at her shoulder, close, always close, because they had no choice.

"No! I don't want you to leave." Elijah's breathing changed; he was near panic.

She couldn't leave him in this state; she didn't want to read him, but perhaps she could impart some of her strength to him. Gently she laid her hand on his face, her fingertips touching his temple. "Be strong," she whispered. "Be brave."

She held her breath, because she had never tried such before. To her amazement, she could immediately feel Elijah calming down. Her words, and her touch, had reached him. Elijah understood.

He leaned his head against her shoulder. "Uncle Bobby can't find me here, can he?"

"No, he can't," Lenna said fiercely.

"And you and Caine are going to make sure he goes to jail or . . . or something."

Or something, more likely, given that Caine was involved. And as far as Lenna was concerned, the sooner, the better.

"Yes," Lenna said. "Until we get the job done, you'll be safe here. You'll fish, play, learn magic tricks, and go swimming in that beautiful water."

He took a deep breath and nodded once, decisively. "Okay. Swear you'll come back for me."

"I swear," Lenna said.

Elijah looked up at Caine, his dark eyes wide. "You, too. Swear."

Caine put his hand on Elijah's chest. "Hunter to Hunter, I so swear."

Chapter 13

"What did you do to Elijah?" Caine asked.

Lenna glanced up at him. His face was half in shadow, sharp and handsome and determined, always determined, though he was beginning to show some fatigue from teleporting her and Elijah so often, as well as constantly maintaining a shield to keep her hidden. The Hunters had incredible strength, but the effort he'd been putting out was also incredible. At some point, he would need time to rest, though she didn't know if he truly could and still keep her shielded.

"I gave him strength," she said simply. "It's what I do."

"You touched him."

Why did that simple statement sound like an accusation?

"I didn't know if I could affect him otherwise. It was . . . a reverse reading, so to speak. Normally I just *am*, but he needed a boost." She wouldn't have left Elijah behind if he'd been frantic at the idea of being separated from them, but she didn't tell Caine that. Yes, he was safe with Caine's friends. Yes, it was for the best that they remove him from the physical danger he might face if he remained here. And still, she wouldn't have caused him more trauma by abandoning him.

They stood in the wooded area behind Elijah's house, just beyond the tree line. Snow hadn't fallen for hours, but the day remained cold, and snow and ice still stuck to the ground and on the roofs of the houses. There were many footprints visible now; the snow wasn't nearly as pretty as it had been when it had been newly fallen.

A lot had happened since she'd stood on almost exactly this same ground a day earlier. Night was falling. The sun would soon set; the day was almost done. One more precious day in this world, gone.

The thought had been that they'd search Elijah's house, looking for photos or any other clue they could find, but that wouldn't be happening right away.

Red and blue lights flashed from the road on the other side of the house, reflecting on the snow and on the houses lining the street. Obviously Elijah's mother's body had been found, and identified.

Anxiously Lenna wondered exactly what was

happening. Were the authorities searching the house? Yes, of course they were; if they had identified Elijah's mother, then they would know about Elijah, know he was missing. They would be scouring the house, looking for clues to what had happened. Had they found the Moon card? She thought about it, and her anxiety eased. Even if they had, it would mean nothing to them. A single card—even the entire deck, if it were there—could have nothing to do with the murder of the woman who had lived in that house. Their focus was on the victim, and the missing child.

Caine nodded in the direction of the house. "Is the deck in there?"

Lenna sighed. Telling him that much wouldn't change anything. "Not really."

Caine looked down at her, a scowl pulling his brows together. "Not really? I asked a yes or no question. I would like a yes or no answer."

His tone annoyed her, but there wasn't any reason not to tell him the truth—part of it, anyway. "I hid one card in Elijah's room."

Caine tensed. They were so close she felt the change in him. "Is the Alexandria Deck scattered about like a handful of bird seed?"

She ignored the testiness in his voice, recognizing that she hadn't made this job easy for him—not that it was her purpose to make things easy for him or anyone else. Her reason for being was to stand strong even in the face of the worst adversity. "I didn't think it would be wise to leave the deck intact. It's too powerful." And too many desired to possess it. She'd acted out of instinct, but Veton had immediately proven her right. "The majority of the deck is . . ." She hesitated, wondered how much she could tell. "The rest of the deck is where I found it." Where Elijah had found it, more rightly. "I hid two cards. Just to be safe."

"One is in Elijah's room. Where is the second hidden card?" he asked.

"I'll tell you when the time is right."

She could see the muscles in his jaw flexing as he ground his teeth. If he hadn't liked her first answer, that one had enraged him. He knew better than to try browbeating her, though; she was Strength, and she was more likely to bring the world down around his ears than she was to capitulate. After several seconds he said in a carefully controlled voice, "We have three days before you must be returned. The deck is necessary for your transport. I'd feel better if it was in my hands."

"Of course you would!" Lenna snapped, her own temper fraying. They'd been over this ground before, and nothing had changed. "That way you could take me home immediately, as you've been instructed."

He didn't deny it. She respected him for that, for not trying to trick her. He was silent as he returned to studying the house and the beehive of activity around it. Then he asked, in a lowered voice, "Why five days? What's the significance?"

The change of subject caught Lenna by surprise, but she was glad of it. They would never agree about some things, including when she was to be returned to her place.

"I don't know," she admitted, a little surprised to realize that was true. Why *was* it five days? "That's how it's always been. The Major Arcana are too powerful to have complete freedom. We are immortal, we possess great powers, we influence the beings of other worlds, even from afar." Even as she explained, she realized that those reasons still didn't answer the significance of the specific number of allowed days. She also realized that she didn't like the restriction at all. The thought of not being able to interact with other worlds, other beings, filled her with sadness. Her attachment to Elijah, her attraction to Caine—they were new to her. They were . . . unexpectedly important. How was she to properly assist the humans of Seven, the Hunters, the beings like Wiley and Chantel, if she didn't fully understand them? The Major Arcana shouldn't be isolated on Aeonia, observing but never experiencing.

"No one has ever tested the limits of that restriction?" Caine asked.

"Of course not." Her heart did an unpleasant dance at the very idea. "Aeonia still stands."

"Things change," he said.

She turned to stare at him. Did he know something she didn't? "How?" Less than two full days on Seven, and already she longed for that change. Since the Alexandria Deck had been rediscovered, would the Arcane be able to travel as they once had? Or would the Emperor destroy or imprison the deck so it could never be used again? She hadn't possessed the ability to travel for more than two thousand years. She'd fed her need for knowledge by constantly losing herself in studies, but . . . it wasn't the same.

She shouldn't crave it now; she shouldn't feel as if she'd been robbed of an important aspect of her life when it had been taken away, but she did.

"I have no idea," Caine growled. "It was an observation. Things always change."

Neither did she have any idea. Perhaps the Emperor, or the Hierophant, or the High Priestess could come up with a solution. How long had it been since the Major Arcana had petitioned the One? How long had they been content to watch the lives they touched from afar? For far too long the Arcane had blindly accepted the rules that bound them. Was that a revolutionary thought? Was she breaking some unknown rule for even considering the idea?

She looked back at the house, already second-guessing her decision to leave the Moon card there. The cards were too important. Perhaps they should—

She pointed to a second-floor window. "Elijah's room is there. We can teleport in, grab the card—"

"No," Caine interrupted sharply. "There are too many people in the house, and I can't locate them all. I can't take the chance that we'll be seen."

"But—"

He shook his head as he looked down at her. "You have your rules to abide by, I have mine. There's too much activity here, and we can't risk being seen. We can't even stay here and watch for much longer. The police will be looking for Elijah, and these woods will be one of the first places they search."

"They won't find him," Lenna said softly. She felt some satisfaction that he was so safely far away. "How long will they search?"

"For a long while. A missing child is a big concern."

"Of course." She tried to imagine that Elijah was truly missing, maybe dead, maybe lost, maybe held captive, and her heart leapt.

"We'll come back tomorrow morning," Caine said

decisively. "We'll retrieve the Moon card, and then we'll concentrate on finding Uncle Bobby."

"What do we do until then?" Lenna asked. The idea of returning to their hotel suite and waiting out the night didn't appeal to her.

Thankfully, Caine had other ideas. "This might be your only chance to see the world, to experience it. What do you want to see?"

Lenna thought of all the things she had seen when she'd connected with Caine, all the beauty, all the wonder of this world. She didn't hesitate a single second with her answer. "I would like to attend a concert, preferably one featuring a pianist. I want to experience a thunderstorm, and I'd like to see the sun come up over the desert. Any desert. And mountains!" she added. "I want to stand atop a mountain."

A slow smile touched his lips. Her heart gave an unaccustomed leap. He didn't smile often, and maybe he should. Or perhaps he shouldn't, because the effect the smile had on her heart rate was too extreme, and the bottom dropped out of her stomach. He slid his arm around her waist and pulled her tight against him. "Piece of cake," he said, and they were off.

Tomorrow they'd continue trying to solve Elijah's problem, they'd argue about who should safeguard the deck, and they'd disagree about how best to accomplish the tasks at hand. For tonight, though, Caine put all that aside to show Lenna the wonders of Seven. She had asked for very specific things, but what she hadn't asked for, what he suspected she needed more than anything else, was to interact with the humans here.

He teleported her to Paris for a concert, as she had asked. She was entranced by the young pianist, a prodigy who wasn't much older than Elijah. Caine listened to the music, but instead of watching the musicians on the stage he watched her face. For someone who had lived such a long time, who possessed so much power, she was amazingly naive about some aspects of life. No, not naive—separate. Distanced.

After the concert ended, he took her to a café where they drank rich coffee drinks and ate decadent pastries. They walked, rather than teleporting. That, too, was an experience for her. He suspected the food on Aeonia was perfection, but she was thrilled with her Parisian snack. Even perfection got old, when it was all you knew. As he had expected she might, Lenna spent much of her time in the café absently nibbling on the pastry while she watched the people, the chattering friends, the teenagers full of life, the lovers young and old. She drank it all in, her hunger for new experiences raw on her face.

She deserved better than paradise.

As soon as he had the thought he mentally laughed at himself, because what was better than paradise?

Except the perfection of Aeonia would drive him crazy, and he knew it. He liked action, he liked being challenged, he liked overcoming obstacles and solving problems, getting his hands dirty, fighting, drinking, and relaxing with some fiercely hungry sex.

The thought of sex made him restless, and he pulled her to her feet, took her to an alley where no one could see them, and whisked her to Australia for a fierce thunderstorm.

They stood upon a stretch of land filled with sunflowers and watched the storm move in, and then he pulled her tightly to him and let the rain and wind rage around them. Lightning struck, thunder rolled. Lenna clung to him, shrieking a little when a bolt of lightning hit close enough to make the air feel as if it had exploded, but she wasn't afraid; she didn't know she should be. She laughed, then threw her head back and screamed, just because she could. There was no one there to hear her but him, and he had brought her to experience this very thing, the elemental power of nature.

Rain soaked both of them; wind blew Lenna's hair into a tangle. The wonder on her face was one of the most beautiful things he had ever seen.

When that was done, he took her to a desert in North Africa to watch the sun rise. She wasn't bothered by the wet clothes she wore, and neither was he, but in any case their clothing dried quickly. The sands turned orange as the sun rose, and silently she watched, entranced. She didn't laugh and scream, as she had in the storm, but remained silent, as if to make a noise in this place would be somehow wrong.

They traveled the world in a single night. They experienced daytime on one continent, dark of night on another, and then they teleported into the sun once more. They walked in the teeming crowds of large cities, and watched children play on suburban playgrounds. They saw farmers and businessmen, mothers and movie stars. In the blink of an eye, they could be anywhere, do anything. He took full advantage.

Caine didn't want to dwell on the hardships that existed here, that existed on every plane except Aeonia, and he didn't want to distress her, but her experience wouldn't be the same without it. They visited a village so poor every man, woman, and child was undernourished. They went to a hospital and walked a hallway crowded with the sick and dying.

While she didn't touch anyone as she had touched Elijah, he could tell when she imparted her strength and will to the humans who had need of it. It was as if a wave only he could see undulated from her hands to touch those around her. In these instances she was no longer Lenna, a woman he desired, but was Strength, of the Arcane. Yes, they were one and the same, but now he could separate them to some degree.

As the night came to an end, he took her to the top of a mountain in Tennessee. It wasn't the highest mountain in the world, not anywhere close, but it was an impressive sight. Before them mountains stretched as far as the eye could see, smoky and blue, undulating across the horizon. They sat until the edge of the sun was visible on the horizon, his arm around her, enveloped by the silence of the winter mountain. Then he took her to a small café there in the mountains, where she ate biscuits and grits like a woman who had never before tasted such wonders.

For most of the night he was able to forget that Lenna was who she was—a powerful being, a goddess to many, a woman out of place, out of time. She was simply a beautiful woman inhaling the wonders of this world in the limited time she had here.

The night was over; it was time to get back to the mission that had brought him here. He teleported them back to the hotel room. They needed to shower and change clothes, and then they needed to get back to the business at hand.

He could've worked last night, hacking into the local police department's computer to snag whatever information they had on Elijah's mother. If the name "Robert" or "Bob" popped up as an acquaintance or a suspect, they would likely have their murderer. The police might also have a list of next of kin. Eventually Elijah would need to be left with someone who would care for him—grandparents, maybe, an aunt or an uncle. If there weren't any relatives, a friend or a couple willing to take in a child would have to suffice. There had to be someone on the world who would welcome Elijah and take care of him, give him a home.

But the computer could wait. He wouldn't have given up the adventures of the night in order to move themselves a few hours closer to their goal.

Elijah was safe. Uncle Bobby wasn't going anywhere. But Lenna's time here was limited, and he'd wanted to share those experiences with her.

He steeled himself not to react as they began stripping off their clothes to take a shower. He'd known shielding her, having to stay permanently, physically close to her, would be a trial, but he hadn't realized the situation would elevate into torture.

If her mind was on being naked with him, it didn't show. "I want more," she said, absently tossing her clothing aside. Caine did the same, his eyes on her, on the slim line of her back, on her shapely ass, on that golden hair and glowing skin. Why the hell couldn't Strength have been a burly blacksmith type? Was it some kind of cosmic joke, to pair unending determination and endurance with . . . this?

"More what?" he asked, forcing himself to look away from her ass.

She spun to face him, throwing her arms out to encompass the world. "More everything! Music, food, people, storms, sunshine, beaches."

"I thought Aeonia was the perfect place," he said. "The perfect world with the perfect music and food and weather."

"Perfection is boring," she replied with heat. "It's perfect. It's all the same. I'm tired of it, and I want more!" Fiercely she seized his face in her hands, rising up on her toes to press her mouth to his. Her lips were parted, her tongue teased at him, then she tilted her head and the kiss wasn't teasing at all.

Caine wondered if he should be insulted that Lenna

apparently considered *him* imperfect, but she was kissing him and he didn't give a damn about insults.

Lenna was giddy with delight, electrified with discovery. She couldn't remember the last time she'd felt so alive, so connected—not simply connected with one being, but with all of creation, with pain and beauty and joy.

She kissed Caine, and he kissed her back. His steely arms wrapped around her, pulling her completely against him. Their tongues danced, and hunger surged between them. Skin to skin, mouth to mouth, they were connected in an entirely different way. She didn't invade his mind, but she didn't need to, to feel connected to him. They melded, their bodies flowing together, skin hot and sensitive to every touch.

The night had been magnificent, but it wasn't yet complete. She wanted him. She needed him, in a way she'd never before needed a man. What she felt for Caine was out of control, for she who was never out of control. This passion, the need she felt for him, went beyond anything she had known in the past.

He lifted her from her feet and turned toward the bed. He laid her there, on sheets still rumpled from the previous night, and kissed her again. Still. More. There were kisses deep and then easy, kisses that aroused and then soothed, kisses that asked and then gave.

He stopped, and lifted his head just enough to give her a narrow-eyed look. "You're not peeking into my head, are you?"

She shifted restlessly, because he'd stopped touching her and she didn't like that. "Of course not. It would be rude to connect without your permission."

"Good. Because what I'm thinking right now might scare you."

She reached for him, stroked her hands over that hard, muscled chest. Her eyes were heavy-lidded as she looked up at him. "I doubt that, but do your best."

This time when he moved in to kiss her, it was even slower, even deeper. In answer, she wrapped her legs around him, pulling him closer. Her entire body trembled and ached, wanting him, wanting to be filled by him in the most intimate way possible.

"Now," she whispered.

Caine scooted them farther onto the bed as he answered, "Not yet." He lowered his head and took a nipple into his mouth, kissing, sucking, nibbling.

Foreplay, any foreplay, was torture right now. The entire night had been foreplay. She had laughed in his arms in the middle of a thunderstorm; she had almost climaxed during the last teleportation. She *wanted* him.

"Now!" she gasped. Her back arched as she tried to lift herself to take his penis, jutting so hard and long from his body. The thick head brushed between her legs and a small, breathless cry broke from her when he twisted just enough to deny her.

"Not yet," he said again. His voice was deep and thick with his own desire, his eyes like obsidian. His mouth moved to her neck, where he kissed and licked, slowly tasting her as if she were the most luscious of desserts. "I taste the night on your skin," he whispered. "I taste rain and sand and sugar. I taste the winds of all corners of Seven."

She wanted to taste the same on him, and as he rose up again she did. She put her mouth on his throat and kissed the flesh. She sucked. She moaned. And one more time, she said, "Now."

"No going back."

She didn't know what he meant, and didn't care. Go back? Return to not knowing how he tasted, how it felt to have his heavy weight bearing down on her? No, a thousand times no. "No going back," she agreed.

He pushed inside her, heavy and thick, connecting in a way she had never before known, because this was Caine, because in just two days he had become so important to her she couldn't find any boundaries to what he meant. It was the way he'd cared for her and Elijah, even against his own instincts. It was the way he'd known what she wanted, and shown her more beauty than she'd imagined existed. It was even that damn flannel nightgown, because it had spoken to how deeply she affected him.

She had her arms and legs curled around him. His hands were under her, gripping her buttocks, lifting her to meet every thrust. At first he was slow, lingering, enjoying every sensation inch by inch as he pushed in and pulled out. But eventually their breaths began to come fast, their hearts were pounding in rhythm with each other, and slow wasn't enough. He was fast, then, pounding into her, and whatever control she might have had left fled, unmourned.

Chapter 14

Derek sat back in his recliner, took a sip of steaming hot coffee—black and strong, not any of that sissy crap from a coffee shop—and watched the local news. Five minutes in, he sat upright with a bang from the footrest slamming down, an impressive stream of foul language exploding from him. If he hadn't just swallowed, coffee would have been included. *Damn* the senator! If there was a bigger fuckup, Derek hadn't met one. Markham couldn't do anything right, not even disposing of a body, which wasn't that difficult if you just put a little thought into it.

He rubbed his forehead. If he'd been in charge of disposing the Tilley woman's body, it wouldn't have been found so soon, if ever. Not only had she been found too soon, she'd been identified very quickly, thanks to her fingerprints being on file. He didn't know why her prints had been in the system, if she had applied for a job that had a strenuous security check or if she had a checkered past that included an arrest. The why didn't matter. If he'd been called in sooner, if the senator hadn't been such an idiot to begin with—

But it was too late to go back. As he liked to say, "It is what it is."

All things considered, the senator's instruction to make the mechanic's death look like a suicide hadn't been a bad idea. Sammy's body hadn't been discovered yet, but when he didn't show up for work someone would go looking for him—if not today, then tomorrow. And they'd find him, in his own bathtub with his wrists slit. The GHB he'd used to knock Sammy out—or, at the least, make him far more manageable—would be long gone from his system by the time he got to a medical examiner's table. And once they connected the idiot to Amber Tilley, the story would become clear. Their love affair had gone wrong, he'd killed her and dumped the body, and then in remorse he'd killed himself.

But what about the kid? Where would Elijah fit into the story?

The kid's last school picture had been plastered all over the news. Every law enforcement officer, victim's group, and friend or friend of a friend was searching for him. Derek mumbled another curse. He probably wouldn't be able to step out his own door without tripping over someone who was looking for the kid.

Derek wondered if the blonde still had Elijah. If she did, why hadn't she come forward? Why hadn't she taken the kid to the police? There was something going on there that wasn't quite right, that just didn't make sense. He hated it when things didn't make sense.

The senator would have a come-apart if Elijah wasn't found—by Derek, not by the police—and soon.

Let the senator stew. Derek scrubbed a hand over his face, disgusted by the senator, and not all that willing to kill a kid. He'd thought he could do the job with no problem, but then he'd looked Elijah in the eye, seen the kid's innocence, his fear, his devastation. The woman the senator had killed had been a cheating whore. Sammy was a moron who was a waste of skin. The kid? The kid hadn't done anything wrong. Elijah hadn't lived long enough to make the kind of mistakes that would bring Derek, or someone like him, to his door. Some people deserved to be taken out of the gene pool, but not a kid who'd just happened to be in the wrong place at the wrong time.

Fuck a duck, maybe he did have a few morals, after all.

Still and alert, Esma crouched in a cluster of overgrown shrubs by the corner of a brick home that was presently unoccupied. The bushes that offered her a place to hide were thick with shiny green leaves so spiny that they would be almost dangerous, if she wasn't covered head to toe, and an abundance of bright red, inedible berries. It was some kind of holly bush, she thought, but she wasn't well-educated on the plant life of all the worlds. All she cared about was the good cover the plants offered.

A For Sale sign posted in the front yard leaned precariously to one side. From her position she could watch the front of the house where she'd found the Moon card, tucked high on a shelf. There was a lot of activity there on this morning. Thank the One she had found the card before the law enforcement entities of Seven had, though they might not have realized exactly what it was. Even if they had, what could they have done with just one card? Nothing, the way she could do nothing. But as long as she had the card, no one else could access the deck's power, either.

She hated to hide in this way. As a Hunter she always preferred a fight to subterfuge. But this moment of this assignment on this world dictated that she stay out of sight and wait patiently. Well, she would wait, but she had never been patient. She didn't belong in the neighborhood and on a day like today if she showed herself she would be noticed. Everyone was on alert and would be alarmed by any and all strangers.

Policemen came and went. Friends and neighbors who had heard the news about murder and a missing child came by to stand and gawk, to find out whatever they could from any officer who would talk to them, to organize search teams or contact anyone who might know where the child was.

That damned old woman who had seen Esma and Stroud and mistaken them for friends of the dead woman was talking her head off. If the detectives weren't in the house interviewing her, then she was standing in her front yard, bundled up in her winter gear, chattering with the neighbors and waving her arms for emphasis. There were moments it was obvious she was genuinely upset, but she also reveled in the attention.

She had probably described the people she'd seen in Amber's backyard in great detail. Nosy old women always remembered everything.

Esma and Stroud had split up, since the neighbor would have the cops looking for a couple. It was their bad luck that the woman had walked out of her back door when she had, to admire the snow. Esma didn't know what Stroud was doing; he'd simply disappeared. He should have informed her of his plans, but he hadn't. Then again, she hadn't told him she'd found the Moon, either.

For all she knew he was hiding out in another world, avoiding both her and Veton.

She slipped two fingers into the right front pocket of her blue jeans and let them slide over the treasure there. The card didn't feel thousands of years old; this kind of paper hadn't even existed on this world when the deck had been created. The magic in the cards had caused them to morph over the years; instead of fading, the colors were more vivid than ever. The writing shifted so that the words were readable by whoever viewed it. The material the cards were made of had become stronger over time, more resilient.

The Alexandria Deck was, in an odd way, a survivor.

It had been good luck that had led Esma to the card that had been hidden in the kid's bedroom, good instincts that had led her to keep the card's existence from Stroud. That in itself was proof that she didn't trust him. She couldn't say why she didn't, because she and Stroud had worked together before and he'd never shown himself to be treacherous. Still . . . this deck of cards was the most important thing she'd ever encountered. If Stroud had found it what would he have done? Would he have killed her so he could seize control of it?

She might as well have the entire deck. Why not? The Alexandria Deck would be worthless without this card, without every card. And shouldn't she be the one in control of it?

It was impossible to mistake what she'd found for anything other than what it was. An instinct had called Esma into the house and up the stairs and to the child's room. A faint glow had marked as otherworldly the card there. It was heavier than a single card should be; she had noticed the heaviness when she'd first lifted the card and she felt that weight as the Moon rested in her pocket.

Fewer than three days, and Lenna had to be back in Aeonia. Or dead. Veton's order to kill Lenna if it became necessary was still shocking.

Then again, he was the Tower. He loved chaos. He *was* chaos.

Esma had enjoyed more than her share of chaos in her life, but she called upon strength and willpower daily. If she considered any one of the Major Arcana cards her own, it would be Strength.

Chaos came and went. Strength was a quality any man or woman would wish to possess for a lifetime.

Esma preferred to see Lenna returned to Aeonia

rather than kill her and watch what disasters might befall all the worlds, but she still wanted to be able to take the deck to Veton. She wanted to fulfill the mission.

So did Caine. It was a part of who they were, an important aspect of their training. There was nothing worse than to fail. The problem was, they weren't working on the same mission, which meant she and Caine were adversaries. That wasn't good, for her, because Caine was Caine and beside him all other Hunters were ordinary, even her.

Which meant she had to be smart. She had to keep on when others would have given up.

Esma crouched so long her legs began to ache, but she ignored the ache and maintained her position. Eventually the house began clearing out, the gathered gawkers began to thin and go home. A police car was parked at the curb, but no police officers were inside the house—which had been designated a crime scene—at the moment. Searchers were in the wooded area behind the house, scanning the ground for the second or third time, looking for a child, terrified that they would find his body.

As soon as she was sure the house was empty, she teleported herself into Elijah's room. The place had been thoroughly searched, as she'd expected.

She needed to be here. If Lenna had hidden the card in Elijah's room—and that was the only explanation that made sense—then she'd be back for it sooner or later. Esma hoped it was sooner.

She stood by Elijah's bed, well away from the window, the card heavy in her pocket, a Hunter's knife equally heavy in her hand. She stretched, working the kinks out of her muscles, preparing herself for confrontation. Lenna and Caine would come here for the Moon card; since the house was now empty, they might pop in at any moment. She was on alert. She didn't want to hurt anyone if it could be helped, and she certainly did not want to remove Strength from this world and every other.

But she wanted the deck. She would complete her mission.

An early-morning visit had verified what Caine had suspected would be true. The street where Elijah lived—had lived—was far too busy for him to be popping in and out. A child going missing was always big news. It was disturbing, as it should be, and the neighbors were all searching, visiting one another to share their concerns, thankful that their own children were safe. They were on alert for anything and anyone they might deem out of place.

Find Uncle Bobby. Find a safe place for Elijah. Collect the Alexandria Deck and return Lenna to her proper place. It all seemed simple enough, but with the time constraints and lack of information it was far from simple.

Normally he would return to his employer—in this case, the Emperor—and ask for further instructions. What was supposed to be a simple task had turned out to be anything but. He couldn't return to Aeonia with Lenna until he had the deck, and leaving her here while he traveled would mean the shield would fall. Not for long, but the Hunters looking for her wouldn't need long. An instant of vulnerability, and they'd be on her.

After realizing Elijah's house wasn't yet clear, they'd returned to the hotel room. There was still work to be done.

Over the years, Caine had become quite good with computers. Anything could be found, if you knew where to look, and he did. He'd made a point of making himself proficient, and he returned to Seven often enough to keep abreast of the newest technology. He'd told Lenna that electronics didn't travel between worlds well, and that was true, but there was another reason he bought new devices when he found himself here and needed something.

What passed as days in other worlds could be years

here, and technology changed so quickly anything he tried to retain was seriously outdated by the time he returned. He managed to catch up quickly, and had no problem learning how to use the updated devices, but it made no sense to keep them when he left Seven.

His search on Elijah's mother was a simple one, but it revealed a lot of information on her. Amber Tilley had been renting her house from a retired couple who kept several rental houses in the area. She had never missed a payment, even though it didn't look as if she earned enough to afford the rent. She'd changed jobs often, going from one low paying job to another, but she had the house, health insurance, cable television, cell phone plan, and a couple of high-end department store credit cards, as well as an American Express. She had everything a woman with a mid-range income might have, except a mid-range income.

Which meant she'd been getting money from another source—a man, most likely. The man who had killed her? Again, likely.

He found no Robert in her easily accessible history. Uncle Bobby, whoever the hell he was, had kept a low profile.

Lenna stood just behind him while he sifted through

data, her arm draped around his shoulder and her hand resting lightly against his neck. It wasn't an invasive touch, not even a possessive touch; it was just . . . comforting. And arousing. *Personal.*

Caine didn't do personal. It was outside his job description.

After coming back to the suite, she'd changed into the white dress she'd been wearing when she'd come to Seven. Because they were alone she didn't have to blend in, and she'd said the dress was much more comfortable than the clothing he'd bought her. In those Walmart clothes, she'd looked *almost* ordinary, or as ordinary as a superbeing could look. In the white dress, though, it was clear that she was unlike any other female in the universe.

He'd do well to remember that. She wasn't a woman to be trifled with.

For now, he needed to keep his mind on the job. Vae, she made that difficult.

"We'll go back in tonight, when the activity in Elijah's neighborhood dies down," he said. At least at night there would be shadows to hide in, if there were prying eyes. "We'll retrieve the card you hid there." It was possible the police had found the card, but it would have no meaning to them, no possible connection to the murder they were investigating. Still, he wouldn't rest easy until it was in his hand. It was one more piece of the puzzle he needed to return Lenna to Aeonia, where she'd be safe.

"What will we do until then?" Lenna asked.

He spun around in the uncomfortable office chair so he faced her. "You can take me to the Alexandria Deck."

Her face darkened. "Not yet."

"I won't take you back to Aeonia immediately. We can—"

"Don't lie to me." He saw a flash of her temper in her eyes; he heard it in her voice. "I know you, Caine. The job is everything to you. Your assignment, any assignment, is more important than anything else. Even a promise to me. The minute you have the deck in your hands, you'll take me home." The temper faded, her expression softened. "I'm not ready to go home."

He stood, wrapped his arms around her, and lifted her so they were nose to nose. "You know me too well." He wouldn't apologize for being focused on the mission.

"And you don't know me at all."

That wasn't entirely true. He did know her. Not as she knew him, but still . . . He had seen so much of her last night—her wonder, her joy, the strength she shared with those who needed it most. He knew her; he liked her. She was an amazing creature who should be protected and cherished.

"Even if we retrieve the deck I won't be able to take you back. Even if we find the Moon right where you left it, I won't be able to take you back—because you hid *two* cards, you damnable woman."

She threw back her head and laughed, and that was all it took. He caught her to him, kissed her, and she kissed him back. He lifted her, and she wrapped her legs around him, her body all hot, sweet welcome.

He carried her to the bedroom. She was right about one thing, though; as soon as he recovered the entire deck, he'd have to return her to Aeonia. As dedicated as he was, as committed as he was to doing his job well, at this moment, he wasn't eager to have this particular assignment finished. He wanted more time with her, as much time as they could squeeze out of fate.

Lenna whipped off her fine, white dress and tossed it aside, and then she started on his clothing. "I don't suppose frequent and amazingly wonderful sex will change your mind about taking me home a moment before it is necessary."

"If anything could . . ."

"That's a no."

"That's a no." He finished undressing, managing the task more efficiently on his own than she could, and then he grabbed her and fell sideways with her onto the bed. "But that doesn't mean you shouldn't try."

Chapter 15

Lenna stood behind Caine's shoulder, watching his fingers tap on the computer he'd placed on the small desk in the suite. He'd explained computers to her, and the technology struck her as loosely related to the way they viewed things on Aeonia. They didn't have computers; they could summon images, but the end result was the same: information came to them. With computers, though, there were traps and passwords and other hazards that had to be negotiated before the information could be accessed.

It puzzled her how Caine could be proficient in such things, and reading him hadn't provided her with any insight, which annoyed her. Normally when she read someone, she knew them completely. With Caine, it was as if he could compartmentalize his knowledge, allowing her access only to those things he wanted her to know. She had no idea if this was something all Hunters could do or if only Caine was this provoking. "How do you know how to do this hacking?"

"I learned online," he absently replied, leaning forward to carefully read something on the screen he'd just accessed. "Hidden service protocol."

"What's that?"

"It's for sites that don't advertise their existence. Some people call it deep web. You have to know the sites are there and how to access them, but there's always a way to find what you want. Every time I come to Seven, I update my skills. I even make special trips just to do that. Technology changes so fast here compared to worlds where time moves slower that if I didn't I'd be lost."

"Is it complicated?" She thought she'd like to have these skills herself, though why bother learning if she would never be back to Seven? The thought made her sad. She wanted to return, she wanted to see other worlds, she wanted to experience instead of just observe. Observing was like this hidden service protocol he mentioned; if she didn't know where to look, how would she know what was there?

"Not really. It's specialized knowledge that requires attention to detail, that's all. Ah."

"*Ah,* what?"

"I've accessed the Lawrenceville police department computer system."

Quickly she pulled a chair over to sit beside him so she, too, could read. He accessed a few more pages before he found the initial report written by the detective who had been assigned to the case. The writing was dry, as if investigators used language as a way of distancing themselves, though perhaps they were required to use certain phrasing. She skimmed over the details of death, not wanting to know more.

"They're looking for a person of interest," Caine muttered. "State Senator Robert Markham. There's a strong possibility he's Elijah's Uncle Bobby." A woman who lived next door had seen the state senator visiting Amber Tilley's house on more than one occasion.

Caine pulled up a photo of Robert Markham; just looking at the picture, Lenna couldn't detect any viciousness in his face, even when she touched it. Nothing came through the screen; she couldn't read him. Still, there was a certain . . . *smugness,* perhaps, or even arrogance, that she disliked. It was there in his eyes, for all to read even without the powers of the Major Arcana.

Caine said, "We'll take this to Elijah, let him look at this picture to tell us if this is Uncle Bobby."

"No!" Lenna said in alarm, without thinking, just knowing that was the wrong thing for Elijah.

Caine's obsidian gaze turned on her. "Why not?" To him this was the most simple thing, and she had to agree with him on that, but a simple solution wasn't most important to her.

"He's terrified of Uncle Bobby. He saw the man kill his mother." She had to feel her way through the tangle of thoughts and emotions, following what her instinct told her was a thread of truth. "His emotions are so fragile now, a reminder will be too traumatic for him. If we can do this without involving him, that is my preference. How certain can we be that this man is Uncle Bobby? Could Elijah's mother have been involved with *two* men named Robert, or Bobby?"

"Not likely, but the only way we can be certain is to ask Elijah."

"No," she said again. "We can find Robert Markham, and ask *him*. If I can touch him, I'll know."

"You'd read him without his consent?"

"Under these circumstances—yes. If there's a price I have to pay for breaking the rules, I'll pay it, and gladly, for Elijah."

He stood and framed her face with his big hands, intently studying her features. "You are Strength—can he not draw from you?"

She sighed. "Perhaps, but he's so young. He deserves every moment of happiness he can have for the rest of his life, to balance this. If I can take some of the burden from him, I will."

After another moment he drew her close to him, his big hands hot on her back, wrapping her in his scent and strength and giving her a sense of being protected. With wonder, she realized that no one ever before had protected *her*; she hadn't needed it, living her pampered and secure life on Aeonia. She hadn't truly known adversity of any kind until Elijah had pulled her here to Seven. He was just a little kid, and in his short life he'd already known more horror and pain than she'd known in her own unending years. She felt . . . humbled.

"We can't give him more pain than what he's already endured," she said into Caine's broad shoulder.

"No," he said gently. "We can't."

It was well after dark before Derek could safely manage a face-to-face with the senator. The meeting hadn't been easy, not to plan or to execute. Derek had watched a while, before making his move. He had to be sure the senator wasn't being followed. Yet.

A friendly contact with the Lawrenceville police, a uniformed cop who was happy to take on the occasional legitimate security job Derek threw his way, had spilled the beans that the senator was a "person of interest." It was juicy gossip, exciting stuff, and the cop had no idea what significance it had for Derek. That tidbit hadn't hit the news yet, but it would. Once it did, there was no way in hell Derek would be able to get close to the man even if he wanted to; the best plan was to make his move now.

Markham had—probably unknowingly—helped his case by dumping the body in a different county from the one in which he'd committed the murder. There was always red tape in those cases, the police department from a town in one county and the sheriff in another comparing penis sizes and blustering over whose case it was. If they managed to connect the senator to the victim, as it looked like they would, the GBI—the good ole Georgia Bureau of Investigation—would be called in, too. One more big penis to throw into the mix. If nothing else, all the measuring would slow the process.

The abandoned building near an industrial park south of Atlanta was perfect for their meeting. Once upon a time something had been made here—textiles of some kind, if his memory didn't fail him. Socks? Flags? T-shirts? Like it mattered. The jobs that had once made this a thriving mill had gone away years ago.

Even on a Monday night, the place was deserted.

There wasn't another car, other than Derek's and the senator's, for a mile or more.

He was glad the cold weather gave him an opportunity to wear his gloves without arousing suspicion. Details were important. Details could mean the difference between life and death.

Derek arrived five minutes late. The asshat had turned on a light in what had once been an administrative office near the main door. Might as well hang out a Come and Get Me sign.

Even though he was sure they were alone, Derek surveyed the area—the hallway, the nearby offices, the dark hole at the end of the hallway where old rusty machines sat unused—before opening the door to the small office and joining the pale, pacing senator.

Markham spun on Derek. "The police contacted my office! I'm supposed to call some detective in the morning to arrange a meeting! What the hell?" He acted as if this was Derek's fault, instead of his own. "Tell me the kid is dead. Tell me you found the little shit."

Derek remained calm. "It's not the little shit who's been talking to the police."

Markham's hands fisted. "Who, then? How did this happen?"

The truth, at least for now. "A neighbor saw you."

Markham stumbled back a step or two. "I was seen Friday night?"

"I don't know if it was Friday or earlier. All I know is that you're a person of interest in this case."

The single, harsh light the senator had turned on made him look pasty green and sickly. "What does that mean? Am I a suspect?"

Probably. Almost surely. But Derek didn't want to be the one to share that news. "I don't know. They connected you to the dead woman, though. Stay calm. Act innocent. Play dumb." Not a stretch, he thought. Playing smart would be an Oscar-worthy performance.

He wondered what kind of evidence the senator might've left for the crime scene investigators. It was unlikely he'd made a clean getaway. "You never did say . . . how did you kill her?"

Again, those clenched fists. "I choked her with my bare hands."

Well, shit. It was an imperfect science, dependent on the environment and the condition of the body, but fingerprints could be taken from skin. "No gloves?"

"No. This isn't some television show where the cops can find a hair or a skin cell or a . . . a . . ."

"Fingerprint?" Derek supplied.

"Yeah," Markham muttered. He turned away,

paced some more, then spun around to face Derek again. "There's no other choice. You'll have to kill this neighbor."

Derek sighed, tired of this already. "I don't know which one saw you." That was the truth. While he had contacts in Atlanta, and Lawrenceville, and Marietta, and in towns and cities all around who would spill a bit of news now and then, they weren't going to hand over all the details.

"Then kill them all," Markham breathed. "All of them. Dead people can't testify."

The direction was so coolly delivered and so irrational, Derek realized the senator was a lost cause.

"I can't do that," he answered.

"You will," Markham said, and then he foolishly added, "If I go down, I'm taking you with me. I assume Sammy is good and dead?"

Derek nodded. "He is."

"Don't think I won't make a deal with the cops, if that's what it takes."

Derek plunged his gloved hands into the pockets of his overcoat. He shrugged his shoulders and pulled out the length of thin nylon rope he'd stuffed in there. "I was afraid you'd say something like that." Actually, he'd kind of been expecting it, hence the rope. Never underestimate stupid.

Markham reeled back, his pasty complexion turning white. Clumsily, panic making him stumble, he turned to run, to *try* to run. He'd have been better off lunging toward Derek, instead of conveniently turning his back.

Derek crossed his wrists, looped the cord around Markham's neck, then straightened his arms to close the loop. The force yanked the senator back, but Derek was careful not to yank so hard the senator fell. Markham gagged and clawed at the rope, then at Derek's gloved hands. Derek pulled harder, tightening the loop, cutting off the senator's air. Markham flailed, completely panic-stricken, which made him even more ineffective.

Now that Derek knew how Elijah's mother had been killed, this method of execution seemed appropriate. He pulled the cord tight. Tighter. Markham was a small man, and had no chance to escape. He attempted to fight, to work himself free. He dropped, which only made the rope pull tighter. He pulled away, but couldn't go far. Derek held on, jerking tighter and tighter, until Markham hung limply by the loop around his neck. Still Derek held him, calmly counting off seconds, because it wouldn't do to let the bastard somehow revive. The brain started dying in four minutes. Derek held him for seven, which didn't seem like a long time unless you were holding someone's dead weight with your arms, in which case seven minutes was a hell of a long time.

When the senator was good and dead, face dusky, not breathing, heart not beating—good enough dead—Derek let his body drop to the floor. He was sweating. The rope was still around that scrawny neck, and that's where it would stay. With the senator's car parked out front, he'd be found soon enough, even here.

Lucky for Derek, Markham had been diligent in his efforts to make certain no one could connect him to the private detective who did his dirty work for him, which meant there was no way to link Derek to the dead senator, no canceled checks, no paperwork that could come back on him. All payment had been in cash, which had actually created a small problem for Derek here and there, because the IRS frowned on large cash deposits. He'd been forced to spread it out, to attribute it to other clients, pay cash when he filled up his car—little things like that eventually added up.

With Markham out of the picture, there was no need at all to try to find Elijah. Once he'd decided that he wasn't going to kill a kid, the path to killing Markham instead had been clear. There was no way the senator would allow his henchman to walk away without doing the job, so the answer to that problem was to take the senator out of the equation.

Derek considered this a life lesson, one the senator would never learn now because he'd died as stupid as he'd lived. The life lesson was to never threaten the person who held the gun. Or the rope.

Elijah was safe. He was a cute little kid; he'd lost his mom—there was no reason to hurt him. But the blonde . . . the blonde who had kicked Derek in the nuts could identify him. He'd been in the house where the Tilley woman had been killed. The cops would at the very least want to question him, if they knew he'd been there. Pretending to be a cop—though that would come down to her word against his.

The problem was, how to find her? She could be anywhere in the world by now. She could also be around the next corner. Since she hadn't turned up with the kid yet, it was possible they were both out of the picture. Possible, but not likely. She had to know the kid's mother had been murdered; she might be staying hidden now, until she could maybe figure out Derek wasn't a cop, after all, but eventually she'd come forward with the kid.

He wanted to catch her before she could do that.

In his experience people always returned to what was familiar; that was what got so many criminals caught, because they couldn't stay away from home, or Mama, or their old buddies.

It wouldn't hurt to keep an eye on the kid's house for a couple of days, just to see what happened.

At last the street was quiet. The search for Elijah would continue in the morning, after sunrise. Those who slept in the houses along this street were restless tonight, made uneasy by the murder of a neighbor, worried about their own children after the disappearance of that neighbor's son. Others didn't sleep at all, their hearts too burdened.

She surveyed the house where Elijah had called her in, where the majority of the Alexandria Deck waited to be reclaimed, but she kept her gaze moving, not allowing herself to linger in the survey for even a split second. She gave the house no more and no less time or attention than she gave to each of them, but she saw some of the windows were bright with light. She wanted to look more closely, see if she could detect for certain whether or not the owners had returned, but Caine was standing right beside her and she didn't dare. She didn't discount a Hunter's acute alertness. He noticed everything she did, everything around him, every movement and every sound. If he hadn't he wouldn't be who he was, wouldn't have lived as long as he had.

She sighed; she couldn't help feeling guilty that she knew Elijah was safe, but was keeping that knowledge from all the searchers and neighbors who cared about him. She had known him such a short while, but she'd be devastated now if he went missing and she didn't know where he was. Ah, well; she wasn't close to feeling guilty enough to tell anyone where he was, at least not yet. When she was certain he was safe, when they found a place for him to live and be loved, that would be the time to let everyone know.

"Ready?" Caine asked, but he might as well have not said a word because his arm was already around her. By the time she grabbed his shoulder, they were there, in Elijah's bedroom where she'd hidden the Moon card. The sensation was still alarming, still electric, and at least half the effect was being in Caine's arms. The sensation was almost as intense as their sexual connection—no, she had to be honest with herself. Their physical chemistry was both explosive and strangely *comfortable*, as if they simply fit together. As surprising as that was, even more surprising was their *emotional* connection. She didn't know what to think about that. The sex was wonderful—she didn't regret a single moment of their time together—but there was more, a more she didn't dare ponder too deeply.

What good could ever come of it? He was a Hunter. She was Strength. They were what they were, with duties and lives that normally would never bisect.

"Where?" he asked, releasing her and focusing immediately to the reason for them being there. He looked around the dark room, lit only by the moonlight coming through the window. They didn't dare turn on a light, or even use Lenna's magic light, because a lot of troubled gazes would be looking at this house tonight; people disturbed by the violence that had happened here would keep searching for a reason *why*, as if that reason were in the house itself, imbued in the brick and masonry. How sad; the *why* of anything outside natural occurrences was always in people, in the decisions they made that piled on top of each other until they eventually culminated in the end of life.

Fortunately, Hunters had excellent night vision and he didn't need artificial light any more than she did. She turned toward the corner shelf where she'd put the Moon; she'd keep it with her own card, then she and Caine would continue in their search for Uncle Bobby until the last possible moment, though now that they had a name she hoped they could quickly take care of that part. Only then, and only when Elijah was safely settled, would she reunite the cards and allow him to return her to Aeonia.

As soon as she turned toward the corner she sensed something wrong, though she didn't know what. The shadows in the corner were darker, but that was to be expected. Caine tensed a half second before Lenna heard a woman's voice from the corner of the dark room.

"About time."

He immediately thrust Lenna behind him and drew his knife, his steely muscles coiling as he prepared to launch himself toward the threat, but Lenna's hand on his back and a softly spoken, "Wait," stilled him. The woman moved out of the corner, darkness detaching itself and approaching until she was revealed. Ah. She was another Hunter, probably one of the party sent to kill Lenna and take the cards to Veton.

But she didn't attack, though she held a knife much like Caine's in one hand. Instead, she lifted her other hand, and in it was a faintly glowing card. Lenna's heart sank. She'd worried that the card might be found by the police; it had indeed been found, by someone much more difficult to retrieve the card from than the police would have been.

"Looking for this?" the woman asked, waving the card in front of her before tucking it securely away in a pocket.

Both Hunters were braced for combat, their gazes never leaving each other. It was clear in their stances, was indeed a part of their very makeup. Hunters weren't negotiators; they didn't bargain—they fought. That was who and what they were.

Lenna's own instincts hummed in alarm. Deep in her bones, she knew that these two shouldn't face one another in battle. It wasn't just that she didn't want Caine hurt, or even possibly be killed—a big dilemma considering what he was—but there was something about Esma that was so familiar . . .

She had to trust her instincts, because there was no time to do otherwise. Swiftly she moved away from the shelter of Caine's body, stepping around him to get closer to the woman. Caine snarled, the sound feral in the night, and immediately closed the difference so he was so close behind her his chest brushed her back when he breathed. She ignored the almost physical blast of his fury and alarm, and focused on the female Hunter. "I know you," she said softly, opening that part of herself that had absorbed so much knowledge, and feeling memories flood her. She knew *exactly* who the Hunter was.

The woman didn't look away from Caine's face. "We have never met."

"That doesn't mean I don't know you," Lenna replied. "Your name is Esma."

The Hunter's startled gaze jerked to Lenna's face. Lenna lifted her brows. She had to admit, she was impressed to meet this woman face-to-face, because she did indeed know her, or know about her. "I've been isolated for millennia, true, but that doesn't mean I haven't watched and studied all the worlds and the beings upon them. I've seen you, I know you. You're a warrior, a rare female Hunter who possesses all the qualities I represent. We aren't acquainted, but I'm well aware of your existence, who you are."

Esma was motionless, staring at Lenna. She appeared stricken. Her lips barely moved as she murmured, "As I am aware of yours."

Lenna started to step even closer but Caine grabbed her arm and jerked her to a halt. Knowing he would protect her from harm—real or imagined—at all costs, she stopped. One wrong word, one wrong move, and the Hunters would be at one another. She didn't want that.

"Did Veton send you to kill her?" he asked tersely.

Esma was silent for a moment, not even the sound of her breathing drifting on the night air. Finally she said, "Yes and no. My job is to kill her if she doesn't give me the Alexandria Deck, but I would prefer not to take this assignment so far."

Caine's body was as tense as if he were pulling with all his might against an invisible tether. His voice ground out from the depths of his chest. "If you think I will allow—"

"I'm not afraid of death," Lenna calmly interjected.

"I've seen this world in all its glory and heartache, such as there isn't on Aeonia. There is *true* life here, life as I have never known it before, life that I wouldn't have seen without all of this happening. I've learned that life isn't truly precious without death."

Esma looked incredulous. "You *wish* to die?"

"No, of course not. There's still so much to see, so much to do. I don't want to die, but I'm not afraid of it." Lenna offered her hand, palm up. "My world needs to change. That can't happen unless I have the deck in my possession. Will you give that card to me, so I may take the deck to the Emperor?"

"I can't," Esma whispered. "I have a job to finish."

"You also have free will," Lenna said, though she already knew that argument was useless. To a Hunter, the mission was always uppermost.

Esma moved so fast Lenna could do nothing but spin out of the way as the female Hunter and Caine met with a monumental clash.

Caine restrained some of his strength; his main purpose, other than protecting Lenna, wasn't to kill Esma, but to retrieve the card. One wasn't more important than the other. Without the card in Esma's pocket, the Alexandria Deck would never be complete. Lenna would be grounded here. In a matter of days, Aeonia would crumble, taking all the Major Arcana down with it.

She said she wasn't afraid to die. He was afraid for her.

Esma was a good fighter. He knew that going in, because even the weakest Hunter was much stronger than a superb fighter of any other species; that was how they essentially served as bounty hunters for the known universe. What surprised him was what almost immediately became evident. She didn't want to kill him any more than he wanted to kill her. They were both after Lenna and the complete deck; only their assignments—their employers—were at odds with one another. He heard Lenna yelling at them both to stop fighting, to be reasonable. He ignored her, and so did Esma.

They crashed into a wall, and Esma went partway through it. Toys fell from a shelf and tumbled to the floor and the bed. The crash was still resounding when Caine grabbed Esma's shirt and pulled her back into the room, spun her and threw her to the ground. She landed with a grunt; the force would have knocked out any other being, but she was only winded.

He grabbed for the card in her pocket. He felt the thickness of it under his fingers—and then she teleported out and left him there on the floor, with no card, and no opponent.

Immediately he searched for Esma's energy, but she had either left this world or had shielded herself. Likely she'd shielded herself and had been doing so before, otherwise he'd have felt her before he brought Lenna here.

Caine flipped to his feet and whirled to face Lenna. She could no longer be allowed to call the shots. The timing was critical; the situation had to be in his control.

He grabbed her and pulled her close, his fingers biting into her arms as he glared into those celestial blue eyes. Even in the dark, he could see into them, into her. "The search for Uncle Bobby won't continue until I have every card of the deck in my hand."

"What I have immediate access to is no good without the card Esma holds."

"Then you lose nothing by allowing me to guard it for you."

Lenna wanted to argue; she almost did. He saw it in her face, felt it in the tension that ran through her body. Her brows snapped together. Much as Caine hated to take the chance that he might rouse her legendary temper, he had to take a stand, for the sake of the mission, for her, and for Elijah. But after a tense moment in which they glared silently at each other, he saw the reluctant acceptance cross her face.

Her jaw set, she unzipped and reached into her red bag, coming out with a card that glowed as the Moon card had done. He took it with a curse—it had been right there, all along, but she'd been so careless with the bag that he hadn't even considered the possibility she had the card with her and thus hadn't checked— and slipped it into his pocket, asking, "The rest?"

There was a moment of complete silence.

"Trust me," he said insistently. "We can't just hope Esma won't find them first. She already has the Moon. If she has the others, then the card you hold will be all that stands between her and success. Don't get between a Hunter and the completion of a mission. She might not want to sacrifice you to get your card, but she'll do it, anyway."

Lenna hesitated, then she sighed in resignation. "I'll take you there."

He kept all sign of victory from his face, and instead pulled her close to him. "Don't you mean, *I'll* take *you*? Just tell me where. And do it now, because it isn't safe here."

Chapter 16

Lenna remembered precisely how many houses down the street Zack's house was, and she conveyed the location to Caine. He held her, and they teleported out of Elijah's bedroom, into the cold night. She found herself holding onto him in the dense shadow of a tall tree that was set between two houses and a bit away from the street. They were, for the moment, effectively hidden.

"There," she said softly, pointing. From the cover of darkness they studied the house; she was surprised to feel a bit of rogue nostalgia.

It was here that Lenna had come into this world, thanks to Elijah and the Alexandria Deck. She couldn't say she'd enjoyed *everything*, but she'd met Elijah, and Caine—most of all, Caine. Just thinking his name gave her a strange sensation in the center of her chest. It wasn't his toughness, though by the One he was certainly tougher than anyone else she'd ever met; it was his heart. When Elijah had been traumatized by watching a man kill his mother, then another man try to kill him and Lenna, then yet another man attack Lenna, Caine had been the man who had undone the evil perpetrated by the others of his sex. He had protected them. Elijah would remember that.

At some point during the past couple of days, the residents had returned. There were lights on in the downstairs part of the house, but all the windows upstairs were dark; she hoped that meant no one was upstairs grieving in solitude, too bereft to turn on a light. She had bolstered too many beings during intense grief not to know that the wounded sought the comfort of darkness and quiet. Would Elijah's friend Zack be crying in his room? He was just a child, like Elijah; surely his parents wouldn't leave him to weep alone.

"I don't like entering an occupied house," Caine murmured, "but we have no choice."

She didn't want to go in that house, either; she could feel the grief from here, a sharp sense of loss not just for the young mother whose life was no more, but for Elijah, who was missing and, they thought, likely as dead as his mother. Grief was always worse when a child was involved.

Want to or not, she had to go with Caine. "The bedroom we want is the one on the right back corner of the house."

No sooner were the words out of her mouth than they were there, with her clinging to his shoulders and wondering if the effect ever faded, if she would ever stop feeling as if she wanted to lie beneath him right now. Teleporting shouldn't be sexual, she thought dizzily. It should be . . . efficient. It was that, too, but she wasn't the only one who felt the sharp zing of desire, if she went by the hard thrust of his erection against her. She rested her head on his chest, allowing herself a moment to revel in the feel of his strong arms around her, in the powerful beat of his heart beneath her ear. Just one moment, though, then she lifted her head and looked up at him.

In the dark room, his eyes were a deeper darkness. "Shhh," he whispered, his voice barely audible even though she stood in his embrace. "There's a dog downstairs. We can't alarm it."

She didn't question his discernment. If he said there was a dog, then there was a dog, though all they could hear was the faint sound of a television coming from downstairs; perhaps the family was trying to distract itself. She gave a brief nod and pointed at the closet where Elijah had called her through, where the rest of the Alexandria Deck patiently waited.

He looked at the door; the closet was only a few steps away, but they were steps that might be heard by the dog. He made a low sound—and then they were in the closet.

Not without some difficulty, however; Caine's head bumped against something, and Lenna's shoulder sent clothing scraping on their hangers along the rail. They both froze, listening for the sound of barking.

It was blessedly silent. Perhaps the television had drowned out the bump and scrape of their in-the-dark landing.

She remembered the light switch Elijah had shown her, on their first meeting, but she didn't remember exactly where it was and didn't want to bump into anything else, so she opened her hand and formed a ball of light on her palm. Her light was silvery, otherworldly; in its glow she gestured toward the light switch, and Caine flipped it on, substituting glare for glow.

Lenna extinguished her light and silently got down on her knees, reaching beneath the hanging clothing into the corner where she'd left the box that held the cards. Her searching hand found shoes and then a folded blanket, but no hard corner of a wooden box. For a brief moment she knew alarm—had the cards been moved? Had Zack's parents seen some evidence of disruption in their closet and searched it for valuables which might be missing? Had they decided to move the box to a safer location?

But why would they? If Zack's father had any idea of the value of the deck, would he have stored it in the closet? The box had to be here. Probably when the family had returned and unpacked, items had been shoved into the closet that pushed the box farther away. She stretched her arm out and her fingers brushed wood. As soon as she touched it she felt the power of the cards within, and she breathed a sigh of relief. Using both hands, she pulled the box toward her.

Kneeling on the closet floor, she opened the box. Nestled inside were tarot cards—mere paintings on paper like so many others—but these had been imbued with great magic, and in her presence they came alive. The images shifted, as did the words. The cards glowed, the edges bright, as the Moon had in Esma's hands, as Strength had for her. She felt their energy all the way to her bones.

And the deck wasn't complete. Would it ever be again? If they couldn't retrieve the Moon from Esma, all of this power was useless.

Worried, Lenna thought about Esma, mining her memories of the female Hunter to see if she had misread the type of person Esma was. She *wasn't* a bad person, but like Caine she took her assignments seriously. She wouldn't give up; literally nothing short of death would stop her from fulfilling her mission.

But Caine would listen to reason . . . in a way. He listened to reason when he had no other choice. Perhaps they could get Esma to listen; after all, the one card she had was useless without the cards *they* had.

She lifted the cards from the box, cradling them in her hands. They were heavy and oddly warm, and simply holding them caused her hands to tingle. She laid them aside, then carefully returned the box to its place, rearranging shoes and other items as she had found them. As she did so, she wondered if Zack's father would ever notice that the contents were gone, if he'd simply brought the box and cards home and then forgotten about them.

For a moment she remained there, on her knees, facing a wall of skirts and pants. What machinations of the universe had brought all this together? Zack's father, these cards, this house, a traumatized child with the ability to call, her surprising transport from Aeonia . . . Caine. Of all the Hunters the Emperor might've sent for her, he was the one who'd been chosen. Had each and every step been directed by the One or was this adventure, this experience, the product of chance? It didn't seem like chance, not to her, who had seen centuries pass as events fell into place and begat other events.

She didn't, couldn't, regret dedicating herself to Elijah's safety, but at the same time . . . logic dictated that she should've given the cards to Caine when he'd first asked, that she should've allowed him to return her to Aeonia. There she'd have petitioned the Emperor for the freedom to travel so that she might see to Elijah's well-being for herself. Perhaps he'd have denied her, but perhaps not. She could be very persuasive, and she didn't give up.

But if she'd given in to logic and returned home, she wouldn't have experienced Caine's amazing tour of this world. She wouldn't have come to love Elijah. She wouldn't have taken Caine as a lover. Did she love him? She had never wondered such a thing before; love wasn't part of her duties. Yet here it was—or she was simply overwhelmed by the raw vibrancy of life the world of Seven had to offer.

If she had immediately handed the precious Alexandria Deck over to Caine when he'd demanded it, nothing would ever have changed. She would have continued to live a perfect life in a perfect world, untouched by the aspects of a real life: the pain, the beauty, the wonder, and the horror. And she wouldn't have known what she was missing.

She stood slowly and turned to face him, the cards held in both hands. Caine was so large the closet was not quite big enough to contain him. There was sufficient physical space, but it was as if he filled the closet from wall to wall, from floor to ceiling. She was accustomed to remaining close to him, to traveling in his arms, to sleeping and bathing and working side by side, and yet now she felt as if she was drowning in his essence.

She liked the feeling more than she'd expected, more than she should.

Lenna held the cards out for Caine to see, and she whispered, "I regret nothing."

Perhaps she didn't have regrets, Caine thought later that night as he worked to locate Robert Markham, but he certainly did. He'd crossed a line for Lenna Frost, one he'd never crossed before. Still—what could he have done differently? He couldn't take her back to Aeonia without the entire deck of cards, and she'd outsmarted him by hiding two of the cards.

He regretted that Lenna wasn't safe; he regretted that he hadn't been able to get the Moon card from Esma. He'd protected Elijah, but he'd made damn

305 • FROST LINE

little progress on doing the same for Lenna. He had
to keep her shielded at all times, which meant keeping
her near, which meant he couldn't tackle the problem
of Robert Markham as . . . vigorously . . . as he
otherwise would have. Had he been on his own, Robert
Markham would already be dead. Teleporting Lenna
everywhere with him was wearing on his strength;
for that matter, popping here and there wasn't how he
usually operated, and that, too, was draining him. He
wasn't exactly weak, but he did need more sleep than
normally he would.

He needed sleep now. He didn't get it, because he was
laboriously following computer links to find Markham.
He knew where the man lived. He knew what kind of
car he drove, and the license plate number on that car.
But Atlanta didn't have the extensive camera network
of New York or London, so finding any particular car
was more hit or miss than he liked. That said, there
were cameras, some of which could be accessed by
the public. He started at the residence, found when
Markham left the house, and then by trial and error
had to pin down the route the man had driven.

Normally his concentration was unbreakable, but
that was before Lenna was forced to stay close to him.
She sat quietly, patiently, but that didn't stop her scent
from surrounding him. It wasn't perfume; it was her

skin. She smelled sweet. She smelled like a woman. He'd never before noticed how a woman smelled, other than when they were having sex, but Lenna's scent stayed with him. He couldn't get it out of his head, couldn't stop himself from responding every time he noticed it.

Then there was the damn deck of cards. He wished they'd all burn to ashes. The deck—minus the Moon card—was in Lenna's red bag. He didn't have her instincts, but even he felt the energy that radiated from that bag. He'd felt the other cards fold Strength back into the deck, and now he felt a *yearning* coming from the bag, as if the cards were a living entity.

They wanted the Moon. They wanted to live again.

Lenna was wilier than he'd expected; when she'd had only her own card in the bag, she'd left the bag lying carelessly around, paying no particular attention to it, not keeping it with her. He'd been fooled into assuming there was nothing important in there, but when he thought about it—what would Lenna have been carrying around? Lipstick? A cell phone? She hadn't had any Seven cosmetics until they'd visited Walmart and he'd bought the lip balm for her. She hadn't had so much as a brush for her hair. He should have realized, but women carried handbags on Seven and he hadn't thought anything of it.

Now—now every card but one was in that bag; she kept it with her at all times. She wasn't taking the chance that someone could pick up the bag and get the cards. Esma couldn't do anything with just the Moon card, so they had the upper hand. If necessary, he thought, he'd take one of the cards himself and put it in *his* pocket, a precaution against letting Esma get the upper hand.

First, he had to find Robert Markham, let Lenna determine if he was indeed the one who had killed Elijah's mother, and take care of that problem. Then he could concentrate on locating Esma and relieving her of the Moon card. Once they had the Moon, he'd complete his task and Lenna would be safe.

He suspected that all he had to do was drop his shield and Esma would appear. She'd be more prepared when they met for a second time; worse, she might not come alone. He'd have to come up with a plan to protect Lenna before he did that. He'd also keep searching for Esma's energy, but she was shielding, too, and if she had a companion—nothing there, either. It was frustrating. He didn't deal well with frustration; he moved in and got the mission accomplished. Not this time.

Priorities, he thought. Lenna was his first priority, but Elijah was hers, therefore the problem of Uncle Bobby was first in line.

It had taken all his computer skills to generate a last-known location for Senator Robert Markham. This sort of research was his least favorite part of any job, but in a world with so many inhabitants jammed together in cities—like Seven—it was often necessary. He couldn't function in this world or any other without fairly in-depth knowledge of technology.

He had a complication in his search for Markham, an urgency that went beyond Lenna's time restraints. The police would also be looking for Markham. Caine wanted to find the murderer first.

For Elijah.

The child would never feel safe so long as the killer was alive. Legal systems moved slowly, and he didn't want Markham in police custody. The Hunters were their own legal system, and there was nothing slow about their methods.

Through traffic cameras and by hacking into a variety of security systems of businesses along the senator's route, Caine was able to track the car—or he thought he had. It wasn't possible to be certain, given that cameras weren't conveniently positioned everywhere he needed them to be, but he was almost positive the man he'd been looking for was in a particular area, south of Atlanta. The location was puzzling, as it was nowhere near Markham's home, and from all Caine knew of the senator, he had no interests—financial or otherwise—in the area. It was an industrial district, and with the downturn in the economy many of the buildings there stood empty.

It looked as if Markham had driven into the area but had not, at least as far as Caine could tell, driven out.

"I think Markham's here," he said to Lenna, circling the area on the computer screen with his finger. "But I can't pinpoint his location. We'll have to check each place. Put on your coat. It's miserably cold tonight."

Without comment she pulled on the coat, putting it on over the bag that was slung crosswise across her body. "I'm ready," she said, looping her arms around his neck and looking up at him with a calm expression. He supposed she was; when had she ever shrank from anything? He gave her a quick kiss, then teleported them to the area where he'd last seen Markham's car.

In the blink of an eye they were standing in a dark, decrepit, and deserted parking lot. The icy wind whistled around them. There was no beauty here to share with her; there were rusting fences, cracked asphalt, winter-dead weeds drooping in those cracks. An empty building loomed beside them, broken windows making silent comment on the desolation.

It was after midnight, but midnight had long since passed for this place; it had been sitting unoccupied a long while. Caine looked around, not just searching for the senator's car, but scanning for any other danger that might be nearby, danger of the feral human type. Snow and ice still made some of the footing treacherous, so they carefully walked around the building. Nothing was there, not any kind of vehicle.

Looking around, he tried to get a better idea of the area. The lots were large, separated by fences or ditches or expanses of weed-choked dirt. There was no car, no vehicles of any type, to be seen from this vantage point. Here and there dusk-to-dawn security lights created pools of light that revealed the desolation in stark, sickly detail. Markham wouldn't necessarily be parked near any light, if he was here at all, because it hadn't been dark when he'd driven to this area. He could be anywhere. He could be across town. He could have taken a flight to a different country.

"This isn't going to be easy," he said against Lenna's hair. "There's going to be a lot of teleporting. How do you feel?" She wasn't a Hunter; she wasn't naturally acclimated to teleporting. All he felt was tired from expending so much energy, but she was likely feeling other effects.

"Dizzy," she murmured against his leather jacket. "But we have to do it. I'm ready."

He took her at her word. She was, after all, Strength.

He was methodical in his search; holding her tightly against him, he teleported to another, similarly desolate plant. Again, there was nothing there, no car, no Markham. And then again. By the fourth relocation, she was literally hanging around his neck, her knees weak, gulping deep breaths with her face buried in the curve of his shoulder.

He didn't mind having her cling to him. What he minded was not being able to strip her naked and thrust his aching penis inside her. He minded the constant push of power from the cards. He minded this whole damn situation.

At the sixth site, they found Markham's car.

"There," he said with satisfaction. "We've found the bastard."

Lenna lifted her head from his shoulder and heaved a big sigh. "Thank the One. The effects accumulate, don't they? I would rather use my feet now, instead of popping here and there."

He still held her close as he searched the surrounding area for any sign of danger; if any threatened, he wanted her *there* so he could whisk her to safety without even a second's delay. But the night was empty and cold, the biting wind keeping most beings under shelter. The sky overhead was brilliant with stars, letting him know it would turn even colder before dawn finally arrived.

Markham's car was parked at the side of the building, close to a rusted metal door. They silently approached, not touching now, but he could feel her tension rising. She put a protective hand over the bag, the move instinctive.

Then she stopped so abruptly her feet made a small skidding sound on the grit and gravel. Caine turned back, his instincts ratcheting into high alert, but he didn't see or hear anything unusual, other than Lenna staring at the door.

"Death," she murmured.

"Where?"

Lenna tilted her head toward the door. "Inside. I feel it, violence and death, the way I felt Elijah's mother's death."

He didn't know much about her capabilities, but he didn't doubt her. She was a powerful being. Not physically powerful, like him; her strength was of the mind. She would feel the things that tested all beings, and that included death.

A test of the door found it locked. "One more time," he said, tugging her close. She pressed her lips together and gave a reluctant nod, and he took them inside.

The interior of the abandoned building was icy cold, the air stale. The electricity was still on; a few dim lights lit the depressing space. There were several doors along the long hallway, but Lenna straightened away from him and without hesitation went to one of them, turned the doorknob and opened the door. Caine briefly thought about fingerprints—assuming she had any, which he didn't know—but even if there were, there was no chance the cops could match them to any file here on Seven.

A desk lamp burned on a rusty metal desk, illuminating the ugly scene.

There was a body on the floor.

Lenna simply stood there looking at it, but Caine stepped past her and squatted by the man's shoulders so he could study the face. Death changed a person's appearance; without the spirit's energy and animation, the facial features became slack and empty, more like a mannequin than a person. Nevertheless, this was undoubtedly Robert Markham, state senator, possible murderer. His death had been neither accident nor suicide, because the thin rope that had been used to strangle him was still around his neck.

Lenna moved closer, her face expressionless as she looked down at the body. "He's the murderer," she said flatly. "Even though he's dead, I feel it on him, not just the violence of his own death but the murder he committed. I sensed his energy in Elijah's house." She glanced up, met Caine's gaze. "I feel her here, around him. Elijah's mother."

Caine rose to his feet. "Then Elijah is safe."

"I think so," Lenna said, but her voice lacked certainty. "But who killed *him*? Who was the man who attacked us at Elijah's house?"

"I don't know and I don't care," Caine said. "The police will sort it out. Elijah saw this man kill his mother. Whoever did this isn't the man Elijah saw. The line of events is broken. He's safe."

"That's an assumption, but a good one," she admitted. She exhaled a weary breath, then gave him a faint smile. "We can collect Elijah now."

"Not just yet," he said, and seized her for one more teleportation—back to their hotel room. Immediately they were surrounded by warmth, and comfort. It wasn't by accident that they were standing next to the bed.

"It's the middle of the night," he continued, as if they hadn't just crossed the city in less time than it took to inhale. "He'll be asleep, and so will Wiley and Chantel. We'll fetch him in the morning, and then we'll get the final card from Esma so I can take you home." Though how he was going to accomplish that he hadn't yet figured out, but he knew he'd have to bait Esma into coming for them.

"So anxious to be rid of me?" she teased, her voice light, but her eyes . . . was that sadness?

"Not anxious, no, but it's a matter of necessity. If we don't get that card—"

He didn't have to finish. She nodded and shrugged out of her coat, lifted the strap of the bag over her head and placed the bag on the bedside table, then began removing her clothes. "Esma won't allow Aeonia to crumble. She'll bring the card to us."

"You don't know that." He could argue and undress at the same time. "She's more likely to try to get the rest of the cards than she is to give us the one she has."

"I *do* know. Esma is . . . she's mine. She's one of my people. I don't know how to explain it, other than to say that she won't let me die."

"Neither will I." He meant what he said, but his mind was barely aware of his words. Both of them were naked now. Caine's heart began pounding with a strong, heavy beat of anticipation, because soon he was going to be inside her. Despite his fatigue, he didn't intend to waste one minute of the night sleeping. He lifted her up, deposited her in the middle of the bed so they'd have plenty of room without being in danger of falling off during some of the more energetic things he intended to do to her, and followed her down to trap her under his weight.

If she felt trapped at all, then she was a willing prisoner.

She kissed him; she wrapped her arms and legs around him and held on tight.

When they were like this, skin to skin and mouth to mouth, he forgot who she was. She was no longer Strength, she was just Lenna: a woman, *his* woman. Those were dangerous thoughts.

There wasn't enough time; there would never be enough time. Soon she would be home and he would be off to the next job, the next mission, the next world. Their lives being what they were he might never see her again.

They had become so attuned to each other that she was as ready for him as he was for her. When he stroked between her legs he felt the warm moisture of her pliant flesh. He pushed inside her, heard her gasp, felt her arch beneath him. He became a part of her as she was a part of him, and everything in all the worlds faded. There was only this, only her.

As the sun rose on what was almost certain to be Lenna's final day on Seven, Caine made love to her like a man who was about to lose everything.

Chapter 17

Too soon, the night was over; Lenna would have made it last forever if she could have, but inevitably the sun rose, and the end of her time here on Seven was drawing to an end one way or another. They got up, showered—a long shower, because Caine made love to her so slowly, all urgency gone, that they both ended up sitting on the shower floor until they gained enough energy to get up and towel off.

Caine ordered room service, and while they waited she sat curled beside him on the couch, watching the early-morning news. She was nestled comfortably against his side, his arm around her, her head resting on his shoulder. She felt relaxed, almost limp, as if all the tension had been wrung from her muscles by their lovemaking. Soon enough they would have to retrieve

Elijah, but until then she was perfectly content to be right where she was.

Then she felt Caine tense against her, and her attention jerked to the television screen.

The news announcer solemnly intoned, "Young Elijah Tilley still remains missing after his mother's murder. Amber Tilley's body was discovered near a roadside park, but there has been no sign of seven-year-old Elijah." Elijah's photo flashed on the screen, looking a little younger than he did now, with those big brown eyes and a happy, mischievous smile. "Elijah's family is pleading for the safe return of the child. If anyone has any information about him, please contact the authorities."

A distraught older couple appeared, tears running down the woman's lined face. The white-haired man said, "We just want Elijah safe. Please, whoever has him, bring him home. We're praying that he's okay, and a lot of other people are praying, too, but we need more, we need help bringing our baby home." His voice broke, and his faded blue eyes welled with tears. "We need him home." Their names were printed across the bottom of the screen: James and Susan Tilley. In a trembling voice, James offered a significant financial reward for any tip leading to Elijah's safe return. Susan Tilley tried to talk, but she couldn't choke out any words and just shook her head. Her face was red and blotchy; she wrung her hands in despair. To Lenna's eye and ear, they were both broken by the events of the past few days.

James took a deep, shuddering breath. "We haven't seen our daughter for four years, and now we've lost her. We don't want to lose our grandson, too. Please— whoever has him, don't hurt him. He's all we have."

The screen flashed back to the news announcer. "Amber Tilley's body hasn't yet been released to her family. Funeral arrangements will be announced at a later date."

Lenna clutched Caine's hand. Part of her had expected something like this, because most people had relatives, but her instinctive response was not what she'd expected from herself. Her heart sank a little. No, her heart sank *significantly*, landing in her stomach, churning there and stirring up butterflies. Her mind could be logical about this, but her heart was with Elijah.

"He doesn't know them," she said softly. "They're strangers to him."

"He doesn't *remember* them," Caine replied in that calm, no-nonsense way he had. "But they know him, and they love him. With time, he'll both know them and love them, as he loved his mother."

"Will he?" Her mind spun around and around, worrying at the subject. Elijah had been through so much, seen things no child should ever see. He'd lost his mother, but she and Caine had been there to step in and hold his young world steady. Would he adjust yet again, when they left and he was with strangers? Would they love him? Would they be good to him? The Tilleys were old—not elderly, not physically incapable, but they were definitely beyond their child-rearing years. Were they too old to take on the care of an active seven-year-old? Take him to the baseball games he loved, be indulgent when he whirled around the room in a cape, waving a magic wand, or a pretend knife? When he tried to tell them about "poofing"? Would they still be alive to see him off to college, to guide him through the social years when he'd be trying to select a mate, to hold *his* children in their arms and fill his heart with joy at seeing that connection of generations?

Caine wrapped his arm around Lenna and tugged her closer. She'd kept her doubts—most of them—to herself, but he saw them in her; they had been forced into closeness, but now he knew her too well.

"You didn't think you could take him back to Aeonia with you, did you?" he asked quietly.

"Well, no, but—" What *had* she thought? He

couldn't go with her, which meant he had to live somewhere here on Seven, with someone.

"Elijah isn't a pet." Caine's voice was less harsh than it could have been as he rubbed her shoulder. "He deserves a real life, here on his own world. He deserves to be loved and cared for by ordinary people, like them." He pointed to the screen, where Elijah's grandparents had been, though they had been replaced by a too-loud car commercial.

"I know." Those two words were soft, and filled with the ache she felt. But she would be what she was, and bear whatever heartache was necessary to do what was best for Elijah.

She had fewer than two days to remain in this world, and if Caine worked efficiently—didn't he always?—he might return her to Aeonia today, well ahead of the deadline. Getting the Moon card from Esma was critical, but they would find a way. Caine probably already had a plan. Just as critical, to Lenna, was seeing Elijah settled. More than that, she wanted to see him happy. He had been through too much, had been too traumatized. Could he ever be happy, or was he forever scarred by what he'd seen?

She looked up at Caine, tightened her grip on his hand. In such a short time he'd become so many things to her: protector, lover, teacher of life. He had shown her such vibrancy, here on Seven. He was also a friend, in a way she'd never before known. Their time together had been intense and too short, and it was coming to an end.

An important part of strength was truth: not just acknowledging it, but facing it.

"I don't want to lose you," she whispered.

He didn't show any emotion, but his dark eyes seemed to grow even darker. She felt him tense, saw the tension in the set of his jaw and the narrowing of his eyes. "What choice do we have?" he asked. "You are who you are, and I am who I am."

And there they were, the inevitable truth of their mutual existences. She was Major Arcana. He was a Hunter. They didn't even live on the same world. It was true that while the Major Arcana did occasionally— the phrase from this time in this world was "hook up," which Lenna found distasteful but also oddly accurate—they didn't form the kinds of bonds she had seen on Seven, and she was absurdly envious. The Arcana didn't mate outside their small circle; it was unheard of to do otherwise. What would the others do, how would they react, if Strength herself formed a life-bond with a Hunter? Was it even possible?

If? It was far too late for *ifs*, at least where her

feelings for Caine were concerned. She loved him. How that would shake her fellow Aeonians!

If she knew nothing else, it was that it was past time for Aeonia to be shaken up, and shaken well.

During breakfast, Caine mulled over the situation. He understood Lenna's doubts, her worries about Elijah. She would rest easier if Elijah was in his grandparents' care before she returned to her place in Aeonia, but she didn't just want to *know* that the child was in good hands; she wanted to see for herself—personally, not in a remote Aeonian viewing, like watching a documentary on Seven's television.

He preferred a different, more direct plan: get the card from Esma, complete his mission by returning the deck and Lenna to the Emperor, and then when that was done, see the boy settled. That was what he'd wanted to do all along. Simple, logical—he'd always preferred a clean, no-nonsense mission.

Instead, there was Lenna, and there was nothing uncomplicated about her, though he had to admit all the difficulties she'd put up were definitely in line with her reason for being. She didn't stop trying; she soldiered on. She never took the easiest path unless she was convinced it was the *right* path. He couldn't reason with a woman whose inner path was so clearly marked for her. Hell, he couldn't even convince himself she was wrong.

The facts were, with Markham dead the threat to the child was past, and there was no reason for Lenna to remain here to see to the child's safety herself. Nevertheless, there was time to do things her way—not a lot of time, but time enough. And he didn't have to like it; he simply had to do it.

Vae, he had never before even considered completing an assignment to someone else's specifications. Then again, he had never before taken his target as a lover.

This was likely his last opportunity to be private with her. When they left the hotel today, the odds were they wouldn't be returning. And because this was likely the last time, he seized the privacy they had now and laid her, naked, on the bed . . . one last time. He lost himself in her, one last time. She wrapped her legs around him as if she could hold them together, as if she could keep them linked and earthbound and caught in a never-ending whirlwind of physical pleasure.

If only . . .

The sex was quick and hard, an almost brutal goodbye expressed with their bodies, in sweat and racing hearts and finally a sharp pleasure they shared.

Lenna shook and sighed and whispered his name. He was silent, because what was the point in speaking what they both already knew?

Did she understand that being close to her for days on end had been torture for him? Did she understand that he would miss her when this job was over?

Vae.

Afterward, they showered again, then Caine quickly dressed and collected his weapons, strapped them on. At first he intended to leave the computer in the hotel room for a maid to find. It wasn't as if he could take it with him; a trip between worlds would fry the circuits. But he thought of another use for it, and all but dragged Lenna with him into the parlor, where he downloaded a video. He was certain there was no Wi-Fi on Wiley's island, and he wanted Elijah to see something.

As he prepared himself for departure, Lenna put on her white dress, the one that made her look like the powerful, regal being she was. He watched her dress, the male part of him scowling as each glowing inch of flesh was covered, but not wanting to miss a single second of having her near. She retrieved a handful of jewelry from the bottom of her bag. Like any woman adorning herself, she sat on the side of the bed and slipped on large, sparkling rings that suited her, as well as a bracelet that was obviously not of this world. The light from the pale green stones danced and splintered, like tiny rainbows.

She was not of this world, and now she looked it. Lenna—Strength—glowed. She sparkled. No matter what world she inhabited, she would draw every eye.

"What about not calling attention to yourself?" he asked wryly.

She smiled as she stood and walked to him, wrapped her arms around his neck, and leaned into him. She came to him so easily now, and he accepted her the same way. His arms automatically adjusted to holding someone so much smaller than he, his head automatically bent to find her scent, to take her lips. They *fit*, as if she belonged here, with him, always close.

"You're one to talk," she chided, glancing pointedly at his laser blaster.

"I know how to avoid detection—it's part of my job." She, on the other hand, screamed, *Look at me!* And it was completely unconscious, a simple grandeur of being, rather than dressing or acting for attention. The attention was already hers. She dressed to please herself, for the joy of a luxurious fabric, for the beauty of the jewels.

"I won't be here on Seven much longer," she explained. "When I go before the Emperor, I need to be myself in all ways. Elijah has already seen me as I am, and there's no need to disguise myself for Wiley and Chantel." She smiled. "Besides, now that I have spent a few days here, I understand that there is no true norm. If anyone else sees me, they'll dismiss me as a . . ." She stopped, searched her brain—what she had of *his* brain—and finally finished with, "An odd duck."

Caine snorted. Lenna was no odd duck. She was a treasure, a goddess, a remarkable woman.

She smiled up at him. With all the turmoil ahead of and behind them, she still managed a radiant smile. "You'd have me wear baggy flannel all the time, if I left the choice to you."

It wouldn't matter what she wore. Flannel or silk— she would always draw his attention, and he'd been a fool to think otherwise.

"You don't deny it," she teased when he didn't respond.

"No, I don't," he said in a low, strained tone.

He didn't want to lose her, either, but he didn't see any point in talking about it. She would soon return to her life, and he would return to his.

With that, he brought himself sharply back to the hardness of reality. "Boots or barefoot?"

She dropped her arms from around his neck and crossed the room to grab the boots she'd been wearing since arriving on Seven. He was, out of necessity, right behind her. She sat down to pull on the boots. Any other woman would look ridiculous, in a flimsy white dress and winter boots, but she didn't, because she didn't care.

It would be a waste of time to tell her how he felt, so he didn't bother.

"Ready?"

"For it all to end? No. To see Elijah? Yes."

He put his arms around her, and took them there.

"You're back!" Elijah shouted from the front porch of Wiley and Chantel's island home. He didn't look at all distressed. In fact, there was a bit of color in his cheeks, as well as a bounce in his step as he ran down the steps to meet them. He was already slightly tanned, a little grubby, totally ecstatic.

Lenna braced herself as Elijah launched himself at her. She caught him and then she laughed, as her heart broke a little—laughter and pain, wrapped together in one important moment. She shouldn't care so much for a human child—she knew the difficulties—but she did. In the fatalistic approach of Seven, it was what it was. Elijah was hers, now and forever, in a way she couldn't explain.

He wiggled in her arms, and she released him.

Evidently finished with her, he turned to Caine, tilting his head as he studied the multitude of weapons Caine wore. The hug he gave was more sedate because he had to avoid touching all the guns and knives, but no less forceful. Caine's big hand rested on the shining dark hair for a moment, stroked down to the thin little shoulder.

"Why are you wearing your weapons again?" Elijah asked as he finally released Caine and backed away. "Are you going to war? You look like you're going to war. I caught a fish, and Chantel cooked it for supper last night! I didn't think I could eat a fish I'd seen while it was still alive, but I did, and it was good. I'm glad I didn't give it a name. She made cookies, too. They had coconut in them. I like coconut." He turned and looked up at Lenna. "You're wearing your nightgown again! How come?"

"It isn't a nightgown," she said, as she had upon arriving in this world.

"It looks like a nightgown, kinda," he said. "But it's pretty. I like it."

Caine put a hand on Elijah's shoulder. "Before we leave here, there's something I'd like you to see."

Wiley and Chantel stood on the porch, watching and smiling at the enthusiastic reunion and Elijah's flood of questions. Probably they'd heard their share of questions from him, too. As they went up the steps Caine nodded to Wiley, and Wiley nodded back. It was as if they used some type of man-communication that didn't need words. *Everything all right? Right as rain. Finished with this mess? Hell, no.*

Or something along those lines.

Inside, Caine placed the laptop on the table and turned it on, waited for it to boot up. He pulled up a chair and sat down, motioned for Elijah to climb on his lap. The child clambered up without a second of reservation, sitting astride one of Caine's muscular thighs, leaning back to rest trustingly against him. "Are we going to watch a movie?"

"No, I'm going to show you some people who know you."

"Know *me*? How? Do I know them? Why are they in a movie?"

Instead of reiterating that it wasn't a movie, as soon as the computer was ready for use, Caine pulled up the clip of the interview with Elijah's grandparents.

Lenna tensed, watching Elijah's face for any sign of upset. She wanted to slam the computer shut, protect him from something he might not be ready to see. His grandparents were strangers, strangers who expected to take him in and attempt to take the place of his mother. How would he feel about that? Would he understand what they wanted? No one could replace his mother. No one could undo what Markham had done to this child.

The man had died too easily, in her opinion. She wished she had been there, at his death; *then* he'd have known suffering.

Caine played the interview. Elijah's grandparents' voices filled the room. Elijah tilted his head to the side, wrinkling his nose, then scratching his ear. Lenna was prepared to snatch him away at any second, at the first sign of a tear. Instead . . . Elijah leaned forward and touched the screen with one grubby little finger. "That's my granny, huh? I dreamed about her, a bunch of times. Mostly I dreamed about sitting on her lap. She smelled like cookies."

Lenna was taken aback. Did Elijah actually *remember* these people he hadn't seen for years? He would've been a toddler, or not much more than that, when Amber and her parents had their falling out. He shouldn't remember much of anything of that time, but the human mind was a wondrous thing. He'd told her he had no grandparents, that he had no one other than his mother, but seeing the Tilleys on the computer screen had apparently jogged a memory, or two.

"I dreamed about him, too!" Elijah said, pointing to his grandfather. "He laughed a lot." Then his expression darkened. "He's not laughing now. They look really sad. Are they sad because they miss me?" He didn't mention his mother, but he had to handle that in his own way. At first it had consumed his every thought. Now he was trying to create a space without sadness. His moment to grieve would come around again, in its own time.

"Yes," Caine said.

Elijah looked up at Lenna, up from his place in Caine's lap. His brow knit in concern. "Will Uncle Bobby hurt them, too?"

She gently touched his head, smoothing a strand of hair that immediately popped back out of place. "Uncle Bobby is gone. He won't bother you or anyone else, not ever again."

"Gone forever?"

"Gone forever," Caine said. "I promise." That was good enough for Elijah; he didn't ask gone how, dead or in jail, because that didn't matter. All that mattered was *gone.*

Caine left the laptop for Wiley and Chantel. It would make a nice paperweight, once the battery discharged, or Wiley could take it somewhere and sell it. Maybe they could keep it charged, somehow.

Chantel knelt to give Elijah a tight hug, rocking back and forth with him in her arms. "Don't forget us, okay? You can't talk about us, but at night look up at the star Wiley showed you and we'll look up at it, too, and think about each other."

"Okay," Elijah said, and kissed her cheek. "Maybe someday you can send me a letter and I'll come visit."

They all said their goodbyes, then Caine gathered her and Elijah to him. Elijah glanced up, his expression one of concern. "Wait, we forgot my magic set." He did not mention the new clothes. Priorities.

Lenna was ready to collect the child's things for him, but Caine had other ideas. "Wiley really needs to work on his magic. Would you mind if we left the set with him? You will have access to others. There is no Walmart here."

Elijah's chin stiffened, and he said, "That's a good idea." Then he lowered his voice and added, "Wiley really does need some practice."

With that, Caine teleported them to the street where Elijah lived. They landed not in or near Amber Tilley's house, but instead were down the street, close to the house where Lenna had entered Seven.

And in that instant, she knew what Caine intended, what he'd intended all along.

"We should be the ones to deliver Elijah to his grandparents," she said, fighting to keep her voice even. Now that the moment was staring her in the face, seeing it through was taking more effort than she'd expected. She swallowed, because she couldn't let Elijah see how upset she was. This was for him, for his future.

"We can't do that, and you know it."

She wanted to argue, but she couldn't. She *did* know it. She and Caine couldn't bring that sort of attention to themselves. Still, her stomach was once more twisting with dread.

As they had last night, they stood back and looked into the home from a shaded side yard. It was still cold, though most of the snow was gone, revealing the brown, winter-dead grass lawns. That house had represented safety to Elijah when he most needed it. The people inside would welcome him joyfully into the warmth.

Caine knelt down on one knee to look Elijah in the eye. "Your friend and his family will take you to your grandparents."

Those big brown eyes apprehensively searched Caine's face, and his bottom lip began to tremble. "Why can't you and Lenna take me? You'd like them! They're nice! I know they're nice!"

"I'm sure they're very nice," Caine said gently, "but Lenna and I have important work to do and we need to get to it."

Lenna saw in Elijah the same kind of pain she felt as he said, "I thought I was important."

"You are!" Lenna said as she dropped down to join them. She hugged Elijah to her, and again, her heart broke. "You're important to me and you always will be." They separated a little bit, and she brushed a strand of hair out of her eyes. "But it would be best if Caine and I didn't meet your grandparents or Zack's family. You see, we don't really belong here."

"Would you get in trouble?"

"Yes, I'm afraid we would. We aren't supposed to be here. We should have gone home a long time ago, but we stayed to help you."

Elijah nodded, but his lip still trembled. "Will you come to see me sometime?"

"If I can," she whispered, knowing it would be next to impossible to return.

Strength was a quality, a force of will; through the eons so many had called for it, pulled it from her when they needed it. She held it for others. Never before had she tried to give it without being asked, but how would a child know to ask? With two fingers she touched Elijah's temple, felt the heat and life of him, and gave. She whispered, "I give to you the strength to be happy." Her eyes stung with tears. She never cried—never! And yet here she was, near to breaking down and sobbing like a . . . like a . . . like an emotional female from this very world.

She dropped her hand. It was done.

"Now, go ring that doorbell," she said. "Your life awaits. We'll wait here until you are safely inside."

Elijah looked up her, then at Caine. He gave them a tiny, uncertain wave. Then he turned to look at his friend's Zack's house, and a glow came to his face. "Bye!" he said. "I love you!"

"I love you, too," she whispered to his back, because he had already turned and was running, running toward the house, toward his friends, toward his life. He stopped once and quickly looked back, and waved. He was smiling. Perhaps her gift of strength was working.

Caine put his arm around her shoulders and pulled her close. They watched as Elijah rang the bell, as Zack's mother answered. They heard the woman's scream—a happy scream—from where they stood. Through the window they saw the family gather around Elijah, though the father didn't wait long before taking a cell phone from his pocket and making a call.

They had to leave, before someone saw them, but Lenna wanted to watch a minute longer. So did Caine apparently, because he didn't whisk them away. She nestled her head into the curve of his shoulder.

"He'll tell them all about us," he said, sounding unconcerned.

"They won't believe him."

"No, I suppose not."

"We sound like one of their fairy tales: a Hunter who can 'poof' and a woman who crossed worlds and appeared in a walk-in closet, wearing her nightgown, in answer to his call for help." She managed a smile. No, his tale would be written off as the overactive imagination of a traumatized child, a mechanism to help him cope.

And eventually even Elijah would forget what was real and what was not.

Elijah would be fine. He had family and friends who loved him, and he had strength, his own and a bit more. Nevertheless, leaving him was wrenching.

Even more, she didn't want to leave this Hunter who had become so important to her. Caine had protected her, and Elijah. He'd shielded her. He had loved her. But it was time.

She put her hand on his cheek and said, "Take me home."

Chapter 18

Derek drove slowly, both hands on the wheel, his eyes straight ahead. The commotion at the other end of the street was impossible to miss. Cop cars, news vans, neighbors—happy smiling neighbors and happy crying neighbors. Shit, there was so much snot running he could probably make a fortune selling tissues.

Well short of the circus, he pulled into the driveway of a house that was up for sale and put his car in Park. Before he could get out, a red sedan sped by behind him and came to a tire-squealing stop at the curb, so close to the excited gathering it almost took out a few people who hadn't been paying enough attention. People scattered, and almost simultaneously the doors of the red Chevrolet flew open and an older couple jumped out. He thought they were pretty spry for their ages, because they went running across the yard.

He knew who they were: Elijah's grandparents. He'd seen them on the news. And because he was thorough, he'd even known their car was red, because he'd driven by their house himself to check them out.

As he watched, the boy everyone had been looking for, the boy he had been looking for, bolted from the house and ran toward the couple. He ran the way some kids did, full out and with perfect form, as if he had been made for running. Derek couldn't see much in the way of detail. Too many people were in the way, including a shitload of photographers—still and video—capturing the reunion for posterity. But now and then the crowd would shift and he'd get a good glimpse.

The Tilleys were on their knees, both of them holding on to Elijah for dear life. He hung on to them, too, first one and then the other and then a tight, three-way hug. Elijah hugged the way he ran, with complete enthusiasm, the way kids do. Everyone else stood back and allowed the little family their reunion. There would be a lot for them to do in the next few days: interviews, legal stuff, investigation. But for now, there was just this, loving grandparents and their grandson.

Derek experienced a rare rush of sympathy, maybe even empathy. His own childhood hadn't been all that great. He'd seen kids who lived a lot worse lives than he had, but seeing other people miserable didn't help your own misery; it just gave you company. He could have done with less company.

Elijah had been through a lot in the last few days, more than he should have. Yeah, better Markham than Elijah. The kid was going to be okay.

Derek looked for the blonde in the crowd, and swore under his breath when he didn't see her. There wasn't anything he could do with so many witnesses around, but he at least wanted to locate her, follow her. There were a lot of women standing around, and a few of them were blond, but that particular one—the kicker—wasn't here. He'd have recognized her right away, even if she'd had a hood pulled over her head. She was the kind of woman who would stand out in a crowd, something about the way she moved, the way she held herself, as if she'd never got over being prom queen or something. He could still clearly remember her face, and he didn't normally pay much attention to a woman's *face*.

She could be anywhere: at the police station, giving a statement, or at a television station, giving an interview. Or she might be in jail, for keeping the kid for so long while everyone and his brother had been looking for him. He liked the idea of that.

But wherever she was, she'd be describing in great detail the man she'd seen in Elijah's kitchen.

If Derek hadn't been forced to kill the senator, he might go on about his business and take his chances. But between Sammy and Markham, the odds were there was some overlooked evidence floating around. Maybe someone had glanced out a window at the wrong time, maybe he'd left a footprint in the dust—something, anything. Sammy wasn't much of a problem. Even if the cops realized that Sammy had been murdered, they probably wouldn't look too hard for his killer.

Markham, though, was another story. He'd been a state senator, well respected even though he was a complete shit—a murdering shit, at that. His killer would be hunted from now until the end of time. Derek didn't think there was anything to connect him to Markham, he had always been certain there was not, but what did he know? How could he be sure? He couldn't, damn it. The senator might have all sorts of paperwork or electronic trails linking him to his own "anything you need, boss" private investigator. Maybe he even had a damning letter somewhere marked, "To be opened in the event of my death." People who were involved in illegal shit sometimes threatened to have such a letter in anonymous hands. Derek suspected that people who really did that wouldn't bother to warn anyone. It would be a surprise.

He hated surprises.

He put his car in Reverse, backed into the street, and headed slowly and cautiously out of the neighborhood. The excitement was behind him—literally and figuratively. Ahead there was an unplanned future, a world of possibilities. It was time to start over, to change his name and embrace the world of semiretirement. Maybe he'd open a small bar somewhere, maybe in Florida. On a beach. Some place where he could see people coming from a good distance. That sounded like a plan, one of the best he'd ever had.

But he knew that, in the back of his mind, he would always be on the lookout for that blonde . . .

"You know what I have to do," Caine said. He wanted Lenna to be prepared. She wasn't helpless, but she wasn't a Hunter. He wouldn't worry so much if she would show some of the legendary temper for which she was famous, but hell, he hadn't seen any real temper in her at all. Maybe it was all a hoax. In general, she was as reasonable as he could have asked; stubborn, but reasonable, so long as he defined reasonable as not being nasty-tempered, because she didn't step back from her chosen position much at all.

"You have to let Esma find me," she said, no fear at all in her blue gaze as she looked up at him. "I know."

"Yes. I'll have to get far enough away from you that

you're unshielded. But we get to choose the place and the time. We get to choose your position, and mine. You have to be ready to fight as hard as you've ever fought."

"I have faith in Esma. I do. She's one of mine."

"She might not *want* to hurt you, but never forget that she's a Hunter first. And what if she isn't the Hunter who first targets your energy? We have no way of knowing how many there are, or who they are. One of us has to retrieve the Moon card from Esma— whatever we have to do—then I'll get to you. Somehow, if I have to destroy everything in my path, I *will* get to you, and we'll teleport to Aeonia."

She nodded, accepting. This could be a death trap, for both of them. It didn't matter, because they had no choice. Lenna had to go back to Aeonia.

"Are you ready?" he asked, though the question was rhetorical. They had talked about this, they'd planned as best they could, and nothing was to be gained by putting off the inevitable. She nodded, made sure the bag that held the cards was securely fastened and draped crosswise across her body. Caine had reinforced the strap so it couldn't be cut, even with a Hunter's knife.

He put his arms around her, kissed her, and while they were still kissing teleported them to one of the abandoned factories they'd searched when they'd been looking for Markham. Not much had changed, though it was daylight now instead of dark. All the snow had melted, but the air was still cold and the empty buildings and lots looked even more decrepit in bright sunlight than they did at night.

So far as they knew, the senator's body hadn't been found yet. If it had been, the police were staying very quiet about it, and given all the hoopla over Elijah and the fact that the senator was a person of interest in Amber Tilley's murder, secrecy wasn't very likely. They were some distance away from where they'd found him, because Lenna hadn't wanted to be anywhere near the ugly energy that had lingered around him.

The inside of the abandoned building was stale and icy cold; dust motes floated in the shafts of sunlight. Caine looked around, selecting their best positions. They each needed not to be taken from behind, and they needed to restrict the directions from which they would be attacked. Neither of them doubted there would be a fight; the biggest unknown was how many Hunters would come.

She stood in his arms, her eyes closed as she nestled against him. He was oddly reluctant to move away from her, and going by the way she clung to him she was just as reluctant. Then she opened her eyes and looked up at him with an expression he couldn't quite read. It might be longing . . . or regret. Or . . . he didn't dare examine all the ors that passed through his mind.

"Don't drop the shield just yet," she murmured. "I have something to say before . . ."

"Before all hell breaks loose?" he finished for her when she stumbled.

She sighed, then nodded. "I don't know what will happen next. I know what I want to happen, but life is uncertain, more uncertain than I ever realized. You . . ."

She stopped speaking again, as if she had lost her words, as if that was even possible for someone like her.

"You . . ." she began again, only to hit the same stumbling block. Judging by the expression on her face, what she wanted to say, what she couldn't bring herself to say, was better left unsaid, anyway.

She took a deep breath, steeled herself, and took a step away from him. Caine held out his hand. "Give me one of the cards." It was a command, not a suggestion.

Her eyebrows lifted slightly.

"If Esma appears and touches you, you have the deck and she has the Moon. Together, you complete the deck. She can teleport you to Veton. Do you trust him with the deck?"

"No."

"A safeguard," he said, waving two fingers impatiently.

She unzipped the bag and reached inside. Without looking, without choosing, she grabbed a card and offered it to him.

He flicked it over and looked at it. The Emperor. Of course; what else would it be? He slipped the card into his front pants pocket, making sure it was firmly and deeply seated there.

She wasn't going anywhere without him.

He put her in the position he wanted, and maintained the shield as he moved away. He'd been telling the truth when he told her he didn't know exactly how far from himself the shield extended, but for the sake of surprise he had to keep himself hidden, though she was exposed. At the same time, he couldn't be *too* far away from her. His strategy was coming down to a matter of crucial inches; too far, and he couldn't get to her in time. Too close, and either the shield would still hide her or he'd have to let it fall completely and expose him, too, thereby losing the element of surprise.

He moved away from her. One step. Two. A couple more, and he was farther away than he had been since he'd first shielded her. There had been times when he'd hated the necessity of having her *right there* all the time, when he'd grumbled about the energy it took to shield her, when he'd wanted nothing more than to be rid of her. But now it felt odd and somehow wrong to be at such a distance. He wanted her closer.

She looked so out of place here, a gentle, warm glow against a harsh, gray backdrop, beautiful otherworldliness against the ugliness of neglected abandonment. She should be in Aeonia, living in comfort and luxury and well away from danger, well away from him.

He couldn't stand the thought of it.

"I've never known anyone like you," she said, blue gaze locked on him.

As he watched, a few snowflakes began to fall—not everywhere, but over and around her, flakes swirling and dancing in the beams of light. It was her, it had to be her. Somehow she—

Esma flashed into existence, practically on top of Lenna.

A few feet away, another form flashed. As he'd more than halfway expected, Esma hadn't come alone. *Stroud.*

Caine had *been right to take one of the cards.* Lenna had that very clear thought as Esma grabbed her and—apparently assuming that the deck was in the bag Lenna wore and protected with one arm—

attempted to teleport them both to Aeonia, to Veton. Surprise flashed across Esma's face when it didn't work, and she cursed.

"Fooled you," Lenna said softly, but her attention was mostly on Caine.

There had been another Hunter, after all, a Hunter who was as big as Caine. To Lenna's eyes, there was no distinguishing between the speed of the blows, whether or not Caine had an advantage. She flinched with every blow that was delivered, with every swing of the knife that was intended for him. Wrenching away from Esma, she started toward the fight.

Esma grabbed her arm and yanked her back. "Where's the deck?"

Lenna swiftly searched her shared memories with Caine for the proper response, and found one that was very satisfying: "Kiss my ass."

The vicious fight between Caine and the other Hunter moved them farther and farther away, one step at a time. Lenna kicked at Esma's knee, trying to break free again. Esma twisted as the kick landed just above her knee, not doing any damage, and wrenched Lenna into a hip roll that dumped her on the floor. Immediately Esma was on her, bearing her weight down.

"Where's the deck?" Esma asked, more harshly than she had before.

Lenna pulled one arm free, threw a punch to Esma's left jaw, but the Hunter shook it off and grabbed her arm again. Lenna knew she was no match physically, not that she'd stop trying, but—

Lenna ground her teeth in frustration and fear. Teleporting her to Veton wasn't possible, but what if Esma decided to teleport her somewhere else on Seven, separate her from Caine, hide her away, and perhaps negotiate with Caine to get the entire deck. Apart, they were much less effective than they were together.

But Esma had to be touching her to teleport her.

Fiercely Lenna bucked, throwing everything she had into the effort; Esma was taken by surprise and fell to the side, rolling so she could flip to her feet, but by then Lenna was also on her feet and darted away to put some distance between them. All Esma had to do was flash to her side, so Lenna didn't stay still, jerking here and there, changing direction, but all the time working closer to the savage battle going on between the two men.

"I could use a hand here, Stroud!" Esma called, circling Lenna as she tried to anticipate her movements.

Stroud didn't answer because he had all he could handle. Esma cursed, disappeared, then flashed directly behind Lenna and grabbed her shoulder.

Lenna growled. Physically she might not be able to match Esma in a fight, but she had other strengths she could call upon, strengths that made her who she was. She ducked and whirled, and when she faced Esma this time her blue eyes were glowing hot, her voice low and throbbing with power. "Don't touch me again."

Esma was a Hunter and no Hunter was a coward, but at the look in Lenna's eyes she reeled back in shock, instinctively holding up her hands as if to ward off what might come her way.

Lenna jerked back and turned her attention to the vicious fight between Caine and the other Hunter. There was blood on both of them now, blood on the floor, blood on the flashing knives. They moved so fast it was impossible to determine who was winning, impossible to truly tell who was where. The metal from their blades flashed like lightning, the air around them shimmered from the speed of their movement.

Caine was wounded. She didn't know how severely, but just knowing he was hurt made her heart swell with panic until she almost choked. Esma wasn't holding her now, but she was helpless. She had no weapon, no power that could help Caine, no way to even swing a piece of metal that wasn't as likely to hit Caine as it was Stroud.

"Let me take you back to Aeonia," Esma said, her voice lower and calmer than it had been before. "You belong there. Tell me where the deck is."

Lenna ignored her, moving closer to the whirling, flashing dance of death. Just as she was about to throw caution to the wind and launch herself into the middle of the battle, Caine heaved Stroud back and for a few seconds they were separated. Caine was bleeding, badly, but Stroud was worse. He would quickly lose strength now.

Stroud must've realized, as Lenna had, that he couldn't win the fight. In a surprise move, likely using all his reserves of strength, he feinted to the side, then reversed and with a well-placed kick swept Caine's feet out from under him. Caine dropped. Stroud turned. He took a solid stance and threw his knife—at Lenna.

A raw, rough sound burst out of Caine and he flashed in front of Lenna, their eyes meeting.

She saw the instant the knife went into his back. She saw the obsidian of his pupils flare, saw the minute flinch of pain. For a split second, the world stopped. It paused, and everything that had happened since Elijah had pulled her from the comforts of home made sense to her. Every joy, every pain, it had all been leading her to this moment.

Caine's body arched. His lips parted, then he stumbled, dropped to the floor, desperation crossing his expression as he tried to force his body to ignore the pain, to react, to turn and face the enemy. She saw him go white, saw his eyes close.

"Nooooo!"

She heard the howl of anguish rising up from deep inside her, bursting from her throat. Fury rose behind the anguish, filling her, exploding through every cell and fiber of her being. She felt herself expanding, felt power gathering in and around her. Without conscious thought one hand snapped up, and she pointed at Stroud. She saw nothing but him, nothing but Stroud and the knife in Caine's back. The world around her shook and went hazy. The icy interior of the abandoned building became impossibly colder, hoarfrost limning every surface. Sleet pelted them, ice pellets like tiny needles.

Stroud's eyes widened, his mouth fell open. His hands up to ward off whatever she sent his way, he stumbled back. He took two steps, then turned and ran. Hunters didn't run away, but this one did—from her.

Lenna howled her fury, and loosed all her anger through her fingers. Pure energy and ice and fire that had been born in her essence took shape, mingled, shot out to catch Stroud in the back like a frozen thunderbolt. He screamed, the sound piercing and inhuman. Lenna blasted him again, and the very earth shook; the remaining windows in the building exploded to rain shards of glass both in and out, as if the power that destroyed them came from the very fabric of the building, of the universe itself.

Caine! She had just found him, and already she'd lost him. Her agony knew no bounds, and fed the urge to blast everything, destroy Seven, take down Aeonia itself. Only the knowledge that Elijah was on Seven stayed her hand.

Frustrated, screaming, she blasted a piece of rusted machinery to smithereens, slammed her hand toward the floor and cratered it, the shock wave almost taking Esma into the hole. Esma threw herself sideways, desperately seeking cover.

Lenna whirled on her, blood rage in her eyes. She lifted her arms, ready to destroy Esma, herself, the cards, everything that had taken Caine from her—

"Vae," came a weak, slurred voice. "You nearly deafened me."

She froze, barely holding back the destruction that surged against her skin, snarling to be released. Or perhaps *she* was snarling. She spun . . . and Caine was looking at her. He was rolled half on his side, because of the knife in his back, and he was utterly white, but part of that was the frost she had caused to cover everything in sight. His black eyes were open. His breathing was fast and shallow, but he was breathing. With an incoherent sound she dropped to her knees beside him, sobbing. "I thought you were dead! I thought—" She didn't finish what she thought, running frantic hands over him. "Where else are you hurt? Your back—I know about your back. Where else?"

"Minor," he murmured, closing his eyes again. "Except for that."

"*Damn* you!" She swiped both cheeks with her hands. "You threw yourself in front of me! Why? *Why*? It makes no sense!"

Those dark eyes slitted open. "Love you."

The words hit her with more power than that she had unleashed on her surroundings. She sank back on her heels, mouth open with wonder. "L-love?" she stuttered.

"After the temper tantrum I just saw, I'm rethinking that."

"Love," she said, and now her tone was achingly gentle. "The temper tantrum was because I thought I'd lost you."

"You still might," Esma said acerbically behind her, "unless you move and let me tend him. The longer the knife is in his back, the worse it will be. Our knives are specially formulated to cause accumulating damage."

Lenna turned her head to look at Esma. The Hunter had regained her feet and stood behind her close enough to touch, but hadn't tried to wrench Lenna away. She held up her hands. "I swear I won't harm him. I don't want you to—" she glanced at Stroud's motionless body "—do to me what you did to him. Whatever it was."

Lenna cast Stroud a dismissive glance. She had no pity for him. She hadn't lost her temper in such a very, very long time that she'd almost forgotten what it felt like, but she wasn't surprised that Stroud wasn't moving.

"If you can help him, do it," she commanded Esma, her voice full of the authority of her position.

Esma knelt beside them, and together she and Lenna eased Caine to a sitting position. He could barely help them, and he ground his teeth to keep from groaning as the movement worked the wicked blade deeper into him.

Lenna saw how deep the knife was, and she remembered how long the blade was. She blanched. This was a death wound; it had to be. No wound could be so deep and not cause mortal damage.

But . . . he was a Hunter, and Hunters were notoriously difficult to kill. She reached for the knife to pull it from his flesh.

"Wait!" Esma put her hand over Lenna's. "It has to be removed a certain way, to avoid further injury. I've done this before, more than once. I promise, I'll take every care. Word of a Hunter."

Lenna glanced at Caine, and he gave her a faint nod. She looked back at Esma. "Do it."

For herself, she trusted Esma, and for some reason always had. But this was Caine, and he had to agree. He knew more about what was going on than she did.

Esma dug in one of her pockets and produced a slim pouch from which she removed two green pellets, handing them to Lenna. "When I pull out the blade, break each pellet and sprinkle the dust over the wound." She slit Caine's clothing, clearing the space around the wound. "Are you ready?"

Again Caine gave a brief nod. Esma gripped the hilt, slowly tilted the blade in a certain way that made the sweat pop out on his forehead, though he didn't make a sound. Then she carefully rotated the blade to the right, just a little, and slid it free. Blood all but gushed from the ugly wound. Swiftly Lenna popped one of the green pellets and carefully sprinkled the contents over the wound, then did the same with the other pellet. Almost miraculously the blood slowed to a trickle, and the open edges of torn flesh seemed to smooth and flatten.

Esma slapped a square of bandage on the wound and it adhered to his flesh. Almost immediately Lenna could feel relief flowing through him, revealed in the relaxing of his muscles. He took a deep, shuddering breath, let his head drop for a few seconds, then he straightened his shoulders and prepared to stand.

Lenna and Esma both gaped at him. "You can't get up yet!" Lenna protested.

He rose to his feet. "I can't?" Gingerly he rolled his shoulders, but already his color was almost normal, and that hard, glinting light was back in his eyes.

Esma said weakly, "I've never seen anyone recover that fast."

But this was Caine, and everything that Hunters were, he was *more*.

Lenna and Esma both stood, too. "How long have you realized you were meant to be on our side?" Lenna asked the other woman.

"Since I decided that it would be foolish to even attempt to kill Strength." Esma sighed, shrugged. "I've never not completed a mission, but . . . I don't trust Veton, not with the deck, and not with you."

"Good call," Caine said as he cleaned his knife and slid it back into the sheath. "He is the Tower, you know."

"I know," Esma said. To Lenna, she said, "If you had possessed the entire deck when I arrived, I'd have taken you to your own home, not to Veton."

Lenna nodded, gave a small smile. "I should have known."

Caine walked over to Stroud's still body, and Esma went with him. Reluctantly Lenna joined them; if she could do harm, she could see the results. "Is he dead?"

To her surprise, Stroud was looking up, frozen but fully aware. The sight gave her the shivers. Caine experimentally nudged him. "He's frozen solid. Can you thaw him?"

No longer surprised at a Hunter's endurance, or differences from normal beings, Lenna held her hands out, palm up, and looked at them. "I don't know how. If I tried, I might cook him. When I lose my temper I don't . . . pull my punches, so to speak."

"I noticed," Caine said. To Stroud, he said, "Guess you'll have to come to room temperature on your own, buddy." He looked around the ice-covered warehouse, everything silver and blue and drifting in snow, a winter wonderland if one overlooked the destruction. "But that might be spring."

Stroud couldn't even blink, but his wide eyes showed comprehension. Caine shrugged. "Here's some free advice: never let me hear of you or see you again. Change your name, live on another world, never cross me or mine again and I'll let you live. Bide by those terms and you'll be safe. Otherwise I'll turn her loose on you again, and next time she won't be merciful."

Stroud's eyes filled with horror.

Lenna didn't feel pity for him. He had almost killed Caine. She glanced down at him once more. Maybe someone would find him, but she simply didn't care.

She pulled Caine and Esma away from Stroud's prone body and held out both hands. "The cards you hold, please."

Esma reluctantly took the Moon from her pocket and slapped it onto Lenna's palm. Caine did the same with the Emperor. Lenna reverently added those two cards to the rest of the deck, in the red bag. The glow of the cards brightened. The bag, which had been heavy while the deck had been incomplete, was suddenly lighter.

She took Caine's hand and then Esma's. "We will finish this task together," she said, and leaned against Caine. "Take us to the Emperor."

The Emperor's castle hadn't changed in the few hundred years since Lenna had last visited . . . or she thought it had been that long. Time didn't matter on Aeonia, the way it did on other planes. Everything was exactly as it had been: the furnishings in his offices, the way the sunlight slanted through the tall windows. Jerrick hadn't changed, either. Like her, he was forever Arcane.

Jerrick rose to his feet and gave Lenna a stern, serious look before dismissing Caine and Esma with a wave of his hand and a single brisk command. "Go."

"No," Lenna said, stepping forward. The Emperor wasn't her superior. He was a . . . spokesperson, a leader, but in the end she held sway over as much of the universe as he did, perhaps more, because if Jerrick was strong he took that strength from her. "I would like a word with you, and I ask that these two Hunters be allowed to stay until I have done what must be done."

Jerrick shook his head, focused on the task at hand. "Hand over the Alexandria Deck—"

Lenna shook her head. "No, not just yet. I have a request. A number of requests actually." Convincing him to join her in what must be done wouldn't be easy, but she needed the cooperation of several of the most powerful Major Arcana, and it all began with Jerrick.

Jerrick's eyebrows arched in surprise. What had he thought she'd do, hand over the deck and go home as if nothing had happened? Maybe he thought she'd be happy to be back, grateful to return to her life of unending perfection. Perhaps she was . . . to a degree. Beyond that degree, though, a lot had changed.

It had been countless years since the Major Arcana had petitioned the One, He who had made them all, He who still guided them all. Now was the time. She knew what needed to be done, but she couldn't do it alone.

"Call everyone here," she said, issuing a command, not a request. "It's time for a full council." Some of the Arcane were close, others were far, but all could be here in short order, with the assistance of a Hunter or two. "Caine and Esma can assist with the transportation, for those who require it."

Jerrick didn't refuse her; he couldn't ignore her, but he was less than enthusiastic. "It has been a very long time since we've had a full council meeting. What possible reason do I give for calling one now? It would be unwise to tell them all about the Alexandria Deck. It would be best for everyone if the deck is destroyed, or locked away."

"I disagree. You lead us, Jerrick. You always have. But this is not a decision for you alone."

Again, that eyebrow.

She continued, confident that he would accede to all her requests. "Before the full council meets, I will require a meeting with you, the Empress, the High Priestess, and the Hierophant. Caine and Esma can collect them first, and then continue with the others."

"A meeting," Jerrick said, again without enthusiasm, though he looked intrigued at the mention of the Empress. Their relationship was . . . interesting.

Lenna reached inside her bag and withdrew the cards that had started this adventure. She used both hands to remove them, to fan the cards out so Jerrick could see them, to display them as a powerful thing of beauty. They glowed more brightly than before, as alive as she was.

"Such beauty and power should not be locked away, not if there is another choice."

Was there? Was there truly another choice? She was about to find out.

Caine's back still hurt like hell, but it was healing, even though it had just been a few hours since Stroud's knife had cut into it. He barely paid attention to it, so fascinated was he by watching Lenna literally remold her world by the strength of her will. Some of the other Major Arcana argued with her, some were wary and unconvinced, but it was evident in their eyes that, strong as they all were, *she* was Strength, and they would do what she wanted or would never again know peace.

A few hours was all that was needed apparently, for Lenna Frost, Strength, a woman, to change her world. She was no longer satisfied with things as they had always been.

In changing her world, she would change all the others, as well.

Her special premeeting accomplished, the One petitioned, she was ready for all the Major Arcana gathered in the Emperor's castle, in a vast ballroom ostentatiously decorated in gold and crimson. The tall, wide windows were uncovered, allowing shafts of bright sunlight to shine through. Even Veton was there, looking displeased with Lenna, casting angry glances at Esma. He had sent three Hunters to Seven, and only one returned—one who had not only not completed the mission he'd given her, but who had evidently thrown in her lot with the others.

Perhaps, back on Seven, enough time had passed for Stroud to thaw, though here on Aeonia very little time had passed. If Stroud had indeed thawed, he'd been wise enough to follow Caine's instructions and disappear.

Caine had never seen the Arcane gathered together in its entirety; not many beings had. It was an impressive sight, and he was not easily impressed. How long had it been since this had happened? A thousand, two thousand years? More? But they were all here now, because they had been called.

"Gather around me," Lenna instructed, and the beings formed a circle around her. Caine studied them all. Some were dressed finely; others preferred plain dress. Several, like Lenna, were beautiful. Others were ordinary, while a few—two of them—might even be called ugly. Together they represented every aspect of life, from birth to death, and on this occasion they were gathered together in this room, so much power, so much potential and knowledge, bound to their physical beings.

Using both hands, Lenna held out the Alexandria Deck. She turned about slowly so all had a chance to see what she possessed. Long ago, they had all had some experience with the cards. They knew what she held; they recognized that which had been lost for so long. No one spoke or stepped forward. It was as if they were in a trance. The glow the cards produced was stronger than before, more constant. Together, complete and alive again, the cards were powerful beyond measure.

"The Alexandria Deck," Lenna said in a soft, reverent voice. "It's been a long time since we've seen it. It wasn't destroyed by fire—the fire Veton caused," she added as an aside, not looking at him but letting her displeasure with him color her words. "We thought it was gone, but it survived. It thrived. It lived. I suspect this deck is more powerful than it has ever been."

Someone—Caine wasn't sure who—called out, "It should be destroyed!"

"No," Lenna responded. "It should be treasured and protected. And changed," she added with a tilt of her head. "The time for a power such as this one has passed."

"Don't destroy it!" Veton called out, his hands fisted, his face showing intense distress.

Lenna ignored him. "In the past few days I have had the opportunity to truly see one of the worlds we influence. Experiencing, touching, feeling . . . it isn't the same as watching from afar." She glanced at Caine, but her strong gaze quickly moved on, as she looked at each of her fellow Aeonians in turn. "I saw such wonderful things on Seven, and I also saw the ugliest mankind has to offer. There is so much love, and there is also hate. I saw disease and violence. I laughed. I experienced the beauty of a magnificent planet, the power of it, and I also saw firsthand the wonder of a child."

"A child," the Empress murmured, her voice full of emotion.

"We see all these things from the safety of Aeonia," the Emperor said, though he seemed less insistent than he had when they'd first arrived.

"Each world has things we should know. Music and laughter must be experienced, not watched from a distance," Lenna explained. "To hold a child, to feel rain on your skin, to experience fear—it's all important. It's not the same to watch from a safe distance. Watching from afar is no substitute for feeling. Whether it's joy or pain, it isn't sufficient to simply observe. And love . . ." She stopped circling, then she turned her head and focused on Caine, let a radiant smile transfuse her features. "I have loved, and I have been loved. We should all know that feeling, at least once in our long lives."

There was an interested murmur from some of her peers, while others were obviously uncertain.

"The Arcana have not been a true part of life for a very long time," she continued. "For too long, we have simply observed the lives we influence. It's time, past time, for a change. Along with a few others among us, I have petitioned the One to make that possible." With that, she tossed the cards into the air. Many gasped at that seemingly impulsive action. Veton even lurched forward, but he stopped when the cards Lenna had tossed into the air did not fall, as they should have, but remained floating.

The cards swirled, much as snow and ice had swirled around Lenna on Seven. They glowed and vibrated and danced, alive with power and joy. "Nothing stays the same forever," she said quietly. "We've been trapped here for too long, insulated and isolated. The One has heard our pleas for change, and He has responded."

One by one, the cards drifted to the Major Arcana they represented. The Fool grabbed his card from the air, laughing with joy as he grasped it in both hands. The others received theirs in much the same way, though some were more solemn than others.

"With your card," Lenna said, "and with the assistance of a Hunter of your choosing, you will have the ability to travel to other worlds, to experience life, perhaps even to touch those who need you most. You don't have to use your card if you don't want to—participate in your own time. It won't always be easy, but we have had it easy for far too long." Again, she looked at Caine. "It takes strength to participate in life."

Veton was disturbingly giddy as he waited his turn. He rubbed his hands together in anticipation. There were two cards left—Strength and the Tower. Lenna's card drifted down to her, twirling as it dropped slowly. She took it and smiled. Only then did the Tower card move toward Veton.

Halfway between Lenna and the Tower, the card stopped moving. It hung in the air, shimmering and hesitant. The glow that marked the cards dimmed briefly, then increased until it was difficult to look directly into the glare.

Then the card burst into flame.

Veton screamed; the room shimmered and shook

on the waves of his distress. The fire burned longer than it should have given the physical substance of the card, but soon enough the flames died, and a few charred wisps of paper drifted to the floor. Veton gave a long, choking moan, then dropped to his knees and screamed.

"The Alexandria Deck will never again be whole," Lenna said. "Our power is great. As we have always known, that power is too great to continue unchecked. Abuse the gift you have been given today, and it can and will be taken away. The One has decreed that the Tower shall not travel."

Veton remained on the ground, a sobbing puddle of a man, and in that moment he looked more like a man than a powerful Aeonian. He was broken. He muttered to himself, nonsense and sorrow spilling from him. The others were full of questions for Lenna, about her adventure, about how this new power would work. Would they still be restricted to five days? Yes, but with the ability to come and go that was not too great a burden. The One had set that time limit for a reason, and whether or not they knew why or agreed with it wasn't important.

Others asked again if they would be required to travel? No, Lenna answered, the choice was theirs.

"Unfair!" Veton howled.

Lenna gave him a cool look. "You're still the Tower, you'll still be able to create chaos from afar, as you have since the beginning of time. You crossed a line when you tried to have me killed, and the One is holding you accountable."

Veton sulked, but chaos never stayed defeated for long. Within minutes he mused aloud that if the One could take his card away, then one day He might return it . . . in a thousand years, or two, or five. . . . Time meant nothing on Aeonia.

Lenna walked toward Caine, a gentle smile on her face. Esma nodded to her, grinned, and then moved into the crowd of Major Arcana to line up some work. She wouldn't be working for Veton again, that was a given, but she had first crack among all the other Hunters at making contact. Lenna suspected that in short order Esma would be a very wealthy Hunter.

"What do you think?" Lenna asked, rubbing her cheek against his arm. "And how are you feeling?"

"I feel fine, and I think you're amazing."

He'd expected that while they were among her peers she would keep her distance from him; she wouldn't want the others to know that she had been intimate with a Hunter. He was wrong. She put her arms around him, went up on tiptoe, and kissed him before saying—loudly enough for those nearby to hear, in case they misunderstood—"I missed being close to you."

He had missed it, too.

She tilted her head and gave him a brilliant smile. "I love you, Caine," she continued in a softer tone. "Discovering love was the most important aspect of my adventure. That night, that wonderful night when you showed me the world . . . I fell in love with you. I don't want to lose that."

A few of the others glanced their way; eyebrows were raised, and not just the Emperor's. Some smiled. Others were shocked. But they all moved on to more important things very quickly, because what Strength did was her business and they really didn't want to make her angry. Once upon a time, so long ago their memories were somewhat foggy, she had lost her temper and no one wanted to see that again.

Caine wrapped his arms around Lenna and lifted her so they were face-to-face. "I love you, I do, but I don't know how we will make this work. I'm a Hunter. You're Strength."

"Which means we're among the most powerful beings in the universe. That won't change. You will continue to be what you are, as will I. Together we will find a way to make it work if we want this badly enough. I do. I want it very much." She kissed him again. "Don't be a wienie," she said, her eyes twinkling her relish at using the Seven term.

He wanted it, too, more than he'd ever wanted anything. He overlooked the wienie remark, and joined in the kissing.

She took her mouth from his and smiled again. "I want to see everything, and I want to see it with you. Not this world, not Seven, not your world, but . . . all of them. There's so much to do and to see. I didn't understand that until I met you."

"You have turned the universe upside down, love," he said.

"Perhaps it was time." She held on to him, standing close, always close. She never wanted to be far from him again.

Perhaps it was. "What do you want?" he asked. He would do everything in his power to give her whatever that might be.

She did not hesitate in delivering her answer. "Show me the universe, Hunter. Help me to make our lives the adventure it was meant to be."

"Starting now," he said, and they were off.

Epilogue

25 Seven-years later

Elijah had always been interested in magic. As a teenager, he'd performed elaborate illusions for school talent shows, which he usually won. He'd tried college, he really had, but even though he'd wanted to make his grandparents proud, he'd dropped out after two years and had gone on the road. There had been more ratty clubs along the way than he could count. At some point—he'd been in Tampa, Florida, at the time—he'd decided Elijah Tilley wasn't snazzy enough and he'd taken a stage name:

Elijah Frost.

He didn't know where the Frost had come from, but it had popped into his head and had seemed right.

It had been a good decision. Shortly after that name change, he'd been booked into a bigger club, and then again, and then he'd found an agent who'd booked him into a small auditorium.

The rest was history. *His* history.

What Elijah knew, what no one else in his circle knew, was that not everything he did on stage was illusion.

Magic was real.

Now here he was, in Vegas. Elijah Frost, Master Illusionist. He played to a packed house every night.

Tonight, *they* were here again.

He had first seen the blond woman and the dark-haired man at a baseball game when he'd been ten years old. For some reason they had drawn his attention. They looked familiar but he couldn't place them. He wasn't alarmed by their familiarity, because deep down he accepted that there was more to life than most people dreamed, and he hadn't approached them or mentioned them to his grandparents.

That night he'd dreamed of them, and he'd awakened almost certain they were the superheroes he had talked about so much after his mother had been killed. He didn't remember much from that time, and he remembered nothing at all from the days he'd been missing, but his grandparents had told him how worried they'd been when he'd kept talking about the Hunter and the Angel who had saved him. Apparently he'd talked a lot about "poofing."

He'd been working on that trick for years, with no success.

He'd seen the couple several times since that baseball game: at his high school graduation, and in a seedy dive of a club in New Orleans. When he'd had that car wreck, a few years back, they had shown up and kept him company until rescuers arrived. If they'd talked he didn't remember, but deep down he felt that they had. There had been a couple of times when he'd thought he saw them out of the corner of his eye, and had turned around to see . . . nothing.

They never changed. They never aged and he never saw one without the other.

He had seen them in this venue before, last year, opening night. And here they were again, on another opening night. Everything felt right in the universe, the way Elijah had always known it could feel.

They were seated in the very center of the audience, not so close that he could see them well, once the houselights went down, but not so far away that they were lost in the crowd.

Elijah was halfway through the show when he added in a new and unplanned trick. He thrust his hand out,